James Patterson is one of the best-known and biggest-selling writers of all time. He is the author of some of the most popular series of the past decade: the Women's Murder Club, the Alex Cross novels and Maximum Ride, and he has written many other number one bestsellers including romance novels and stand-alone thrillers. He has won an Edgar Award, the mystery world's highest honour. He lives in Florida with his wife and son.

Praise for James Patterson:

'The man is a master of this genre. We fans will have one wish for him: write even faster'　　*USA Today*

'Pacy, sexy, high-octane stuff'　　*Guardian*

'Packed with white-knuckled twists'　　*Daily Mail*

'A novel which makes for sleepless nights'　　*Daily Express*

'Breakneck pacing and loop-the-loop plotting'
Publishers Weekly

'Reads like a dream'　　*Kirkus Reviews*

'Murder mystery at its best'　　*Mirror*

'Ticks like a time bomb – full of threat and terror'
Los Angeles Times

'Absolutely terrific'　　*Bookseller*

'Patterson's action-packed story keeps the pages flicking by'　　*The Sunday Times*

'A fine writer with a good ear for dialogue and pacing. His books are always page-turners'　　*Washington Times*

'Patterson is a phenomenon'　　*Observer*

'Keeps the adrenaline level hi

JAMES PATTERSON

CROSS

headline

First published in Great Britain in 2006
by HEADLINE PUBLISHING GROUP

This edition published in 2010
by HEADLINE PUBLISHING GROUP

1

Cataloguing in Publication Data is
available from the British Library

ISBN 978 0 7553 4940 1

Typeset in Palatino Light by Palimpsest Book Production Ltd,
Grangemouth, Stirlingshire

Printed and bound in Great Britain by
Clays Ltd, St Ives plc

Headline's policy is to use papers that are natural, renewable
and recyclable products and made from wood grown in
sustainable forests. The logging and manufacturing processes
are expected to conform to the environmental regulations of
the country of origin.

HEADLINE PUBLISHING GROUP
An Hachette UK Company
338 Euston Road
London NW1 3BH

www.headline.co.uk
www.hachette.co.uk

Dedicated to the Palm Beach Day School;
Shirley and Headmaster Jack Thompson.

PROLOGUE

WHAT IS YOUR NAME, SIR?

THOMPSON: *I'm Dr Jack Thompson, with the Berkshires Medical Center. How many shots did you hear?*

CROSS: *Multiple shots.*

THOMPSON: *What is your name, sir?*

CROSS: *Alex Cross.*

THOMPSON: *Are you having trouble breathing? Experiencing any pain?*

CROSS: *Pain in my abdomen. Feel liquid sloshing around. Shortness of breath.*

THOMPSON: *You know that you were shot?*

CROSS: *Yes. Twice. Is he dead? The Butcher? Michael Sullivan?*

THOMPSON: *I don't know. Several men are dead. Okay, guys, give me a nonrebreather mask. Two wide-base IV lines, stat. Two liters IV saline solution. Now! We're going to try to move you, get you to a*

	hospital immediately, Mr Cross. Just hold on. Can you still hear me? Are you with me?
CROSS:	*My kids . . . tell them I love them.*

PART ONE

NO ONE WILL EVER LOVE YOU THE WAY I DO

Chapter One

'I'm pregnant, Alex.'
Everything about the night is so very clear to me. Still is, after all this time, all these years that have passed, everything that's happened, the horrible murderers, the homicides solved and sometimes not.

I stood in the darkened bedroom with my arms lightly circling my wife Maria's waist, my chin resting on her shoulder. I was thirty-one then, and had never been happier at any time of my life.

Nothing even came close to what we had together, Maria, Damon, Jannie, and me.

It was the fall, a million years ago it seems to me now.

It was also past two in the morning, and our baby Jannie had colic something terrible. Poor sweet girl had been up for most of the night, most of the last few nights, most of her young life. Maria was gently rocking Jannie in her arms, humming 'You Are So Beautiful,' and I had my arms around Maria, rocking her.

I was the one who'd gotten up first, but I couldn't seem to get Jannie back to sleep no matter what tricks I tried. Maria had come in and taken the baby after an hour or so. We both had work early in the morning. I was on a murder case.

'You're pregnant?' I said against Maria's shoulder.

'Bad timing, huh, Alex? You see a lot more colic in your future? Binkies? More dirty diapers? Nights like this one?'

'I don't like this part so much. Being up late, or early, whatever this is. But I love our life, Maria. And I love that we're going to have another baby.'

I held on to Maria and turned on the music from the mobile dangling over Janelle's crib. We danced in time to 'Someone to Watch Over Me.'

Then she gave me that beautiful partly bashful, partly goofy smile of hers, the one I'd fallen for, maybe on the very first night I ever saw her. We had met in the emergency room at St Anthony's, during an emergency. Maria had brought in a gangbanger, a gunshot victim, a client of hers. She was a dedicated social worker, and she was being protective – especially since I was a dreaded metro homicide detective, and she didn't exactly trust the police. Then again, neither did I.

I held Maria a little tighter. 'I'm happy. You know that. I'm glad you're pregnant. Let's celebrate. I'll get some champagne.'

'You like being the big daddy, huh?'

'I do. Don't know why exactly. I just do.'

'You like screaming babies in the middle of the night?'

'This too shall pass. Isn't that right, Janelle? Young lady, I'm talking to you.'

Maria turned her head away from the wailing baby and gave me a sweet kiss on the lips. Her mouth was soft, always inviting, always sexy. I loved her kisses – anytime, anywhere.

She finally wriggled out of my arms. 'Go back to bed, Alex. No sense both of us being up. Get some sleep for me, too.'

Just then, I noticed something else in the bedroom, and I started to laugh, couldn't help myself.

'What's so funny?' Maria smiled.

I pointed, and she saw it too. *Three apples* – each one with a single childlike bite out of it. The apples were propped on the legs of three stuffed toys, different-colored Barney dinosaurs. Toddler Damon's fantasy play was revealed to us. Our little boy had been spending some time in his sister Jannie's room.

As I got to the doorway, Maria gave me that goofy smile of hers again. And a wink. She whispered – and I will never forget what she said – 'I love you, Alex. No one will ever love you the way I do.'

Chapter Two

Forty miles north of DC, in Baltimore, two cocksure long-haired hit men in their mid to late twenties ignored the MEMBERS ONLY sign and sashayed into the St Francis social club on South High Street, not far from the harbor. Both men were heavily armed and smiling like a couple of stand-up comedians.

There were twenty-seven capos and soldiers in the club room that night, playing cards, drinking grappa and espresso, watching the Bullets lose to the Knicks on TV. Suddenly the room was quiet and on edge.

Nobody just walked into St Francis of Assisi, especially not uninvited and armed.

One of the intruders in the doorway, a man named Michael Sullivan, calmly saluted the group. This was some funny shit, Sullivan was thinking to himself. All these goombah tough guys sitting around chewing their cud. His companion, or *compère*, Jimmy 'Hats' Galati, glanced around the room from under the brim of a beat-up black fedora, like the one worn by Squiggy on *Laverne & Shirley*. The social club was pretty typical – straight chairs, card tables, makeshift bar, guineas coming out of the woodwork.

'No welcoming committee for us? No brass bands?' asked Sullivan, who lived for confrontation of any kind, verbal or physical. It had always been him and Jimmy Hats against everybody else, ever since they were fifteen and ran away from their homes in Brooklyn.

'Who the hell are you?' asked a foot soldier, who rose like steam from one of the rickety card tables. He was maybe six two, with jet-black hair, and weighed 220 or so, obviously worked with weights.

'He's the Butcher of Sligo. Ever hear of him?' said Jimmy Hats. 'We're from New York City. Ever hear of New York City?'

Chapter Three

The buffed-up mob soldier didn't react, but an older man in a black suit and white shirt buttoned to the collar raised his hand like the Pope or something and spoke slowly and deliberately in heavily accented English. 'To what do we owe this honor?' he asked. 'Of course we've heard of the Butcher. Why are you here in Baltimore? What can we do for you?'

'We're just passing through.' Michael Sullivan spoke to the old man. 'Have to do a little job for Mr Maggione in DC. You gentlemen heard of Mr Maggione?'

Heads nodded around the room. The tenor of the conversation so far suggested that this was definitely serious business. Dominic Maggione controlled the Family in New York, which ran most of the East Coast, down as far as Atlanta anyway.

Everybody in the room knew who Dominic Maggione was and that the Butcher was his most ruthless hit man. Supposedly, he used butcher knives, scalpels, and mallets on his victims. A reporter in *Newsday* had said of one of his murders, 'No human being could have done this.' The Butcher was feared in mob circles and by the police. So it was a surprise to those in the room that the killer was so young and that he looked like a movie actor, with his long blond hair and striking blue eyes.

'So where's the respect? I hear that word a lot, but I don't see any in this club,' said Jimmy Hats, who, like the Butcher, had a reputation for amputating hands and feet.

The soldier who had stood up suddenly made his move, and the Butcher's arm shot forward in a blur. He sliced off the tip of the man's nose, then the lobe of an ear. The soldier grabbed at his face in two places and stepped back so fast he lost his balance and fell hard on the wood-plank floor.

The Butcher was fast, and obviously as good as promised with a knife. He was like the old-time assassins from Sicily, and that's how he had learned knife play, from one of the old soldiers in South Brooklyn. Amputation and bone-crunching had come easily to him. He considered them his trademark, symbols of his ruthlessness.

Jimmy Hats had a gun out, a .44-caliber semi-automatic. Hats was also known as 'Jimmy the Protector,' and he had the Butcher's back. Always.

Now Michael Sullivan slowly walked around the room. He kicked over a couple of card tables, shut off the TV, and pulled the plug on the espresso machine. Everyone suspected that somebody was going to die. But why? Why had Dominic Maggione unleashed this madman on them?

'I see some of you are expecting a little show,' he said. 'I see it in your eyes. I *smell* it. Well, hell, I don't want to disappoint anybody.'

Suddenly Sullivan went down on one knee and stabbed the wounded mob soldier where he lay on the floor. He stabbed the man in the throat, then in the face and chest until there was no movement in the body. It was hard to count the strokes, but it must have been a dozen, probably more.

Then the strangest thing of all. Sullivan stood up and took a bow over the dead man's body. As if this was all a big show to him, all just an act.

Finally, the Butcher turned his back on the room and walked unconcerned toward the door. No fear of anything or anyone. He called over his shoulder, 'Nice meetin' you, gentlemen. Next time, show some respect. For Mr Maggione – if not for myself and Mr Jimmy Hats.'

Jimmy Hats grinned at the room and tipped his fedora. 'Yeah, he's *that* good,' he said. 'Tell you what, he's even better with a chain saw.'

Chapter Four

The Butcher and Jimmy Hats laughed their asses off about the St Francis of Assisi Social Club visit for most of the ride down I-95 to Washington, where they had a tricky job to do in the next day or two. Mr Maggione had ordered them to stop in Baltimore and make an impression. The don suspected that a couple of the local capos were skimming on him. The Butcher figured he'd done his job.

That was a part of his growing reputation: not just that he was good at killing, but that he was reliable as a heart attack for a fat man eating fried eggs and bacon.

They were entering DC, taking the scenic route past the Washington Monument and other important la-di-da buildings. 'My country 'tis of V,' sang Jimmy Hats in a seriously off-key voice.

Sullivan snorted out a laugh. 'You're a corker yourself, James m'boy. Where the hell did you learn that? My country 'tis of V?'

'St Patrick's parish school, Brooklyn, New York, where I learned everything I know about the three Rs – readin', 'ritin', 'rithmetic – an' where I met this crazy bastard named Michael Sean Sullivan.'

Twenty minutes later they had parked the Grand Am and joined the late-night youth parade traipsing along M Street in Georgetown. Bunch of mopey-dopey college punks, plus him and Jimmy, a couple of brilliant professional killers, thought Sullivan. So who was doing better in life? Who was making it, and who wasn't?

'Ever think you shoulda gone to college?' asked Hats.

'Couldn't afford the cut in pay. Eighteen, I was already making seventy-five grand. Besides, I love my job!'

They stopped at Charlie Malone's, a local watering hole popular with the Washington college crowd for no good reason Sullivan could figure. Neither the Butcher nor Jimmy Hats had gone past high school, but inside the bar, Sullivan struck up an easy conversation with a couple of coeds, no more than twenty years old, probably still in their late teens. Sullivan read a lot, and remembered most of it, so he could talk with just about anybody. His repertoire tonight included the recent shootings of American soldiers in Somalia, a couple hot new movies, even some Romantic poetry – Blake and Keats, which seemed to appeal to the college ladies.

In addition to his charm, though, Michael Sullivan was a looker, and he knew it – slim but nicely toned, six one, longish blond hair, a smile that could dazzle anybody he chose to use it on.

So it was no major surprise when twenty-year-old Marianne Riley from Burkittsville, Maryland, started making none-too-subtle goo-goo eyes at him and touching him in the way forward girls sometimes do.

Sullivan leaned in close to the girl, who smelled like wildflowers. 'Marianne, Marianne . . . there used to be a song. Calypso tune? You know it? "Marianne, Marianne"?'

'Before my time,' the girl said, but then she winked at him. She had the most gorgeous green eyes, full red lips, and the cutest little plaid bow planted in her hair. Sullivan had decided one thing about her right away – Marianne was a little cock tease, and that was all right with him. He liked to play games too.

'I see. And Mr Keats, Mr Blake, Mr Byron, weren't they before your time?' he kidded her, with his endearing smile turned on bright. Then he took Marianne's hand, and he lightly kissed it. He pulled her away from her barstool and did a tight Lindy twirl to the Stones song playing on the jukebox.

'Where are we going?' she asked. 'Where do you *think* we're going, mister?'

'Not too far,' said Michael Sullivan. 'Miss.'

'Not too far?' questioned Marianne. 'What does that mean?'

'You'll see. No worries. Trust me.'

She laughed, pecked him on the cheek, and laughed some more. 'Now how could I resist those killer eyes of yours?'

Chapter Five

Marianne was thinking that she didn't really want to resist this cute guy from New York City. Besides, she was safe inside the bar on M Street. What could go wrong in here? What could anybody try to pull? Play a New Kids on the Block tune on the jukebox?

'I don't much like the spotlight,' he was saying, leading her toward the back of the bar.

'You think you're another Tom Cruise, don't you? Does that big smile of yours always work? Get you what you want?' she asked.

She was smiling too, though, daring him to bring his best moves.

'I don't know, MM. Sometimes it works okay, I guess.'

Then he kissed her in the semidarkened hallway at the back of the bar, and the kiss was as good as Marianne could have hoped, kind of sweet actually. Definitely more on the romantic side than she'd expected. He didn't try to cop a feel along with the kiss, which might have been all right with her, but this was better.

'*Whooo.*' She exhaled and waved a hand in front of her face like a fan. It was a joke, only not totally a joke.

'It is a little hot in here, isn't it?' Sullivan said, and the coed's smile blossomed again. 'A little close, don't you think?'

'Sorry – I'm *not* leaving with you. This isn't even a date.'

'I understand,' he said. 'Never thought you would leave with me. Never crossed my mind.'

'Of course not. You're too much of a gentleman.'

He kissed her again, and the kiss was deeper. Marianne liked that he didn't give up too easily. It didn't matter, though – she wasn't going anywhere with him. She didn't do that, not ever – well, not so far anyway.

'You are a pretty good kisser,' she said. 'I'll give you that.'

'You're holding up your end,' he said. 'You're a great kisser actually. That was the best kiss of my life,' he kidded.

Sullivan pushed his weight against a door – and suddenly they were stumbling inside the men's room. Then Jimmy Hats stepped up to watch the door from the outside. He always had the Butcher's back.

'No, no, no,' Marianne said, but she couldn't keep from laughing at what had just happened. *The men's room?* This was pretty funny. Crazy funny – but funny. The kind of stuff college kids did.

'You really think you can get away with anything, don't you?' she asked him.

'The answer is yes. I pretty much do what I want, Marianne.'

And suddenly he had a scalpel out, the gleaming razor-sharp blade not far from her throat, and everything changed in a heartbeat. 'And you're right, this isn't a date. Now don't say a word, Marianne, or it will be your last on this earth, I swear on my mother's eyes.'

Chapter Six

'There's already blood on this scalpel,' the Butcher said in a throaty whisper meant to scare her out of her wits. 'You see it?'

Then he touched his jeans at the crotch. 'Now *this* blade won't hurt so much.' He brandished the scalpel in front of her eyes. 'But *this* one will hurt a lot. Disfigure your pretty face for life. I'm not kidding around, college girl.'

He unzipped his jeans and pressed the scalpel against Marianne Riley's throat – but he didn't cut her. He lifted up her skirt, then pulled aside her blue panties.

He said, 'I don't want to cut you. You can tell that, can't you?'

She could barely speak. 'I don't know.'

'You have my word on it, Marianne.'

Then he pushed himself inside the college girl slowly, so as not to hurt her with a thrust. He knew he shouldn't spend a lot of time here, but he didn't want to give up her tight insides. *Hell, I'll never see Marianne, Marianne after tonight.*

At least she was smart enough not to scream or try to fight him with her knees or nails. When he was finished with his business he showed her a couple of photographs he carried around. Just to be sure she understood her situation, understood it perfectly.

'I took these pictures myself. *Look* at the pictures, Marianne. Now, you must never speak of tonight. Not to anyone, but especially not to the police. You understand?'

She nodded without looking at him.

'I need you to *speak* the words, little girl. I need you to look at me, painful as that might be.'

'Understood,' she said. 'I'll never tell anybody.'

'Look at me.'

Her eyes met his, and the change in her was amazing. He saw fear and hatred, and it was something he enjoyed. It was a long story why, a growing-up-in-Brooklyn story, a father-and-son tale that he preferred to keep to himself.

'Good girl. Strange to say – I like you. What I mean

is, I have *affection* for you. Good-bye, Marianne, Marianne.'

Before leaving the bathroom, he searched through her purse and took her wallet. 'Insurance,' he said. 'Don't talk to anybody.'

Then the Butcher opened the door and left. Marianne Riley let herself collapse to the bathroom floor, shaking all over. She would never forget what had just happened – especially those horrifying photographs.

Chapter Seven

'Who's up so early in the morning? Well, my goodness, look who it is. Do I see Damon Cross? Do I spy Janelle Cross?'

Nana Mama arrived promptly at six thirty to look after the kids, as she did every weekday morning. When she burst through the kitchen door, I was spoon-feeding oatmeal to Damon, while Maria burped Jannie. Jannie was crying again, poor little sick girl.

'Same children who were up in the middle of the night,' I told my grandmother as I aimed a brimming spoon of gruel in the general direction of Damon's twisting mouth.

'Damon can do that himself,' Nana said, huffing as she put down her bundle on the kitchen counter.

It looked as if she had brought hot biscuits and – could it possibly be? – homemade peach jam. Plus her usual assortment of books for the day. *Blueberries for Sal, The Gift of the Magi, Goodnight Moon.*

I said to Damon, 'Nana says you can feed yourself, buddy. You holding out on me?'

'Damon, take your spoon,' she said.

And, of course, he did. Nobody goes up against Nana Mama.

'Curse you,' I said to her, and took a biscuit. Praise the Lord, a hot biscuit! Then came a slow, delicious taste of heaven on this earth. 'Bless you, old woman. Bless you.'

Maria said, 'Alex doesn't listen too well these days, Nana. He's too busy with his ongoing murder investigations. I told him that Damon is feeding himself. Most of the time anyway. When he's not feeding the walls and ceiling.'

Nana nodded. 'Feeding himself all of the time. Unless the boy wants to go hungry. You want to go hungry, Damon? No, of course you don't, baby.'

Maria began to gather together her papers for the day. Last night she'd still been laboring in the kitchen after midnight. She was a social worker for the city, with a caseload from hell. She grabbed a violet scarf off the hook by the back door, along with her favorite hat, to go with the rest of her outfit, which was predominantly black and blue.

'I love you, Damon Cross.' She flew over and kissed our boy. 'I love *you*, Jannie Cross. Even after last night.' She kissed Jannie a couple of times on both cheeks.

And then she grabbed hold of Nana and kissed her. 'And I love you.'

Nana beamed as if she'd just been introduced to Jesus himself, or maybe Mary. 'I love you too, Maria. You're a miracle.'

'I'm not here,' I said from my listening post at the kitchen door.

'Oh, we already know that,' said Nana.

Before I could leave for work, I had to kiss and hug everybody too, and say 'I love you's'. Corny maybe, but good in its way, and a pox on anybody who thinks that busy, scarily harassed families can't have fun and love. We certainly had plenty of that.

'Bye, we love you, bye, we love you,' Maria and I chorused as we backed out the door together.

Chapter Eight

Just as I did every morning, I drove Maria to her job in the Potomac Gardens housing project. It was only about fifteen or twenty minutes from Fourth Street anyway, and it gave us some alone time.

We rode in the black Porsche, the last evidence of some money I'd made during three years of private practice as a psychologist, before I switched full-time into the DC police department. Maria had a white Toyota Corolla, which I didn't much like, but she did.

It seemed as though she was someplace else as we rode along G Street that morning.

'You okay?' I asked.

She laughed and gave me that wink of hers.

'Little tired. I'm feeling pretty good, *considering*. I

was just thinking about a case I consulted on yesterday, favor to Maria Pugatch. It involves a college girl from GW University. She was raped in a men's bathroom in a bar on M Street.'

I frowned and shook my head.'Another college kid involved?'

'She says no, but she won't say much else.'

My eyebrows arched. 'So she probably knew the rapist? Maybe a professor?'

'The girl definitely says no, Alex. She swears it's no one she knows.'

'You believe her?'

'I think I do. Of course, I'm trusting and gullible anyway. She seems like such a sweet kid.'

I didn't want to stick my nose too far into Maria's business. We didn't do that to each other – at least we tried hard not to.

'Anything you want me to do?' I asked.

Maria shook her head. 'You're busy. I'm going to talk to the girl – Marianne – again today. Hopefully I can get her to open up a little.'

A couple minutes later, I pulled up in front of the Potomac Gardens housing project on G, between Thirteenth and Penn. Maria had volunteered to come here, left a secure and much cushier job in Georgetown. I think she volunteered because she lived in the

Gardens until she was eighteen, when she went off to Villanova.

'Kiss,' Maria said. 'I need a kiss. Good one. No pecks on the cheek. *On the lips.*'

I leaned over and kissed her – and then I kissed her again. We made out a little in the front seat, and I couldn't help thinking about how much I loved her, about how lucky I was to have her. What made it even better: I knew that Maria felt the same way about me.

'Gotta go,' she finally said, and wriggled out of the car.

But then she leaned back inside. 'I may not look it, but I'm happy. I'm so happy.'

Then that little wink of hers again.

I watched Maria walk all the way up the steep stone stairs of the apartment building where she worked. I hated to see her go, and it was the same thing just about every morning.

I wondered if she'd turn and see if I'd left yet. Then she *did* – saw me still there, smiled and waved like a crazy person, or at least somebody crazy in love. Then she disappeared inside.

We did the same thing almost every morning, but I couldn't get enough of it. Especially that wink of Maria's. *No one will ever love you the way I do.*

I didn't doubt it for a minute.

Chapter Nine

I was a pretty hot detective in those days – on the run, on the move, in the know. So I was already starting to get more than my fair share of the tougher prestige cases. The latest wasn't one of them, unfortunately.

As far as the Washington PD could tell, the Italian Mafia had never operated in any major way inside DC, probably because of deals struck with certain agencies like the FBI and CIA. Recently, though, the five Families had met in New York and agreed to do business in Washington, Baltimore, and parts of Virginia. Not surprisingly, the local crime bosses hadn't been too thrilled about this development, especially the Asians who controlled the cocaine and heroin trade.

A Chinese drug overlord named Jiang An-Lo had executed two Italian mob emissaries a week before. Not a good move. And reportedly the New York mob had dispatched a top hit man, or possibly a hit team, to deal with Jiang.

I'd learned that much during an hour-long morning briefing at police headquarters. Now John Sampson and I drove to Jiang An-Lo's place of business, a duplex row house on the corner of Eighteenth and M Streets in Northeast. We were one of two teams of detectives assigned to the morning surveillance, which we dubbed 'Operation Scumwatch.'

We had parked between Nineteenth and Twentieth and begun our surveillance. Jiang An-Lo's row house was faded, peeling yellow and looked decrepit from the outside. The dirt yard was littered with trash that looked as if it had burst from a piñata. Most of the windows were covered with plywood or tin. Yet Jiang An-Lo was a big deal in the drug trade.

The day was already turning warm, and a lot of neighborhood people were out walking or congregating on stoops.

'Jiang's crew is into what? Coke, heroin?' Sampson asked.

'Throw in some PCP. Distribution runs up and

down the East Coast – DC, Philly, Atlanta, New York. It's been a profitable operation, which is why the Italians want in. What do you think of Louis Freeh's appointment at the Bureau?'

'Don't know the man. He got *appointed* though, so he must be wrong for the job.'

I laughed at the truth in Sampson's humor; then we hunkered down and waited for a team of Mafia hitters to show up and try to take out Jiang An-Lo. That was if our information was accurate.

'We know anything about the hit man?' Sampson asked.

'Supposed to be an Irish guy,' I said, and looked over at John for a reaction.

Sampson's eyebrows arched; then he turned my way. 'Working for the Mafia? How'd that happen?'

'Guy is supposed to be good. And crazy too. They call him the Butcher.'

Meanwhile, an old, bowed-down guy had begun to cross M Street with deliberate glances left and right. He was slowly dragging on a cigarette. He crossed paths with a skinny white guy who had an aluminum cane cuffed at the elbow. The two stragglers nodded solemn hellos in the middle of the street.

'Couple of characters there,' Sampson said, and smiled. 'That'll be us someday.'

'Maybe. If we're lucky.'

And then Jiang An-Lo chose to make his first appearance of the day.

Chapter Ten

Jiang was tall and looked almost emaciated. He had a scraggly black goatee that hung a good six inches below his chinny-chin-chin.

The drug lord had a reputation for being shrewd, competitive, and vicious, often unnecessarily so, as if this was all a big, dangerous game to him. He'd grown up on the streets of Shanghai, then moved to Hong Kong, then Baghdad, and finally to Washington, where he ruled several neighborhoods like a new-world Chinese warlord.

My eyes shifted around M Street, searching for signs of trouble. Jiang's two bodyguards seemed on the alert, and I wondered if he'd been warned – and if so, by whom? Someone on his payroll in the police department? It was definitely possible.

I was also wondering how good this Irish killer was.

'Bodyguards spot us yet?' Sampson said.

'I expect they have, John. We're here as a deterrent more than anything else.'

'Hit man spot us too?'

'If he's here. If he's any good. If there *is* a hit man, he's probably seen us too.'

When Jiang An-Lo was about halfway to a shiny black Mercedes parked on the street, another car, a Buick LeSabre, turned on to M. It accelerated, the engine roaring, tires squealing as they burned against the pavement.

Jiang's bodyguards spun around toward the speeding car. They both had their guns out. Sampson and I shoved open the side doors of our car. 'Deterrent my ass,' he grumbled.

Jiang hesitated, but only for an instant. Then he took long, gangly strides, almost as if he was trying to run wearing a full-length skirt, heading back toward the row house he'd just come out of. He would have correctly figured he'd still be in danger if he kept going and reached the Mercedes.

Everybody had it wrong, though. Jiang, the bodyguards, Sampson and I.

The shots came from *behind* the drug dealer, from the opposite direction on the street.

Three loud cracks from a *long* gun.

Jiang went down and stayed there on the sidewalk, not moving at all. Blood poured from the side of his head as if there were a spout there. I doubted he was alive.

I spun around and looked toward the rooftop of a brownstone connected to more roofs lining the other side of M.

I saw a blond man, and he did the strangest thing: *He bowed in our direction.* I couldn't believe what he'd just done. Taken a bow?

Then he ducked behind a brick parapet and completely disappeared from sight.

Sampson and I sprinted across M and entered the building. We raced upstairs, four flights in a hurry. When we got to the roof, the shooter was gone. No one in sight anywhere.

Had it been the Irish hitter? The Butcher? The mob hit man sent from New York?

Who the hell else could it have been?

I still couldn't believe what I'd seen. Not just that he'd gotten Jiang An-Lo so easily. But that he'd taken a bow after his performance.

Chapter Eleven

The Butcher found it easy to blend in with the hot-shit college students on the campus of George Washington University. He was dressed in jeans and a gray, rumpled tee that said 'Athletic Department,' and he carried around a beat-up Isaac Asimov novel. He spent the morning reading *Foundation* on various benches, checking out the coeds, but mostly tracking Marianne, Marianne. Okay, he was a little obsessive. Least of his problems.

He *did* like the girl and had been watching her for twenty-four hours now, which was how she came to break his heart. She'd gone and shot her mouth off. He knew it for sure because he'd heard her talking to her best friend, Cindi, about a counselor she'd spoken to a few days before. Then she'd gone back for a second counseling session, against his explicit order and warning.

Mistake, Marianne.

After her noon class in hoity-toity eighteenth-century British literature, Marianne, Marianne left the campus, and he followed her in a group of at least twenty students. He could tell right away that she was headed to her apartment. *Good deal.*

Maybe she was done for the day, or maybe she had a long break between classes. Didn't matter either way. She'd broken the rules, and she had to be dealt with.

Once he knew where she was going, he decided to beat her there. As a senior, she was allowed to live off campus, and she shared a small two-bedroom off of Thirty-ninth Street on Davis with young Cindi. The place was a fourth-floor walk-up, and he had no trouble getting inside. The front door had a key lock. What a joke that was.

He decided to get comfortable while he waited, so he stripped down, took off his shoes and all his clothes. Truth was, he didn't want to get blood on his duds.

Then he waited for the girl, read some more of his book, hung out. As soon as Marianne walked inside her bedroom, the Butcher wrapped both arms around her and placed the scalpel under her chin.

'Hello, Marianne, Marianne,' he whispered. 'Didn't I tell you not to talk?'

'I didn't tell anyone,' she said. 'Please.'

'You're lying. I told you what was going to happen. Hell, I even *showed* you.'

'I didn't tell. I promise.'

'I made a promise too, Marianne. Made it on my mother's eyes.'

Suddenly he sliced left to right across the college girl's throat. Then he cut her again, going the other way.

While she writhed on the floor, choking to death, he took some photos.

Prizewinners, no doubt about it. He didn't ever want to forget Marianne, Marianne.

Chapter Twelve

The next night the Butcher was still in DC. He knew exactly what Jimmy Hats was thinking, but Jimmy was too much of a coward and a survivor to ask, *Do you have any idea what the hell you're doing now? Or why we're still in Washington?*

Well, as a matter of fact, he did. He was driving a stolen Chevy Caprice with tinted windows through the section of DC known as Southeast, searching out a *particular* house, getting ready to kill again, and it was all because of Marianne, Marianne and her big mouth.

He had the address in his head and figured he was getting close now. He had one more hit to take care of, then he and Jimmy could finally blow out of Washington. Case closed.

'Streets around here remind me of back home,' Jimmy Hats piped up from the passenger seat. He was trying to sound casual and unconcerned about their hanging around DC so long after the shooting of the Chinaman.

'Why's that?' asked the Butcher, his tongue planted firmly in his cheek. He knew what Jimmy was going to say. He almost always did. Truth be told, Jimmy Hats's predictability was a comfort to him most of the time.

'Everything's fallin' to shit, y'know, right before our eyes. Just like in Brooklyn. And *there's* your reason why. See the shines hanging out on every other street corner? Who the hell else is gonna live here? Live like that?'

Michael Sullivan smiled, but it wasn't a happy smile. Hats could be moronic and irritating at times. 'Politicians wanted to, they could fix this whole mess. Wouldn't be so hard, Jimmy.'

'Aw, Mikey, you're such a bleedin' heart. Maybe you should run for political office.' Jimmy Hats shook his head and turned to face the side window. He knew not to push it too far.

'And you're *not* wondering what the hell we're doing here? You're not thinking that I'm crazier than the last of the Coney Island shithouse rats? Maybe you want to jump out of the car. Head over to Union Station, hop on a train back to New York, Jimmy my boy.'

The Butcher was smiling when he said it, so Hats knew it was probably okay for him to laugh too. *Probably.* But in the past year he'd seen Sullivan kill two of their 'friends,' one with a baseball bat, one with a plumber's wrench. You had to be careful at all times.

'So what *are* we doing here?' Hats asked. 'Since we should be back in New York.'

The Butcher shrugged. 'I'm looking for a cop's house.'

Hats shut his eyes. 'Aw, Jeezus. Not a cop. Why a cop?' Then he pulled his fedora down over his face. 'See no evil,' he muttered.

The Butcher shrugged, but he was amused. 'Just trust me. Did I *ever* let you down?' Did I *ever* go too far over the top?'

They both started to laugh at that one. Did Michael Sullivan ever go too far over the top? Did he ever *not* go too far over the top was the better question.

It took another twenty minutes to find the house he was looking for. It was a two-story A-frame, looked as if it had been painted recently, flowers in the window boxes.

'Cop lives here? Not too bad a place actually. He fixed it up okay.'

'Yeah, Jimmy. But I'm tempted to waltz in and create a little havoc. Maybe use my saw. Take some photographs.'

Hats winced. 'Is that such a good idea? Really, I'm bein' serious here.'

The Butcher shrugged. 'I know you are. I can see that, James. I feel the heat from your brain working overtime.'

'Cop have a name?' asked Hats. 'Not that it matters.'

'Not that it matters. Cop's name is Alex Cross.'

Chapter Thirteen

The Butcher parked a block or so up Fourth Street, then he got out of the car and walked quickly back toward the cozy house where the cop had the bottom-floor flat. Getting the correct address had been easy enough for him. The Mafia had ties with the Bureau, after all. He loped around the side, trying not to be seen, but not concerned if he was. People in these neighborhoods didn't talk about what they saw.

This job was going to happen fast now. In and out of the house in a few seconds. Then back to Brooklyn to celebrate his latest hit and get paid for it.

He stepped through a thick patch of pachysandra surrounding the back porch, then boosted himself up. He walked right in through the kitchen door, which whined like a hurt animal.

No problem so far. He was inside the place easy enough. He figured the rest would be a snap too.

Nobody in the kitchen.

Nobody home?

Then he heard a baby crying and took out his Luger. He fingered the scalpel in his left-hand pocket.

This was a promising development. Babies in the house made everybody careless. He'd killed guys like this before, in Brooklyn and in Queens. One mob stoolie he'd cut into little pieces in his own kitchen then stocked the family fridge to send a message.

He passed down a short hall, moving like a shadow. Didn't make a sound.

Then he peeked into the small living room, family room, whatever the hell it was.

This wasn't exactly what he'd expected to see. Tall, good-looking man changing diapers for two little kids. The guy seemed to be pretty good at it too. Sullivan knew because years ago he'd been in charge of his three snot-nosed brothers in Brooklyn. Changed a lot of stinking diapers in his day.

'You the lady of the house?' he asked.

The guy looked up – *Detective Alex Cross* – and he didn't seem afraid of him. Didn't even seem surprised that the Butcher was in the house, even though he *had* to be shocked, and probably scared. So the cop had some brass balls on him anyway. Unarmed, changing his kids' diapers, but showing some attitude, some real character.

'Who are you?' Detective Cross asked, almost as if he was in charge of the situation.

The Butcher folded his arms, keeping the pistol out of sight from the children. Hell, he liked kids okay. It was adults he had a problem with. Like his old man – to take one flagrant example.

'You don't know why I'm here? No idea?'

'Maybe I do. I guess you're the hit man from the other day. But why are you *here*? At my house? This isn't right.'

Sullivan shrugged. 'Right? Wrong? Who's to say? I'm supposed to be a little crazy. So people tell me anyway. That could be it. You think? They call me the Butcher.'

Cross nodded. 'So I've heard. Don't hurt my kids. No one else is here but me. Their mother's not home.'

'Now why would I do that? Hurt your kids? Hurt you in front of your kids? Not my style. Tell you what. I'm outta here. Like I said – *crazy*. You lucked out. Bye, bye, kiddies.'

Then the hit man took another bow, like he had after he shot down Jiang An-Lo.

The Butcher turned away, and he left the apartment

the way he came in. Let the hotshot detective try to figure that one out. There *was* a method to his madness though – always a method to every move he made. He knew what he was doing, and why, and *when*.

Chapter Fourteen

That night with the Butcher shook me more than anything that had happened to me before as a policeman. *A killer inside my house. Right in the living room with my kids.*

And what was I supposed to make of it? That I'd been warned? That I was lucky to be alive? Oh, lucky me? The killer had spared my family. But why had he come after me in the first place?

The next day was one of my worst on the police force. While a squad car watched over the house, I was called into three separate meetings about the screwup at Jiang An-Lo's. There was talk of a departmental review, the first I'd been involved in.

On account of all the unscheduled meetings, plus the extra paperwork and my regular workload, I was late picking up Maria at Potomac Gardens that night. I felt guilty about it. I hadn't gotten used to her spending time inside a project like Potomac Gardens, especially once it got dark. It was dark now. And Maria was pregnant again.

It was a little past seven fifteen when I got to the projects that night. Maria wasn't waiting out front as she usually was.

I parked and got out of the car. I started to walk toward her office, which was located near maintenance, on the ground floor. Finally, I began to jog.

Then I saw Maria coming out the front door, and everything was suddenly right with the night. Her satchel was filled with so much paperwork that she couldn't get it closed. She had an armful of folders that wouldn't fit in the bag.

She still managed to wave and smile when she saw me coming her way. There was almost never anger from her over mistakes I made – like being more than half an hour late to pick her up.

I didn't care how corny or old-fashioned it was, but I was excited to see her, and that's the way it always was with us. My priorities had shifted to Maria and our family first and *then* my job. It felt good to me, the right balance.

Maria had this excited way of calling out my name.

'*Alex! Alex!*' she shouted, and waved one hand as I jogged to meet her in front of the building. A couple of neighborhood gangbangers leaning on the front fence turned our way and got a laugh at our expense.

'Hey, beautiful,' I called. 'Sorry I'm late.'

'No problem. I was working too. Hey, *Reu-ben*! You jealous, chico?' she called to one of the bangers propped against the fence.

He laughed and called back, 'You wish, Maria. You wish you had me 'stead of him.'

'Yeah, sure. In your dreams.'

We kissed – not a big show because we were in front of where she worked, and the bangers were there watching, but enough of a kiss to show we meant it. Then I took her work folders, and we started to the car.

'Carrying my books,' Maria teased. 'That's so cute, Alex.'

'I'll carry *you* if you want me to.'

'I missed you all day. Even more than usual,' she said, and smiled again. Then she tucked her face into my shoulder. 'I love you so much.'

Maria sagged in my arms first, and then I heard the gunshots. Two distant pops that didn't sound like much of anything. I never saw the shooter, no sign. I wasn't even sure which direction the shots had come from.

Maria whispered, 'Oh, Alex,' and then she got quiet and very still. I couldn't tell if she was breathing.

Before I realized what was happening, she slid away from me, down onto the sidewalk. I could see that she'd been hit in the chest, or high on her stomach. It was too dark and confusing to tell anything else for certain.

I tried to shield her, but then I saw a lot of blood pumping from her wound, so I picked her up in my arms and began to run.

Blood was all over me too. I think I was shouting, but I'm not sure exactly what happened after I realized Maria had been shot, and how bad it looked.

Close behind me, a couple of the gangbangers were tagging along. One of them was Reuben. Maybe they wanted to help. But I didn't know if anything could help Maria now. I was afraid she was dead in my arms.

Chapter Fifteen

St Anthony's Hospital wasn't far away, and I was running as fast as I could with Maria bundled and sagging heavily in my arms. My heart, the rushing blood, created a loud roar in my ears, like being caught under or maybe inside an ocean wave that was about to crash over both of us and drown us on these city streets.

I was afraid I might trip and fall because my legs were wobbly and weak. But I also knew I couldn't go down, couldn't stop running until I was at the ER.

Maria hadn't made a sound since she had whispered my name. I was afraid, maybe in shock, and definitely affected by tunnel vision. Everything around me was a fuzzy blur that made the moment seem even more unreal.

But I was definitely running.

I reached Independence Avenue and finally saw St Anthony's glowing red EMERGENCY ROOM sign less than a block away.

I had to stop for traffic, which was heavy and moving fast. I began to shout for help. From where I was standing, I could see a clique of hospital attendants huddled together, talking among themselves, but they hadn't seen me yet and couldn't hear me over the traffic noise.

There was no other choice, so I edged my way out onto the busy street.

Cars swerved and skidded around me, and a silver station wagon stopped completely. An exasperated father was at the wheel, kids leaning forward from the backseat. No one honked, maybe because they could see Maria in my arms. Or maybe it was the look on my face. Panic, despair, whatever it was.

More cars braked to let me through.

I was thinking to myself, *We're going to make it.* I told Maria, 'We're at St Anthony's. You're going to be all right, sweetheart. We're almost there. Hang on, we're almost at the hospital. I love you.'

I reached the other side of the street, and Maria's eyes suddenly blinked wide open. She looked at me, peered deeply into my eyes. At first she seemed confused, but then she focused on my face.

'Oh, I do love you, Alex,' Maria said, and she gave me that wonderful wink of hers. Then my sweet girl's eyes closed for the last time, and she was gone forever from me. Even while I was standing there holding on to her for dear life.

Chapter Sixteen

Maria Simpson Cross died in my arms – which was something I told almost no one, except Sampson and Nana Mama.

I didn't want to talk about our last few moments together; I didn't want anyone's pity, or their prying. I didn't want to satisfy some people's need for petty gossip, the latest dramatic story to whisper in hushed tones. All through the murder investigation over the next several months, I never discussed what had happened in front of St Anthony's. That was between Maria and me. Sampson and I talked to hundreds of people, but nobody gave us a lead on her killer. The trail went cold fast and stayed that way. We checked out the crazy mob killer but discovered he'd been on a flight back to New York the previous night – apparently he left town shortly after he left my kitchen. The FBI helped us there because a cop's wife had been shot. The killer wasn't the Butcher.

At two o'clock the morning after she died, I was inside our apartment, still wearing my holster and gun, pacing the living room with a screaming Janelle in my arms. I couldn't get the idea out of my head that our baby girl was crying for her mother who had died that night, just outside St Anthony's, where Jannie had been born six months before.

Suddenly tears were rolling from my eyes, and I felt overwhelmed by what had happened, both the reality and the unreality of it. I couldn't deal with any of this, especially the baby girl I was holding, and whom I couldn't get to stop crying.

'It's all right, baby. It's all right,' I whispered to my poor girl, who was being tortured by an insidious case of colic and who probably wanted to be in her mother's arms rather than mine. 'It's all right, Jannie, it's all right,' I repeated, though I knew it was a lie. I was thinking, *It's not all right! Your mama is gone. You'll never see her anymore. Neither will I.* Dear, sweet Maria, who had never hurt another person that I could remember and whom I loved more than my own life. She had been taken away from us so suddenly and for no reason anyone – not even God – could ever explain to me.

Oh, Maria. I spoke to her as I walked back and forth carrying our baby, *how could this have happened? How can I do what I have to do from now on? How can I do it without you? I'm not feeling sorry for myself. I'm just crazed right now. I'll get it together. I'll get it together, I promise. Just not tonight.*

I knew she wouldn't answer me, but it was strangely comforting to imagine that Maria could talk back, that maybe she could hear me at least. I kept hearing her voice, the exact sound of it and the words. *You'll be fine, Alex, because you love our kids so much.*

'Oh, Jannie, you poor baby. I do love you,' I whispered against the top of our baby's damp, overheated head.

And then I saw Nana Mama.

Chapter Seventeen

My grandmother was standing in the doorway of the hall leading to the apartment's two small bedrooms. Arms folded, she'd been watching me all this time. Had I been talking to myself? Talking out loud? I had no idea what I'd been doing.

'I woke you, didn't I?' I said in a whisper that was hardly necessary given the crying baby.

Nana was calm, and she seemed in control of herself. She'd stayed at the apartment to help with the kids in the morning, but now she was up, and that was my fault, and little Jannie's.

'I was awake,' she said. 'I was up thinking that you and the kids have to come back to my house on Fifth Street. It's a big enough house, Alex. Plenty big. That's the best way for this to work from now on.'

'For *what* to work?' I asked, a little confused by what she was saying, especially as Jannie was wailing loudly in my other ear.

Nana's back arched. 'You need me to help you with these children, Alex. It's as obvious as the nose on your face. I accept that. I want to do it, and I will.'

'Nana,' I said. 'We'll be fine. We'll do this ourselves. Just give me a little time to get my bearings.'

Nana ignored me as she continued to bring me in on her thinking. 'I'm here for you, Alex, and I'm here for the babies. That's the way it has to be now. I don't want any more back talk on it. So just stop, please.'

She walked toward me then and put her thin arms around me, hugged me tighter than it looked like she could. 'I love you more than I love my own life.' Then she said, 'I loved Maria. I miss her too. And I love these babies, Alex. Now more than ever.'

We were both tearing up now – all *three* of us were crying in the close, cramped living room space of the apartment. Nana was right about one thing: this place couldn't be our home anymore. Too many memories of Maria lived here.

'Now give me Jannie. Give her over,' she said, and it wasn't exactly a request. I sighed and handed over the baby to this five-foot-tall warrior of a woman who had raised me from the time I was ten and already orphaned.

Nana began to pat Jannie's back and to rub her neck, and then the baby produced a righteous belch. Nana and I both laughed in spite of ourselves.

'Not very ladylike,' Nana whispered. 'Now, Janelle, you stop this awful crying. You hear me? You just stop it right now.'

And Jannie did as she was told by Nana Mama, and that was the beginning of our new life.

PART TWO

COLD CASE – 2005

Chapter Eighteen

A letter from that psychopath Kyle Craig arrived for me today, and it blew my mind. *How could he get a letter to me?* It came to the house on Fifth Street. As far as I knew, Kyle was still locked away in the max-security facility out in Florence, Colorado. Even so, getting a message from him was disturbing.

Actually, it made me sick to my stomach.

Alex,

I've been missing you a great deal lately – our regular talks and whatnot – which is what prompts this little missive. To be honest with you, what I still find distressing is how beneath me you are, in terms of both intellect and imagination. And yet you were the one to catch me and put me in here, weren't you? The circumstances and ultimate result might lead me to believe in divine intervention, but of course I'm not quite that incapacitated yet.

At any rate, I know that you are a busy boy (no slur intended), so I won't keep you. I just wanted you to know that you're constantly in my thoughts, and that I hope to see you soon. In fact, you can count on it. I plan to kill Nana and the kids first, while you watch. Can't wait to see all of you again. I'm going to make it happen – promise.

K

I read the note twice, then I shredded it and tried to do the opposite of what Kyle obviously wanted me to do. *I put him out of my mind.*

Sort of.

After I called the max-security facility out in Colorado and told them about the letter – and made certain that Kyle Craig was still there in his padded cell.

Chapter Nineteen

Anyway, it was Saturday. I was off from work. No crime and punishment today. No psychopaths on the horizon, at least none that I knew about yet.

The Cross family car these days was an ancient Toyota Corolla that had been Maria's. Other than the obvious sentimental value, and its longevity, I didn't think much of the vehicle. Not in terms of form *or* function – not the off-white paint job, not the various pockmarks on the trunk and hood. The kids had given me a couple of bumper stickers for my last birthday – I May Be Slow, but I'm Still Ahead of You and Answer My Prayer, Steal This Car. They didn't like the Corolla either.

So on that bright and sunny Saturday, I took Jannie,

Damon, and little Alex out to do some car shopping.

As we rode along, Twista was on the CD player, 'Overnight Celebrity,' followed by Kanye West's 'All Falls Down.' All the while, the kids never stopped making wild and crazy suggestions about the new car we needed to buy.

Jannie was interested in a Range Rover – but that wasn't going to happen for all sorts of good reasons. Damon was trying to talk me into a motorcycle, which of course *he* would get to use when he turned eighteen in four years, which was so absurd it didn't even get a response from me. Not unless a grunt qualifies as communication nowadays.

Little Alex, or Ali, was open to any model of car, as long as it was red or bright blue. Intelligent boy, and that just could work as a plan, except for the 'red' or 'bright' part.

So we stopped at the Mercedes dealer out in Arlington, Virginia, which wasn't that far from the house. Jannie and Damon ogled a silver CLK500 Cabriolet convertible, while Ali and I tested out the spacious front seat of an R350. I was thinking family car – safety, beauty, resale value. *Intellect and emotion.*

'I like this one,' Ali said. 'It's blue. It's beautiful. Just right.'

'You have excellent taste in automobiles, buddy.

This is a six-seater, and *what* seats they are. Look up at that glass roof. Must be five feet or so.'

'Beautiful,' Ali repeated.

'Stretch out. Look at all this leg room, little man. This is an automobile.'

A salesperson named Laurie Berger had been at our side the whole time without being pushy or unnecessarily obtrusive. I appreciated that. God bless Mercedes.

'Questions?' she asked. 'Anything you want to know?'

'Not really, Laurie. You sit in this R350, you want to buy it.'

'Makes my job kind of easy. We also have one in obsidian black, ash upholstery. They call the R350 a crossover vehicle, Dr Cross. The station wagon meets the SUV.'

'And combines the best of both,' I said, and smiled congenially.

My pager went off then, and I groaned loud enough to draw stares.

Not on Saturday! And not during car shopping. Not while I was sitting in this beautiful Mercedes R350.

'Uh-oh,' said Ali, and his eyes went wide. 'Daddy's pager!' he called loudly across the showroom to Damon and Jannie. 'Daddy's pager went off.'

'You squealed on me. You're a dirty, rotten squealer,' I said, then kissed him on the top of his head. This is something I do at least half a dozen times a day, every day.

He giggled and slapped my arm and giggled some more. He always got my jokes. No wonder the two of us get along so well.

Only this pager message probably wasn't funny. Not in the least. I recognized the number immediately, and I didn't think it would be good news.

Ned Mahoney from Hostage Rescue? Maybe inviting me to a barbecue and dance out at Quantico? Probably not a barbecue though.

I called Ned back on my cell. 'This is Alex Cross. I got your call, Ned. *Why* did I get your call?'

Ned got right to it. 'Alex, you know Kentucky Avenue, near Fifteenth in Southeast?'

'Of course I do. It's not too far from my house. But I'm out in Arlington right now. I'm with the kids. We're looking to buy a new family car. Can you say *family*, Ned?'

'Meet me there, Kentucky and Fifteenth. I need your help, your local knowledge. I don't want to say too much more on my cell.' Ned told me a couple more details – but not all of it. Why was that? What was he keeping to himself?

Oh man, oh man, oh man. 'How soon? I'm with my kids, Ned.'

'Sorry about that. My team will be there in about ten, fifteen minutes at the most. I'm not kidding, all hell's broken loose, Alex.'

Of course it had. Why else would the FBI's Hostage Rescue Team be involved inside Washington city limits? And why else would Ned Mahoney call me on a Saturday afternoon?

'What's up?' Ali asked, looking at me.

'I have to go to a barbecue.' *I think I'm the main course on the spit, little man.*

Chapter Twenty

I promised Laurie Berger I would be back for the *cross*over vehicle soon; then I drove the kids home, and they were quiet and cranky for the ride. Same as me. Most of the way I was behind a station wagon with the bumper sticker FIRST IRAQ, THEN FRANCE. I'd been seeing that one all over Washington lately.

Hoobastank was blasting irritatingly from the CD player, so that kept everything near chaos, and in perspective. They were the kids; I was the father; I was abandoning them to go off to work. It didn't matter to them that I needed to earn a living, or that I might have a serious duty to perform. What the hell was going on at Kentucky and Fifteenth? Why did it have to happen today – whatever it was? Not something good!

'Thanks for the great Saturday, Daddy,' Jannie said as she was getting out of the car on Fifth Street. 'Really good. A memory.' Her uppity, sarcastic tone of voice kept me from apologizing, as I'd planned to do for most of the ride home.

'I'll see you guys later,' I said instead. Then I added, 'Love you.' Which I did – intensely.

'Yeah, Daddy, *later*. Like maybe next week, if we're lucky,' Jannie continued, and flipped an angry salute my way. It went like a spear through my heart.

'Sorry,' I finally said. 'I'm sorry. *Sorry*, guys.'

Then I headed over to Kentucky Avenue, where I was supposed to meet up with Ned Mahoney and his crack team from Hostage Rescue and find out more about whatever emergency was going on there.

As it turned out, I couldn't even get *close* to Kentucky and Fifteenth. DC police had every street blockaded within ten blocks. It certainly looked serious.

So I finally got out and walked.

'What's going on? You heard anything?' I asked a man loitering along the way, a guy I recognized from a local bakery, where he was a counterman and where I sometimes bought jelly donuts for the kids. Not for myself, of course.

'Pigfest,' he said. 'Cops everywhere. Just look around you, brother.'

It occurred to me that he didn't know I'd been a homicide detective, and was FBI now. I nodded at what he said, but you never get used to that kind of resentment and anger, even if sometimes it's justified. 'Pigs,' 'bacon,' whatever some people choose to call us, we put our lives on the line. A lot of folks don't really understand what that's like. We're not anything close to perfect and don't claim to be, but it's dangerous out here.

Try getting shot at on your job, bakery-man, I wanted to say to the guy, but didn't. I just walked on, sucked it up one more time, played the Happy Warrior again.

At least I was worked up when I finally spotted Ned Mahoney. I flashed my FBI creds so I could get closer. I still didn't know what the hell was going on, just that unidentified hostages had been taken inside a dealer's lab, where drugs were being manufactured and cut. It didn't sound half as bad as it looked. So what was the catch? There had to be one.

'Now aren't you a sight for sore eyes,' Mahoney said as he saw me heading his way. 'Alex, you're not going to believe this shit. Trust me, you're not.'

'Wanna bet?' I said.

'Ten dollars says you haven't seen this one before. Put your money up.'

We shook on it. I really didn't want to lose this bet.

Chapter Twenty-One

Ned scratched and rubbed at his blondish day-or-two-old facial stubble while he talked in his usual animated nonstop nobody-else-gets-a-word-in manner. I couldn't help staring at his chin. Ned is fair-skinned, and I think it impresses the hell out of him that he can grow a semblance of a beard now that he's in his forties. I *do* like Ned Mahoney, obnoxious as he can be at times. I like the man a lot.

'Some guys, maybe a half dozen – well armed – came down here to rob the dealer's lab,' he said. 'They ran into some major problems, got hung up inside. Also, there are some neighborhood people who work in the lab, around a dozen or so from what we can gather. They're trapped in there too. That's another problem we have to deal with eventually. Then—'

I put up a hand to stop Ned's hyperintense ramble.

'The people you mentioned who work at the lab? People who package the drugs? They would be mostly women, mothers, grandmothers? That the case? Dealers like workers they can trust with the product.'

'See why I wanted you here?' Mahoney said, and grinned – at least he showed me his front teeth. His tone reminded me of Jannie's rant earlier. A little bit of a wiseass masking his vulnerability about being such a 'man's man.'

'So the drug hijackers *and* the drug dealers are trapped inside? Why don't we just let them shoot each other?'

'Already been suggested,' Mahoney deadpanned. 'But now we get to the good part, Alex. Here's why you're here. The very well-armed guys who came to jack the lab are DC SWAT. Your old compadres are the *other* bad guys in today's episode of "Anything Can Happen and Probably Will!" You owe me ten bucks.'

I felt sick again. I knew a lot of guys with SWAT. 'You're sure about this?'

'Oh, yeah. Couple of patrolmen heard shots in the building. They went to investigate. One uniform got gut-shot. They recognized the guys from SWAT.'

I moved my head around in circles. Suddenly my

neck felt a little tight. 'So the FBI's HRT team is here to fight it out with DC SWAT?'

'Kind of looks that way, my man. Welcome to the suck and all that. You got any bright ideas so far?'

Yeah, I thought: *Leave here right now. Go back to the kids. It's a Saturday. I'm off.*

I handed Ned the ten dollars from our bet.

Chapter Twenty-Two

I sure didn't see any way out of this sticky mess, and neither did anyone else. That's why Mahoney had called me in, hoping I might have an idea to bail him out.

And of course, misery loves company, especially on a sunny afternoon when everybody wants to be anywhere but in the middle of a potential shoot-'em-up where people would probably die.

The first situation briefing took place in a nearby grade-school auditorium. It was jam-packed with Washington police personnel, but also FBI agents, including key members from the Hostage Rescue Team. HRT was ready to roll if it came to that, and it looked like it might happen soon.

Near the end of the briefing, Captain Tim Moran,

the head of SWAT for the metro police, restated the facts as he knew them. He had to be in a highly emotional state, for obvious reasons, but he appeared calm and in control. I knew Moran from my years on the force and respected his courage. Even more, I respected his integrity, and never more than I did that afternoon when he might have to go against his own men.

'To sum up the situation, the target is a four-story building where black-tar heroin was being turned into powder and a lot of cash. We have at least a dozen drug-lab workers inside, mostly women. We have the lab's guards – well armed and on at least three floors. Looks like about a dozen of them, too. And we have six SWAT members who attempted a robbery and got trapped inside.

'They apparently have a quantity of the heroin and cash in their possession. They're pinned down between drug dealers and other personnel on the top floors, and about half a dozen more armed guards who showed up while the robbery was in progress. At this point we're in a Mexican standoff. We've made initial contact with both sides. Nobody wants to give in. I guess they figure, what do they have to lose, or gain? So they're just sitting tight.'

Tim Moran continued in a calm voice. 'Because there

are members of SWAT inside, given the complications of it, the Hostage Rescue Team will take the lead here. Metro will give our full cooperation to the FBI.'

Captain Moran's summation was clear and concise, and it had taken some guts to hand the operation over to the FBI. But it was the right thing to do if somebody had to go inside and possibly fire on the SWAT guys. Even if they were bad cops, they were still cops. It didn't sit well with any of us to have to shoot at our brothers.

Ned Mahoney leaned in close to me. 'Now what do we do, Einstein? HRT is caught in the middle of a shit sandwich. See why I wanted you here?'

'Yeah, well, excuse me if I don't fall all over myself thanking you.'

'Ah, you're welcome anyway,' said Mahoney, and he punched my arm in a bullshit gesture of cama-raderie that made us both laugh.

Chapter Twenty-Three

*I*t was in his blood.

The Butcher was in the habit of monitoring metro police communications whenever he was in DC, and it was hard to miss this baby. What a royal cluster-fuck, he couldn't help thinking to himself. SWAT against Hostage Rescue. He loved it.

For the last few years he'd been cutting back on the kinds of jobs he did, 'working less, charging more.' Three or four major hits a year, plus a few favors for the bosses. That was more than enough to pay the bills. Besides, the new don, Maggione Jr, wasn't exactly a fan of his. The only real problem was that he missed the thrills, the adrenaline punch, the constant action. So here he was at the Policeman's Ball!

He was laughing as he parked his Range Rover a

dozen blocks from the potential firefight scene. Yes indeedee, the neighborhood was sure jumping. Even on foot, he couldn't get much closer than several blocks away on Kentucky Avenue. On his walk toward the crime scene, he'd already counted more than two dozen metro DC police department buses parked on the street. Plus dozens more squad cars.

Then he saw blue FBI Windbreakers – probably the Hostage Rescue boys up here from Quantico. Damn! They were supposed to be hot shits, right up there with the best in the world. Just like him. This was good stuff, and he wouldn't miss it for anything, even if it was a little dangerous for him to be here. He spotted several command-post vehicles next. And at the 'frozen zone,' or inner perimeter, he thought he picked out the 'incident commander.'

Then Michael Sullivan saw something that gave him pause and made his heart race a little. A dude in street clothes talking to one of the FBI agents.

Sullivan knew this guy, the one in civvies. His name was Alex Cross, and well, he and Sullivan had something of a history. And then he remembered something else – *Marianne, Marianne.* One of his favorite kills and photographs.

This was getting better and better by the minute.

Chapter Twenty-Four

I could definitely see why Ned Mahoney wanted me here.

A heroin factory estimated to have more than a hundred and fifty kilos of poison, street value at seven million. Cops versus cops. It looked like a no-win situation for everybody involved. I heard Captain Moran say, 'I'd tell you to go to hell, but I work there and I don't want to see you every day.' That sort of summed things up.

No one inside was showing signs of surrendering – not the drug dealers, not the guys from SWAT. They also weren't allowing any of the lab workers trapped on the fourth floor to leave. We had the names and approximate ages for some of the lab workers, and most of them were women, between fifteen and eighty-one. They were neighborhood people who couldn't find other jobs, usually because of language and education barriers, but who needed and wanted to work.

I wasn't doing a whole lot better than anybody else at figuring out a possible solution or an alternative plan. Maybe that was why I decided to take a walk outside the barricades at around ten. Try to clear my head. Maybe an idea would come if I physically put myself outside the box.

By now there were hundreds of spectators, including dozens of reporters and TV camera crews. I strolled a few blocks along M Street, my hands dug deep into my pockets.

I came to a crowded street corner where people from the neighborhood were being interviewed for TV. I was starting to walk by, lost in my thoughts, when I heard one of the women talking between wrenching sobs. 'That my flesh and blood trapped inside. Nobody care. Nobody give a damn!'

I stopped to listen to the interview. The woman couldn't have been more than twenty, and she was pregnant. From the look of her, she was due any day. Maybe tonight.

'My gramma is seventy-five. She inside to make money so my kids can go to Catholic school. Her name Rosario. She a beautiful lady. My gramma don't deserve to die.'

I listened to a few more emotional interviews, mostly with family members of the lab workers – but also a couple with the wives and kids of the drug crew trapped inside. One of the runners in there was just twelve years old.

Finally, I headed back inside the barricades, the inner perimeter, and I went looking for Ned Mahoney. I found him with some administrative types, suits, and Captain Moran outside one of the command-post vans. They were discussing shutting off the building's power.

'I've got an idea,' I told him.

'Well, it's about time.'

Chapter Twenty-Five

The Butcher was still hanging around the police barricades in Washington, and he knew he shouldn't be there. He was supposed to be home in Maryland hours ago. But this was worth it. The craziness of it all. He wandered through the crowd of looky-loos, and he was feeling like a kid let loose at a state fair, or at least what he thought a kid at a state fair would feel like.

Hell, they even had ice cream and hot dog vendors at the scene. People's eyes glistened with excitement; they wanted to see some real-life action. Well, hell, so did he, so did he.

He definitely was a crime-scene junkie, and he thought it stemmed from the days spent with his old man in Brooklyn. When he was little, his father used to take him on fire and police calls that he intercepted on his two-way. It was about the only good thing he ever did with the old man, and he figured it was because his father thought he'd look like less of a freak if he dragged a kid along beside him.

But his father *was* a freak. He liked to see dead bodies, any kind – on a slab of pavement, inside a crashed car, being hauled out of a smoldering building. His crazy old man was the *original* Butcher of Sligo – and much, much worse. Of course, *he* was the Butcher now, one of the most feared and sought-after assassins in the world. He was the Man, wasn't he? He could do whatever he wanted to, and that's what he was up to now.

Michael Sullivan was pulled out of his reverie by the sound of somebody talking into a mike at the hostage scene. He looked up, and it was the detective again – Alex Cross. It almost seemed like fate to him, like ghosts calling to the Butcher from the past.

Chapter Twenty-Six

I figured my idea was a long shot, and definitely out of left field, but it was worth it if it could save some lives. Plus, nobody had come up with anything better.

So at midnight we set up microphones behind a solid row of police cars and transport buses parked on the far side of Fifteenth. It looked impressive, if nothing else, and the TV cameras were all over it, of course.

For the next hour, I led family members up to tell their stories into the mikes, to reason and plead with the men inside to put down their weapons and leave the building, or at the very least to let the lab workers out. The speakers stressed that it was hopeless not to surrender and that many of those inside would die if they didn't. Some of the stories told at the mikes were heartbreaking, and I watched spectators tear up as they listened.

The best of the moments were anecdotes – a Sunday soccer game a father was supposed to referee; a wedding less than a week away; a pregnant girl who was supposed to be on bed rest but who came to plead with her drug-runner boyfriend. Both of them were eighteen.

Then we got an answer from inside.

It came while a twelve-year-old girl was talking about her father, one of the dealers. Gunshots erupted in the building!

The gunfire lasted for about five minutes, then stopped. We had no way of telling what had happened. We knew only one thing – the words of their loved ones had failed to move the men inside.

No one had come out; no one had surrendered.

'It's all right, Alex.' Ned took me aside. 'Maybe it bought us a little more time.' But that wasn't the result either of us was looking for. Not even close.

At one thirty, Captain Moran turned off the mikes outside. It looked like nobody was coming out. They had made their decision.

A little after two o'clock, it was decided by the higher-ups that the FBI's Hostage Rescue Team would go into the building first. They would be followed by a wave of DC police – but no one from SWAT. It was a tough-minded decision, but that's the way it was these days in Washington – maybe because of the terrorist activity over the past few years. People didn't seem to want to try to negotiate their way out of crisis situations anymore. I wasn't sure what side of the argument I was on, but I understood both.

Ned Mahoney and I would be part of the first assault team to go inside. We were assembled out on Fourteenth Street, directly behind the building under siege.

Most of our guys were pacing, restless, talking among themselves, trying to stay focused.

'This is a bad one,' Ned said. 'SWAT guys know how we think. Probably even that we're coming in tonight.'

'You know any of them? The SWAT team inside?' I asked.

Ned shook his head. 'We don't usually get invited to the same parties.'

Chapter Twenty-Seven

We dressed up in dark flight suits with full armor, and both Ned and I had MP5s. You could never predict too much about a night assault, but especially this one, with SWAT types on the inside and HRT as the force coming to get them.

Ned got a message on his headset, and he turned to me. 'Here we go, Alex. Keep your head down, buddy. These guys are as good as we are.'

'You do the same.'

But then the unexpected happened. And this time, it wasn't such a bad thing.

The front door to the building opened. For a few seconds, there was no activity at the door. What was going on in there?

Then an elderly woman dressed in a lab smock

wandered out into the bright lights aimed at the building. She held her hands up high and kept saying, 'Don't shoot me.'

She was followed by more women in lab coats, young and old, as well as two boys who looked to be twelve or thirteen at the most.

People behind the barricades were screaming out names. They were weeping for joy, clapping wildly.

Then the front door slammed shut again.

The exodus was over.

Chapter Twenty-Eight

The release of eleven lab workers stopped the full Hostage Rescue Team assault and opened up communications again. The police commissioner and the chief of detectives appeared on the scene and talked with Captain Moran. So did a couple of ministers from the community. Late as it was, the TV crews were still here shooting film.

At around three, we got word that we were going inside after all. Then there was another delay. *Hurry up and wait, hurry up and wait.*

At half past, we got the go. We were told it was final.

A few minutes past three thirty, Ned Mahoney and I were up and racing toward a side entrance into the building; so were a dozen other guys from HRT. The good thing about protective gear is that it might stop a fatal or damaging bullet; the bad thing is that it slows you down, makes it harder to run as fast as you need or want to, and forces your breath to come in gulps and gasps.

Snipers were taking out windows, trying to keep resistance from inside as low as possible.

Mahoney liked to call this drill 'five minutes of panic and thrills,' but I always dreaded it. To me, it was more like 'five minutes closer to heaven or hell.' I didn't need to be here, but Ned and I had done a couple of assaults together and I couldn't stay away.

A booming, earsplitting explosion took out the back door.

Suddenly, there were swirling clouds of black smoke and debris everywhere; then we were both running through it. I was hoping not to catch a bullet to the head or some other exposed body part in the next couple of minutes. I was hoping nobody had to die tonight.

Ned and I took fire right away, and we couldn't even tell who the hell was shooting at us. Drug dealers or the SWAT guys. Maybe both.

The sound of machine-guns and then grenades was deafening in the hallways and as we inched up a set of winding stairs. There was a whole lot of firepower inside the building now, maybe too much for it to hold together. The noise level made it hard to think straight or keep any focus.

'Hey! Assholes!' I heard somebody shout from above us. A volley of gunshots followed. Flashes of blinding light in the darkness.

Then Ned grunted and went down hard on the stairway.

I couldn't tell where he was hit at first; then I saw a wound near his collarbone. I didn't know if he'd been shot or struck with flying debris. There was a lot of blood spilling from the wound though.

I stayed right there with him, called for help on the radio. I heard more blasts, shouts, male and female screams coming above us. Chaos.

Ned's hands were shaking, and I hadn't seen him show fear of anything before. The firefight raging in the building only added to the terror and confusion. Ned's face had lost its color; he didn't look good.

'They're coming for you,' I told him. 'Stay with me, Ned. You hear me?'

'Stupid,' he finally said, groaning. 'Walked right into it.'

'You feeling it yet?'

'Could be worse. Could be better too. By the way,' he said, '*you're* hit too.'

Chapter Twenty-Nine

'I'll live,' I told Ned as I huddled over him on the stairwell.

'Yeah, me too. Probably, anyway.'

A couple of minutes later, the paramedics were with us in the cramped space. By the time they got Ned out of there, the gunfight seemed to be over. Just like he always said – *five minutes of panic and thrills.*

Reports started to come in. Captain Tim Moran gave the latest to me himself. The assault on the heroin factory seemed to have had mixed results. Most of us felt we shouldn't have gone in so soon – but it wasn't our decision. Two metro officers and two from HRT were wounded on our side. Ned was headed into surgery.

There were six casualties among those inside the

building, including two men from SWAT. A seven-teen-year-old mother of two was one of the dead. For some reason she'd stayed inside when the lab workers came out. The girl's husband had died too. He was sixteen.

I finally got home at a little past six in the morning. I was dragging, wasted, bone tired, and something about coming in so late, or early, seemed surreal.

It only got worse. Nana was up waiting in the kitchen.

Chapter Thirty

S he was sitting over toast and a cup of tea, looking infirm, but I knew better.

The hot beverage was steaming, and so was she. She hadn't gotten the kids up yet. Her small TV was tuned to the local news reports on last night's police action at Kentucky and Fifteenth. It felt unreal to see the footage right here in our kitchen.

Nana's eyes fixed on the scrape on the side of my forehead – the *bandage* there.

'It's a scratch,' I said. 'Not a big deal. It's all good. I'm fine.'

'Don't give me that ridiculous nonsense answer, Alex. Don't you dare condescend to me like I'm somebody's fool. I'm looking at the line of trajectory taken by a bullet that came an inch from splattering your brains and leaving your three poor children orphans. No mother, no father. Am I wrong about that? No, of course not!

'I am *so* sick of this though, Alex. I have been living with this sort of terrible dread every single day for over ten years. This time I've had it. Up to *here.* I've truly had enough. I'm done with it. I'm through! I quit! Yes, you heard me *correctly.* I quit you and the children! *I quit!'*

I put up both my hands in defense. 'Nana, I was out with the kids when I got an emergency call. I had no idea the call was coming. How could I? There was nothing I could do to stop what happened.'

'You accepted the call, Alex. Then you accepted the assignment. You always do. You call it dedication, duty. I call it total insanity, madness.'

'I. Didn't. Have. An. Option.'

'You do have an option, Alex. That's my whole point. You could have said no, that you were out with your kids. What do you think they would do, Alex – fire you for having a life? For being a father? And if by some accident of good fortune they did fire you, then so be it.'

'I don't know what they *could* do, Nana. Eventually I suppose they would fire me.'

'And is that such a bad thing? Is it? Oh, forget it!'

she said, and banged her mug down hard against the tabletop. 'I'm leaving!' she said.

'Oh, for God's sake, this is ridiculous, Nana. I'm totally exhausted. I was shot. *Almost* shot. We'll talk about it later. I need to sleep right now.'

Suddenly Nana stood up, and she moved in my direction. Her face was wild with outrage, her eyes tiny black beads. I hadn't seen her like this in years, maybe not since I was growing up, and a little on the wild side myself.

'*Ridiculous?* You call this ridiculous? How dare you say that to me?'

Nana struck me in the chest with the heels of both her hands. The blows didn't hurt, but their intent did, the truth of her words did. 'I'm sorry,' I said. 'I'm just tired.'

'Get yourself a housekeeper, a nanny, whatever you can get for yourself. *You're* exhausted? *I'm* exhausted. I'm fed up and exhausted and sick to death of worrying about you!'

'Nana, I'm sorry. What else do you want me to say?'

'Nothing, Alex. Don't say anything. I'm tired of listening to you anyway.'

She stomped off to her room without another word. Well, at least that was over, I thought as I sat down at the kitchen table, tired and depressed as hell now.

But it wasn't over.

Minutes later, Nana reappeared in the kitchen, and she was lugging an ancient leather suitcase and a smaller traveling bag on wheels. She walked past me, through the dining room, and then right out the front door without another peep.

'Nana!' I called, struggling up from my seat, then starting to jog after her. 'Stop. Please, stop and talk to me. Let's talk.'

'I'm *through* talking!'

I got to the door and saw a dented and gashed pale-blue DC Cab throwing off exhaust fumes and plumes of smoke out front on the street. One of her many cousins, Abraham, drove for DC Cabs. I could see the back of his retro Afro from the porch.

Nana climbed into the ugly blue taxi, and it immediately sputtered away from the house.

Then I heard a small voice. 'Where's Nana going?'

I turned and lifted Ali, who had snuck around behind me on the porch. 'I don't know, little man. I think she just quit on us.'

He looked aghast. 'Nana quit our family?'

Chapter Thirty-One

Michael Sullivan woke with an awful shudder and a start and knew immediately he wouldn't be able to get back to sleep. He'd been dreaming about his father again, the scary bastard, the boogeyman of all his nightmares.

When he was a little kid, the old man had brought him to work at his butcher shop two or three times a week in the summer. This went on from the time he was six until he was eleven, when it ended. The shop took up the ground floor of a two-story redbrick building on Quentin Road and East Thirty-sixth Street. KEVIN SULLIVAN, BUTCHER was known for having the best meats in all of the Flatlands section of Brooklyn, but also for his skill in catering not just to the Irish but to Italian and German tastes.

The sawdust on the floor was always thick and swept clean every day. The glass in the windows of the cases sparkled. And Kevin Sullivan had a trademark – after he presented a customer's meat for inspection, he smiled, and then took a polite bow. His little bow got them every time.

Michael, his mother, and his three brothers knew another side of his father though. Kevin Sullivan had massive arms and the most powerful hands imaginable, especially in the eyes of a young boy. One time he caught a rat in the kitchen and crushed the vermin in his bare hands. He told his sons he could do the same thing to them, crush their bones to sawdust, and their mother seldom went a week without a purplish bruise appearing somewhere on her frail, thin body.

But that wasn't the worst of it, and it wasn't what had woken Sullivan that night and so many other times during his life. The real horror story had begun when he was six and they were cleaning up after closing one evening. His father called him into the shop's small office, which held a desk, a file cabinet, and a cot. Kevin Sullivan was sitting on the cot, and he told Michael to sit next to him. 'Right here, boy. By my side.'

'I'm sorry, Dad,' Michael said immediately, knowing

this had to be about some dumb mistake he'd made during his chores. 'I'll make up for it. I'll do it right.'

'Just sit!' said his father. 'You have plenty to be sorry for, but that's not it. Now you listen. You listen to me good.'

His father put his hand on the boy's knee. 'You know how badly I can hurt you, Michael,' he said. 'You know that, right?'

'Yes, sir, I know.'

'And I *will*,' his father continued, 'if you tell a single living soul.'

Tell them what? Michael wanted to ask, but he knew better than to say a word, to interrupt his father once he had begun to speak.

'Not a solitary soul.' His father squeezed his son's leg until tears formed in Michael's eyes.

And then his father leaned forward and kissed the boy on the mouth, and did other things that no father should ever do to his son.

Chapter Thirty-Two

His father had been dead for a long time now, but the creepy bastard was never far enough away from Sullivan's thoughts, and in fact he had devised unusual ways to escape from his childhood demons.

Around four the next afternoon he went shopping at Tysons Galleria in McLean, Virginia. He was looking for something very special: just the right girl. He wanted to play a game called Red Light, Green Light.

During the next half hour at the Galleria, he approached a few possible game players outside Saks Fifth Avenue, then Neiman Marcus, then Lillie Rubin.

His pitch was straightforward and didn't vary. Big smile, then: 'Hi. My name is Jeff Carter. Could I ask you a couple of questions? You mind? I'll be quick, I promise.'

The fifth or sixth woman he approached had a very pretty, innocent face – a Madonna's face – and she listened to what he had to say. Four of the women he'd hit on before her were pleasant enough. One was even flirty, but they had all walked away. He had no problem with that. He liked bright people, and the women were just being cautious about the pickup game. What was the old saying? *Don't pick that up, you have no way of knowing where it's been.*

'Well, not exactly questions,' he went on with his sales pitch to the Madonna of the Galleria. 'Let me put it another way. If I say anything that bothers you, I'll stop and walk away. That sound fair enough? Like Red Light, Green Light.'

'That's a little weird,' said the dark-haired girl. She had a truly gorgeous face and a nice body from what he could tell. Her voice was somewhat monotone – but hey, nobody's perfect. Other than maybe himself.

'But it's harmless,' he went on. 'I like your boots, by the way.'

'Thanks. It doesn't bother me to hear that you like them. I like 'em too.'

'You have a nice smile too. You *know* that you do, right? Sure you do.'

'Careful now. Don't lay it on too thick.'

They both laughed, hitting it off okay, Sullivan was

thinking to himself. The game was on anyway. He just had to avoid getting a red light.

'Okay if I go on?' he asked. *Always ask their permission.* That was a rule he had whenever he played. *Always be polite.*

She shrugged, rolled her soft brown eyes, shifted her weight from one booted foot to the other. 'I guess. We've gone this far, haven't we?'

'A thousand dollars,' Sullivan said. This was where you usually won or lost the game. Right . . . now.

The Madonna's smile disappeared – but she didn't walk away. Sullivan's heart started to pound. He had her going, leaning his way. Now he just had to close the sale.

'Nothing funny. I promise,' Sullivan said quickly, pouring on the charm without being too obvious about it.

The Madonna frowned. 'You promise, huh?'

'One hour,' Sullivan said. The trick here was *how* you said it. It had to sound like no big deal, nothing threatening, nothing out of the ordinary. *Just an hour. Just a thousand dollars. Why not? What's the harm?*

'Red light,' she said, and walked away from him in a huff, never even looked back. He could tell she was pissed too.

Sullivan was mad, his heart still beating hard, and

something else was rock hard as well. He wanted to grab the Madonna and strangle her in the middle of the mall. Really mess her up. But he loved this little game he'd invented. Red Light, Green Light.

Half an hour later, he was trying his luck outside the Victoria's Secret at the nearby Tysons Corner Mall – he got to 'one hour' with a dreamy blonde in a Jersey Girl T-shirt and short shorts. No luck though, and he was really getting hot and bothered now. He needed a win, needed to get laid, needed an adrenaline hit.

The next girl he approached had beautiful, shimmering red hair. Great body. Long legs and small, lively tits that moved around in rhythm when she talked. At the 'one hour' prompt, she folded her slender arms over her chest. Talk about body language, wow! But Red didn't walk away from him. Conflicted? Sure. He loved that in a woman.

'You're in control the whole time. You choose the hotel or your place. Whatever you want, whatever seems right. It's all up to you.'

She looked at him for a moment, silent, and he knew that she was sizing him up – they stared right into your eyes at this point. He could tell that this one trusted her instincts. *It's all up to you.* Plus, she either wanted, or needed, the thousand dollars. And, of course, he was cute.

Finally, Red spoke in a quiet voice, because nobody else was supposed to hear this, right? 'You have the cash on you?'

He showed her a roll of hundreds.

'They all hundreds?' she asked.

He showed her that they were. 'You mind if I ask you your name?' he said.

'Sherry.'

'That your real name?'

'Whatever, *Jeff.* Let's go. The clock is running. Your hour's already begun.'

And off they went.

After his hour with Sherry was over, closer to an hour and a half actually, Michael Sullivan didn't have to give her any money. Not a thousand, not a nickel. All he had to do was show Sherry his picture collection – and a scalpel he had brought along.

Red Light, Green Light.

Hell of a game.

Chapter Thirty-Three

Two days after she walked out on us, Nana was back at the house, thank God and the heavenly choir, who had to be watching over us. The whole family, but especially me, had learned a lesson about how much we loved Nana and needed her; how many small, often unnoticed and thankless things she did for us every day; how totally indispensable she was, and the sacrifices she made.

Not that Nana ever really let us forget her contributions under ordinary circumstances. It was just that she was even better than she thought she was.

When she waltzed in the kitchen door that morning, she caught Jannie eating Cocoa Puffs and let her have it in her own inimitable style: 'My name is Janelle Cross. *I am a substance abuser,*' Nana said.

Jannie raised both arms over her head in surrender; then she went and emptied the chocolate cereal right into the trash. She looked Nana in the eye, said, 'If you're a vehicle traveling at the speed of light, what happens when you switch on the headlights?' Then she hugged Nana before she could try to answer the unanswerable.

I went and hugged Nana too and was smart enough to keep my mouth shut but my powder dry.

When I got home from work that night, my grand-mother was waiting for me in the kitchen. Uh-oh, I thought, but the second she saw me, Nana put her arms out for a hug, which surprised me. 'Come,' she said.

When I was in her arms, she continued, 'I'm sorry, Alex. I had no right to run away and leave you all like that. I was in the wrong. I missed all of you as soon as I was in the cab with Abraham.'

'You had every right—' I started to say.

Nana cut me off. 'Now don't argue with me, Alex. For once, quit while you're ahead.'

I did as I was told, and shut up.

Chapter Thirty-Four

*B*ig stuff – *now here we go.* On Friday morning of that week, at a few minutes past nine o'clock, I found myself all alone in the alcove outside Director Ron Burns's office on the ninth floor of the Hoover Building, FBI headquarters.

The director's assistant, Tony Woods, peeked his round, deceptively cherubic face out of Burns's outer office.

'Hey, Alex, there you are. Why don't you come on in. Good job the other day on Kentucky Avenue. Under the circumstances especially. The director's been wanting to talk to you about it and some other things he has on his mind. I heard Ned Mahoney's going to make a full recovery.'

Terrific job – I almost got myself killed, I thought as

I followed Woods into the inner office. Ned Mahoney got shot in the neck. He could have died too.

The director was there waiting for me in his sanctum sanctorum. Ron Burns has a kind of funny way about him: He's a hard-charging guy, but he's learned to make meaningless small talk and smile a lot before he gets down to business. That's pretty much a requirement in Washington, especially if you have to deal with as many sneaky politicians as he does. Like many A-type business-minded men, though, Burns is pretty awful at small talk. But we chatted about local sports and the weather for a good ninety seconds before we got into the real reason for my visit.

'So what's on your mind these days?' Burns asked. 'Tony said you wanted to see me, so I take it this isn't purely a social call. I have a few things to go over with you too. A new assignment for starters: a serial up in Maine and Vermont of all places.'

I nodded and let Burns rattle on. But suddenly I was feeling tense and a little unsure of myself. Finally, I had to cut him off. 'There's no good way to ease into this, Director, so I'll just say it. I'm here to tell you that I'm going to be leaving the Bureau. This is very difficult, and it's embarrassing. I appreciate everything you've done for me, but I've made a decision for my family. It's final. I'm not going to change my mind.'

'*Shit*,' Burns said, and he hit his desk hard with the palm of his hand. 'Damn it all to hell, Alex. Why would you leave us now? It makes no sense to me. You're on a very fast track at the Bureau. You know that, right? Tell you what, I'm *not* going to let you do it.'

'Nothing you can do to stop me,' I told him. 'I'm sorry, but I'm sure I'm doing the right thing. I've thought this through a hundred times in the last few days.'

Burns stared into my eyes, and he must have seen something resolute there, because he stood up behind his desk. Then he came around it with his hand outstretched.

'You're making a terrible mistake, and an atrociously bad career move, but I can tell there's no point in arguing with you. It's been a real pleasure, Alex, and an education,' he said as we shook hands. We made some more uncomfortable chitchat for the next couple of minutes. Then I got up to leave his office.

As I reached the door, Burns called, 'Alex, I hope I can still call on you from time to time. I can, can't I?'

I laughed in spite of myself, because the remark was so typical of Burns's never-say-die attitude. 'You can call on me *eventually*. But why don't you give it a few months, okay?'

'Couple of days anyway,' said Burns, and at least he winked when he said it.

We both laughed, and suddenly it sank in – my brief, somewhat illustrious career with the FBI was over and done with.

Also, I was unemployed.

Chapter Thirty-Five

I'm not a big fan of looking back on the stages of my life with anything like regret, and anyway, my time at the FBI had been mostly very good and probably even valuable in the long run. I'd learned things, accomplished a fair amount – like stopping a Russian Mafia psycho called the Wolf. And I'd made some good friends – the head of Hostage Rescue, maybe even the director – which couldn't hurt and might even help me out someday.

Still, I wasn't prepared for the incredible feeling of relief I experienced as I carried a cardboard box stuffed full of my possessions out of the FBI building that morning. It felt as if at least a couple of hundred pounds of dead weight had been lifted off my shoulders, a burden I hadn't even known was there. I didn't know for sure if I'd just made a good decision, but it sure felt like it.

No more monsters, human or otherwise, I was thinking to myself.

No more monsters ever.

I headed toward home at a little before noon. Free at last. I had the car windows open and was listening to Bob Marley's 'No Woman, No Cry,' the words blasting from the radio. I was singing along. I didn't have a plan for what I was going to do next, not even for the rest of the day – and it felt pretty terrific. Actually, I liked the idea of doing nothing for a while, and I was beginning to think I might be pretty good at it too.

There was something I needed to do right now, while I was in the mood. I drove out to the Mercedes dealership and found the salesperson Laurie Berger. I took a test drive in the R350, and all that leg room was even more fun on the open highway than it had been in the showroom. I liked the vehicle's zip and also the dual-dash zone climate control, which would keep everybody happy, even Nana Mama.

But even more important, it was time for the family and me to move away from Maria's old car. It was time, I had money from my books in savings, and so I bought the R350 and felt wonderful about it.

When I got home, I found a note from Nana on the kitchen table. It was meant for Jannie and Damon, but I read it anyway.

Go out and get some fresh air, you two. There's coq au vin in the Crock-Pot. Delicious! Set the table for me, please. And get a start on your homework before dinner. Damon has choir tonight. Remember to 'support your breath,' young man. Aunt Tia and I have taken Ali to the zoo, and WE'RE LOVING IT.

Your Nana isn't here, but I'm watching you anyway!

I couldn't help smiling. This woman had saved me a long time ago, and now she was saving my kids.

I'd been hoping to hang out with Ali, but there would be plenty of time for that in the near future. So I fixed myself a leftover pork and coleslaw sandwich, and then for some strange reason I made popcorn for one.

Why? Why not! I don't even like popcorn that much, but suddenly I was in the mood for some hot, buttered junk food. Free to be me; free to be stupid if I wanted to.

I ate the freshly popped popcorn and played the piano for a couple of hours that afternoon – Duke

Ellington, Jelly Roll Morton, Al Green. I read several chapters from a book called *The Shadow of the Wind.* And then I did the truly unthinkable – I took a nap in the middle of the day. Before I drifted off, I thought about Maria again, the best of times, our honeymoon at Sandy Lane in Barbados. What a blast that had been. How much I still missed her and wished she was here right now to hear my news.

For the rest of the afternoon, the phone never rang once. I didn't have a pager anymore, and in the words of Nana Mama – *I was loving it.*

Nana and Ali came home together, then came Jannie, and finally Damon. Their staggered arrivals gave me the chance to show off our new car three times, and to get their praise and applause *three times.* What a fine, fine day this was turning out to be.

That night at dinner we chowed down on Nana's delicious Frenchified chicken, and I kept the big news to myself until the end of the meal – pumpkin ice cream and café au lait.

Jannie and Damon wanted to eat and run, but I kept everybody sitting at the table. Jannie wanted to get back to her book. She was tripping out on *Eragon* these days, which was okay, I guess, but I didn't understand why it is that kids have to read the same book half a dozen times.

'What now?' she asked, rolling her eyes as though she already knew the answer.

'I have some news,' I said to her, and to everybody else.

The kids looked at one another, and Jannie and Damon shared a frown and a head shake. They all thought they knew what was coming next – that I was leaving town on a new murder investigation, probably a serial. Maybe even tonight, just like I always did.

'I'm not going anywhere,' I said, and grinned broadly. 'Quite the opposite actually. In fact, I'm going to attend Damon's choir practice tonight. I want to listen to that *joyful noise.* I want to see how well he *supports his breath* these days.'

'You're going to choir practice?' Damon exclaimed. 'What, is there some *killer* in our singing group?'

I was purposely stretching it out some, my eyes methodically going from face to face. I could tell that none of them had a clue what was coming next. Not even our crafty, know-it-all Nana had figured it out yet.

Jannie finally looked down at Ali. 'Make him tell us what's going on, Ali. Make him talk.'

'C'mon, Daddy,' said the little man, who was already a skillful manipulator. 'Tell us. Before Janelle goes crazy.'

'All right, all right, all right. Here's the deal. I'm afraid I have to tell you that I'm now unemployed, and that we're practically destitute. Well, not really. Anyway, this morning I resigned from the FBI. For the rest of the day I did nothing. Tonight, it's the rehearsal of "Cantante Domino" for me.'

Nana Mama and the kids went wild with applause. 'Des-ti-tute! Des-ti-tute!' the kids began to chant.

And you know what? It had a nice ring to it.

So did *no more monsters.*

Chapter Thirty-Six

The next beat in the story went like this. John Sampson was a star in the Washington PD these days. Ever since Alex left the department and moved over to the FBI, Sampson's reputation had been rising, not that it hadn't been on a high level before, not that Sampson didn't get a lot of respect for all sorts of reasons. The curious thing, though, was that Sampson couldn't have given a rat's ass. Peer approval had never meant much of anything to the Big Man. Unless maybe it was Alex's, and even that was a hit-and-miss thing.

His latest case was definitely a challenge. Maybe because he hated the bad actor he was trying to bring down. The scum in question, Gino 'Greaseball' Giametti, operated strip joints and massage parlors as far south as Fort Lauderdale and Miami. His sideline was catering to pervs who needed adolescent girls, sometimes prepubescent ones. Giametti himself was obsessed with the so-called Lolita complex.

'*Capo*,' Sampson muttered under his breath as he drove up Giametti's street in the ritzy Kalorama section of DC. The self-important term referred to *capitano*, a captain in the Mafia. Gino Giametti had been a significant earner for years. He'd been one of the first mobsters to figure out that big money could be made bringing in pretty young girls from the former Soviet bloc, especially Russia, Poland, and the Czech Republic. That was his specialty, and it was the reason Sampson was riding his ass now. His one regret was that Alex couldn't be with him on this bust. This was going to be a sweet takedown.

At a little past midnight, he pulled up in front of Giametti's house. The mobster didn't live too extravagantly, but all his needs were met. That was how the Mafia took care of its own.

Sampson peered into his rearview and saw two more cars ease up against the curb directly behind him. He spoke into a mike sticking out from his shirt collar. 'Good evening, gents. I think this is going to be a fine night. I can feel it in my bones. Let's go wake up the Greaseball.'

Chapter Thirty-Seven

Sampson's partner these days was a twenty-eight-year-old detective named Marion Handler, who was almost as big as Sampson was. Handler was certainly no Alex Cross, though. He was currently living with a large-breasted but small-minded cheerleader for the Washington Redskins, and he was looking to make a name for himself in Homicide. 'I'm fast-tracking, dude,' he liked to say to Sampson, without a hint of humor or self-effacement.

Just being around the cocky detective was exhausting, and also depressing. The man was plain stupid; worse, he was arrogant about it, flaunting his frequent logic lapses.

'I'll take the point on this one,' Handler announced as they reached the front porch of Giametti's house.

Four other detectives, one holding a battering ram, were already waiting at the door. They looked to Sampson for direction.

'Take the lead? No problem, Marion. Be my guest,' he said to Handler. Then he added, 'First in, first to the morgue.' He spoke to the detective holding the battering ram: 'Take it down! Detective Handler goes in first.'

The front door collapsed in two powerful strikes with the ram. The house alarm system began to wail, and the detectives hurried inside.

Sampson's eyes took in the darkened kitchen. Nobody there. New appliances everywhere. An iPod and CDs scattered on the floor. Kids in the house.

'He's downstairs,' Sampson told the others. 'Giametti doesn't sleep with his wife anymore.'

The detectives hurried down steep wooden stairs on the far side of the kitchen. They hadn't been inside more than twenty seconds. In the basement, they burst in the first door they came to. 'Metro Police! Hands up. Now, Giametti,' Marion Handler's voice boomed.

The Greaseball was up quickly. He stood in a protective crouch on the far side of the king-size bed. He was a short, potbellied, hirsute man in his mid-forties. He looked groggy and still out of it, maybe drugged up. But John Sampson wasn't fooled by his physical appearance – this man was a stone-cold killer. And much worse.

A pretty, naked young girl with long blond hair and fair skin was still on the bed. She tried to cover her small breasts and shaved genital area. Sampson knew her name, Paulina Sroka, and that she was from Poland originally. Sampson had known she would be here and that Giametti was rumored to be madly in love with the blond beauty he'd imported from Europe six months ago. According to sources, the Greaseball had killed the girl's best friend because she'd refused to have anal sex with him.

'You don't have to be afraid,' Sampson said to Paulina. 'We're the Washington police. You're not in any trouble. *He* is.'

'Just shut the hell up!' Giametti yelled at the girl, who looked both confused and scared. 'Don't say a word to them! Not a word, Paulie! I'm warning you!'

Sampson moved faster than it looked like he could. He threw Giametti on the floor, then cuffed him like a steer at a rodeo.

'Don't say a word!' Giametti continued to yell, even though his face was pressed into the shag rug. 'Don't talk to them, Paulie! I'm warning you! You hear me?'

The girl looked pathetic and lost as she sat among

the rumpled bedsheets, attempting to cover herself with a man's shirt she'd been given by the detectives.

She finally spoke in the softest whisper. 'He make me do anything he say. He do everything bad to me. You know what I am saying – everything you could imagine. I can hardly walk . . . I am fourteen years old.'

Sampson turned to Handler. 'You can take it from here, Marion. Get him the hell out of here. I don't want to touch the slime.'

Chapter Thirty-Eight

An hour later, Gino Giametti was basted, then grilled until he was well done under bright lights in Investigation Room No. 1 at the First District station house. Sampson wouldn't take his eyes off the vicious gangster, who had a disturbing habit of scratching his scalp compulsively, hard enough to make it bleed. Giametti didn't seem to notice it himself.

Marion Handler had carried the show so far, done most of the preliminary questioning, but Giametti didn't have much to say to him. Sampson sat back and observed, sizing up *both* men.

So far, Giametti was getting the best of it. He was a lot smarter than he looked. 'I woke up and Paulie was sleeping in my bed. *Sleeping* – just like when you busted in. What can I tell you? She has her own bedroom upstairs. She's a scared little girl. Crazy some-times, too. Paulie does housekeeping and shit like that for my wife. We wanted to put her in the local schools. The best schools. We were letting her work on her English first. Hey, we were trying to do the right thing by that kid, so why are you busting my balls?'

Sampson finally pushed himself forward in his seat. He'd heard enough bullshit for tonight. 'Anybody ever tell you you could do stand-up?' he asked. *And, Marion, you could be his straight man.*

'Matter of fact, yeah,' Giametti said, and smirked. 'Couple of people told me that exact same thing. You know what? I think they were cops too.'

'Paulina has already told us she saw you kill her friend Alexa. Alexa was sixteen years old when she died. The girl was garroted!'

Giametti slammed his fist down on the table in front of him. 'The crazy little bitch. Paulie is lying through her teeth. What'd you do, threaten to send her back? Deport her to Poland? That's her biggest fear.'

Sampson shook his head. 'No, I said we'd help her stay in America if we could. Get her into school. The best. Do the right thing by her.'

'She's lying, and she's nuts. I'm telling you, that pretty little girl is two kinds of crazy.'

Sampson nodded slowly. 'She's lying? All right, then how about Roberto Gallo? Is he lying too? He saw you kill Alexa and stuff the body in the trunk of your Lincoln. He made that up?'

'Of course he made it up. That's total bullshit; it's complete crap. You know it. I know it. Bobby Gallo knows it. Alexa? Who the hell is Alexa? *Paulie's imaginary friend?'*

Sampson shrugged his broad shoulders. 'How would I know Gallo's story is bullshit?'

'Because it *never* happened, that's how! Because Bobby Gallo probably made a deal with you.'

'You mean – it didn't happen that way? Gallo wasn't actually an eyewitness? But Paulina was. Is that what you're saying?'

Giametti frowned and shook his head. 'You think I'm stupid, Detective Sampson? I'm not stupid.'

Sampson spread his hands to indicate the small, very bright interview room. 'But here you are.'

Giametti thought about it for a few seconds. Then he gestured toward Handler. 'Tell Junior here to go take a nice long walk off a short pier. I want to talk to you. Just you and me, big man.'

Sampson looked over at Marion Handler. He shrugged and rolled his eyes. 'Why don't you take a break, Marion?'

Handler didn't like it, but he got up and left the interrogation room. He made a lot of noise on the way out, like a petulant high school kid who'd just been given detention.

Sampson didn't say anything once he and Giametti were alone. He was still observing the mobster, trying to get under the punk's skin. The guy was a murderer – that much he knew. And Giametti also had to know that he was up shit creek right now. *Paulina Sroka was fourteen years old.*

'The strong, silent type?' Giametti smirked again. 'That your act, big boy?'

Still not a word from Sampson. It went on that way for several minutes.

Giametti finally leaned forward, and he spoke in a quiet, serious voice. 'Look, you know this is bullshit, right? No murder weapon. No body. I didn't clip any little Polack girl named Alexa. And Paulie *is* crazy. Trust me on that one. She's young in years, but she's no little girl. She was hooking in the old country. You know about that?'

Sampson finally spoke. 'Here's what I know, and what I can prove. You were having sex with a four-teen-year-old in your own house.'

Giametti shook his head. 'She's not fourteen. She's a little *whore*. Anyway, I have something for you, something to trade. It's about a friend of yours – *Alex Cross*. You listening, Detective? Hear this. I know who killed his wife. I know where he is now too.'

Chapter Thirty-Nine

John Sampson got out of his car slowly. He trudged along the familiar stone walkway, then up the front stairs of the Cross family house on Fifth Street.

He hesitated at the door, trying to collect his thoughts, to calm himself down if he could. This wasn't going to be easy, and no one would know this better than he did. He knew things about Maria Cross's murder that even Alex didn't.

Finally, he reached forward and rang the bell. He must have done this a thousand times in his life, but it never felt like it did now.

No good would come of this visit. Nothing good whatsoever. It might even end a long friendship.

A moment later, Sampson was surprised that it was Nana Mama who came to the door. The old girl was dressed in a flowery blue robe and looked even tinier than usual, like an ancient bird that ought to be worshiped. And in this house, she surely was, even by him.

'John, what's the matter now? What is it? I'm almost afraid to ask. Well, come inside, come inside. You'll scare all the neighbors.'

'They're already scared, Nana,' Sampson drawled, and attempted a smile. 'This is Southeast, remember?'

'Don't try to make a joke out of this, John. Don't you dare. What are you here for?'

Sampson suddenly felt like he was a teenager again, caught in one of Nana's infamous stern glares. There was something so damn familiar about this scene. It reminded him of the time he and Alex got caught stealing records at Grady's while they were in middle school. Or the time they were smoking weed behind John Carroll High School and got busted by an assistant principal, and Nana had to come to get them released.

'I have to talk to Alex,' Sampson said. 'It's important, Nana. We need to wake him up.'

'And why is that?' she asked, tapping one extended foot. 'Quarter past three in the morning. Alex doesn't work for the city of Washington anymore. Why can't everybody just leave him be? You of all people, John

Sampson. You know better than to come around here now, middle of the night, looking for his help again.'

Sampson didn't usually argue with Nana Mama, but this time he did. 'I'm afraid it can't wait, Nana. And I don't need Alex's help this time. He needs mine.'

Then Sampson walked right past Nana and into the Cross house – uninvited.

Chapter Forty

It was almost 4:00 a.m., and Sampson and I were riding back to the First District station house in his car. I was wide awake now, and wired. My nervous system felt like it was vibrating.

Maria's murderer? After all these years? Was it even a faint possibility that the killer could be caught so many years after my wife was shot down? The whole thing felt unreal to me. Back then, I'd been all over the case for a year, and I'd never completely given up the chase. And now we might suddenly find the killer? Was it possible?

We arrived at the station house on Fourth Street and hurried inside, neither of us talking. A precinct house during the night shift can be a lot like an emergency room: you never know what to expect when you step inside. This time, I didn't have a clue, but I couldn't wait to talk to Giametti.

It seemed unusually quiet when we walked in the front door – but that all changed in a hurry. It was obvious to both Sampson and me that something was wrong when we got down to the holding cells. Half a dozen detectives and uniforms were standing around. They looked way too alert and anxious for this time of morning. Something was definitely up.

Sampson's new partner, Marion Handler, spotted us and hustled over to John. Handler ignored me, and I did my best to pay him no mind, either. I'd talked to him a couple of times, and I thought the detective was a showy punk. I wondered why John put up with him the way he did. Maybe he saw something in Handler that I didn't, or maybe Sampson was finally mellowing just a little.

'You're not gonna believe this shit. It's off the charts,' he said to Sampson. 'Somebody got to Giametti. I shit you not, Sampson. He's over there dead in his cell. Somebody got to him in here.'

I was feeling numb all over as Handler led us back to the last holding cell on the block. I couldn't believe what I'd just heard. First we had a lead on Maria's killer's whereabouts, and then the man who gave us that lead was murdered? In here?

'He even had a private room,' Handler said to Sampson. 'How could they get to him in here? Right under our noses?'

Sampson and I ignored the question as we stepped inside the last cell on the right. There were two evidence techies working around the body, but I could see all I needed to. An ice pick had been driven right up Gino Giametti's nose. It looked like the pick had been used to gouge out his eyes first.

'See no evil,' said Sampson in his deep, flat voice. 'Has to be the mob.'

Chapter Forty-One

When I got home later that morning, I knew I wouldn't be able to sleep very well. So what was new about that? The kids were off at school, Nana was out; the house was quiet as a tomb.

Nana had put up another of her goofy 'mistake' newspaper headlines on the fridge: JUVENILE COURT TO TRY SHOOTING VICTIM. Pretty funny, but I wasn't in the mood for smiles, even at the expense of journalists. I played the piano on the sunporch and drank a glass of red wine, but nothing seemed to help.

I could see Maria's face and hear her voice inside my head. I wondered, Why do we begin to forget, then sometimes remember with such clarity people we've lost? Everything about Maria, about our time together, seemed to have been stirred up inside me again.

Finally, around ten thirty, I went upstairs to my room. There had been too many days and nights like this. I would make my way up to bed and sleep there alone. What was that all about?

I lay down on the bed and shut my eyes, but I didn't really expect to sleep, just rest. I'd been thinking about Maria since I left the station house on Fourth Street. Some of the images I saw were of Maria and me when the kids were little – the good and the hard parts, too, not just selective memories of the sentimental stuff.

I tensed up in bed thinking about her, and I finally understood something useful about the present – that I wanted my life to make sense again. Simple enough, right? But could it still happen? Could I move on?

Well, *maybe*. There was somebody. Somebody I cared about enough to make some changes for. Or was I just fooling myself again? I finally drifted off into a restless, dreamless sleep, which was about as good as it got these days.

Chapter Forty-Two

All I had to do was move on, right? Make some intelligent changes in my life. I'd gotten rid of Maria's old junker and moved onward and upward to our cross-vehicle. What could be so hard about making some other changes? And why did I keep failing at it?

Alex has a big date, I told myself at various times during the following Friday. That's why I'd picked the New Heights Restaurant on Calvert Street over in Woodley Park. New Heights was a big-date sort of place. Dr Kayla Coles was meeting me there after she finished work – early by her standards anyway – at nine.

I took a seat at our table, partly because I was afraid they might give it away if Kayla showed up late – which she did, at around quarter after.

Her being late didn't matter to me. I was just happy to see her. Kayla is a pretty woman, with a radiant smile, but more important, I like spending time with her. It seems like we always have something to talk about. Just the opposite of a lot of couples I know.

'*Wow,*' I said, and winked when I saw her gliding across the dining room. She had on flats, possibly because she's five foot ten without them, or maybe just because she's sane and can't stand the discomfort of heels.

'Wow, yourself! You look good too, Alex. And this *view.* I love this place.'

I had asked to be seated at a bank of windows overlooking Rock Creek Park, and it was kind of spectacular, I had to admit. The same could be said for Kayla, who was decked out in a white silk jacket with a beige camisole, long black pants, and a pretty gold sash tied around her waist, gently falling off to the side.

We ordered a bottle of Pinot Noir and then had a terrific meal, highlighted by a black-bean-and-goat-cheese pâté that we shared; her arctic char, my rib eye au poivre; and bittersweet chocolate praline crumble for two. Everything about the New Heights Restaurant worked great for us: the cherry trees out front, in bloom in the fall; some pretty interesting local art up on the walls; delicious cooking smells – fennel, roasted garlic – permeating the dining room; candle-light just about everywhere our eyes went. Mostly, though, my eyes were on Kayla, usually on her eyes, which were deep brown, beautiful, and intelligent.

After dinner, she and I took a walk across the Duke Ellington Bridge toward Adams Morgan and Columbia Road. We stopped at one of my favorite stores in Washington, Crooked Beat Records, and I bought some Alex Chilton and Coltrane for her from Neil Becton, one of the owners and an old friend who once wrote for the *Post*. Then Kayla and I wound up in Kabani Village, just a few steps from the street. We had mojitos and watched a theater workshop for the next hour.

On the walk back to my car we held hands and continued to talk up a storm. Then Kayla kissed me – on the cheek.

I didn't know *what* to make of that. 'Thank you for the night,' she said. 'It was perfect, Alex. Just like you.'

'It was nice, wasn't it?' I said, still reeling a little from the sisterly kiss.

She smiled. 'I've never seen you so relaxed.'

I think it was the best thing she could have said, and it sort of made up for the kiss on the cheek. Sort of.

Then Kayla kissed me on the mouth, and I kissed her back. That was much better, and so was the rest of the night at her apartment in Capitol Hill. For a few hours anyway, it felt like my life was starting to make some sense again.

Chapter Forty-Three

The Butcher had always felt that Venice, Italy, was kind of overrated, to be honest.

But nowadays, with the unending onslaught of tourists, especially the rush of arrogant, hopelessly naive Americans, anyone with a quarter of a brain would have to agree with him. Or maybe not, since most people he knew were complete imbeciles when you came right down to it. He'd learned that by the time he was fifteen and out on the streets of Brooklyn, after he'd run away from home for the third or fourth time as an adolescent, a troubled youth, a victim of circumstances, or maybe just a born psychopath.

He had arrived outside Venice by car and parked in the Piazzale Roma. Then, as he hurried to catch a water taxi to his destination, he could see the excitement, or maybe even reverence for Venice, on nearly every face he passed. *Dumbasses and sheep.* Not one of them had ever entertained an original idea or come to a conclusion without the aid of a stupid guidebook. Still, even he had to admit that the cluster of ancient villas slowly sinking into the swamp could be visually arresting in the right light, especially at a distance.

Once he was on board the water taxi, though, he thought of nothing but the job ahead – *Martin and Marcia Harris.*

Or so their unsuspecting neighbors and friends in Madison, Wisconsin, believed. It didn't matter who the couple *really* were – though Sullivan knew their identity. More importantly, they represented a hundred thousand dollars already deposited in his Swiss account, plus expenses, for just a couple days' work. He was considered one of the most successful assassins in the world, and you got what you paid for, except maybe in LA restaurants. He'd been a little surprised when he was hired by John Maggione but it was good to be working.

The water taxi docked at Rio di San Moisè, off the Grand Canal, and Sullivan made his way past narrow shops and museums to sprawling St Mark's Square. He was in radio contact with a spotter, and he'd learned that the Harrises were walking around the square, taking in the sights in a leisurely fashion. It was nearly eleven at night, and he wondered what would be next for them. A little clubbing? A late-night dinner at Cipriani? Drinks at Harry's Bar?

Then he saw the couple – *him,* in a Burberry trench; *her*, in a cashmere wrap and carrying John Berendt's *City of Falling Angels.*

He followed them, hidden in the midst of the festive, noisy crowd. Sullivan had thought it best to dress like an average Joe – khaki Dockers, sweatshirt, floppy rainhat. The pants, shirt, and hat could be discarded in a matter of seconds. Underneath, he wore a brown tweed suit, shirt and tie, and he had a beret. Thus, he would become the Professor. One of his favored disguises when he traveled in Europe to do a job.

The Harrises didn't walk far from St Mark's, eventually turning on to Calle Tredici Martiri. Sullivan already knew they were staying at the Bauer Hotel, so they were heading home now. 'You're almost making this too easy,' he muttered to himself.

Then he thought, *Mistake.*

Chapter Forty-Four

He followed Martin and Marcia Harris as they walked arm in arm through a dark, narrow, and very typical Venetian alleyway. They entered a gateway into the Bauer Hotel. He wondered why John Maggione wanted them dead, but it didn't really matter to him.

Moments later, he was sitting across the bar from them on the hotel terrace. A nice little spot, cozy as a love seat, it overlooked the canal and the Chiesa della Salute. The Butcher ordered a Bushmills but didn't drink more than a sip or two, just enough to take the edge off of things. He had a scalpel in his pants pocket, and he fingered it while he watched the Harrises.

Quite the lovebirds he couldn't help thinking as

they shared a long kiss at the bar. Get a room, why don't you?

As if he were reading the Butcher's mind, Martin Harris paid the check, and then the couple left the crowded, subdued terrace lounge. Sullivan followed. The Bauer was a typical Venetian palazzo, more like a private home than a hotel, lavish and opulent at every turn. His own wife, Caitlin, would have loved it, but he could never take her here, or ever come back himself.

Not after tonight and the unspeakable tragedy that was going to happen here in a matter of minutes. Because that's what the Butcher specialized in – tragedies, the unspeakable kind.

He knew that there were ninety-seven guest rooms and eighteen suites in the Bauer, and that the Harrises were staying in one of the suites on the third floor. He followed them up the carpeted stairs and immediately thought, *Mistake.*

But whose – mine or theirs? Important question to consider and be ready to answer.

He turned out of the stairwell – and it all went wrong in a hurry!

The Harrises were waiting for him, both with guns drawn, and Martin had a nasty smirk on his face. Most likely they were going to take him to their room and kill him there. It was an obvious setup . . . by two professionals.

Not too shabby a job, either. An eight out of ten.

But who had done this to him? Who had set him up to die in Venice? Even more curious – why had he been targeted? Why him? And why now?

Not that he was thinking about any of that now, in the dimly lit corridor of the Bauer, with dueling guns pointed toward him.

Fortunately, the Harrises had committed several mistakes along the way. They'd made following them too easy; they'd been careless and unconcerned; and too romantic, at least in his jaded opinion, for a couple married twenty years, even one on holiday in Venice.

So the Butcher had come up the stairs with his own pistol drawn – and the instant he saw them with guns out, he fired.

No hesitation, not even a half second.

Chauvinist pig that he was, he took out the man first, the more dangerous opponent in his estimation. He got Martin Harris in the face, shattered the nose and upper lip. A definite kill shot. The man's head snapped back, and his blond hairpiece flew off.

Then Sullivan dove, rolled to the left, and Marcia Harris's shot missed him by a foot or more.

He fired again – and got Marcia in the side of her

throat; then he put a second shot into her heaving chest. And a third in her heart.

The Butcher knew the Harrises were dead in the hallway, just lying there like sides of meat, but he didn't run out of the Bauer.

Instead, he whipped out his scalpel and went to work on their faces and throats. If he'd had the time, he would have stitched up the eyes and mouths too – to send a message. Then he took a half dozen photographs of the victims, the would-be assassins, for his prized picture collection.

One day soon, the Butcher would show these photos to the person who had paid to have him killed and *failed* and who was now as good as dead.

That man was John Maggione, the don himself.

Chapter Forty-Five

In his Michael Sullivan persona, he had the habit of thinking things through several times, and not just his hit jobs. The lifelong habit included things about his family, small details like how and where they lived, and who knew about it. Also, images from his father's butcher shop in the Flatlands were always with him: an awning of wide stripes with the orange, white, and green of the Irish flag; the bright whiteness of the shop on the inside; the loud electric meat grinder that seemed to shake the whole building whenever it was turned on.

For this new life of his, far away from Brooklyn, he had chosen affluent, and mostly white-bread, Montgomery County in Maryland.

Specifically, he had picked out the town of Potomac.

Around three on the afternoon that he arrived back from Europe, he drove at exactly twenty-five miles an hour through Potomac Village, stopping like any other good citizen at the irritatingly long light at the corner of River and Falls Roads.

More time to think, or obsess, which he usually enjoyed.

So who had put a hit out on him? *Was* it Maggione? And what did it mean to him and his family? Was he safe coming home now?

One of the general appearances, or disguises, that he had carefully selected for his family was that of the bourgeois bohemian. The ironies of the lifestyle choice gave him constant amusement: *nonfat butter*, for example, and NPR always on the radio of his wife's trendy SUV; and bizarre foods – like olive-wheatgrass muffins. It was patently absurd and hilarious to the Butcher: the joys of Yuppie life just didn't stop.

His three boys went to the private Landon School, where they hobnobbed with the mostly well-mannered, but often quite devious, children of the middle rich. There were lots of rich doctors in Montgomery County, working for NIH, the FDA, and Bethesda Naval Medical Command. So now he headed out toward Hunt County, the ritzy subdivision where he lived, and what a private hoot that was – 'Hunt County, home of the Hunter.'

And finally, there was his home, sweet home, purchased in 2002 for one point five million. Six large bedrooms, four and a half baths, heated pool, sauna, finished basement with media room. Sirius satellite radio was the latest rage with Caitlin and the boys. Sweet Caitlin, love of his straight life, who had a life coach and an intuitive healer these days – all paid for by his dubious labors on the Hunt.

Sullivan had called ahead on his cell, and there they were on the front lawn to meet and greet – waving like the big happy family that they thought they were. They had no idea, no clue that they were part of his disguise, that they were his cover story. That's all it was, right?

He hopped out of the Caddy, grinning like he was in a fast-food commercial, and sang his theme song, the old Shep and the Limelites classic, 'Daddy's Home.' 'Daddy's home, your daddy's home to stay.' And Caitlin and the kids chorused, 'He's not a thousand miles a-waaay.'

His life was the best, wasn't it? Except that some-body was trying to kill him now. And of course there was always his past, the way he grew up in Brooklyn, his insane father, the Bone Man, the dreaded back room at the shop. But the Butcher tried not to think about any of that right now.

He was home again, he'd made it – and he took a nice big bow in front of his family, who, of course, cheered for their returning hero.

That's what he was, yeah, a hero.

PART THREE

THERAPY

Chapter Forty-Six

'*Alex!* Hey, you! How you been? Long time no see, big guy. You're looking good.'

I waved to a petite, pretty woman named Paula Leed and kept on running. Paula was a fixture in the neighborhood, kind of like me. She was around the same age as I am and owned the newspaper store where the two of us used to spend our allowances on candy and soda when we were kids. Rumor had it that she liked me. Hey, I liked Paula too, always had.

My flapping feet kept me headed north on Fifth Street like they knew the way, and the neighborhood scrolled by. Toward Seward Square I hung a right and took the long way around. It didn't make logical sense to go that way, but I didn't do it for logical reasons.

The news about Maria's murderer was the one

thing holding me back these days. Now I was avoiding the block where it had happened and, at the same time, working hard to remember Maria as I had known her, not as I had lost her. I was also spending time every day trying to track down her killer – now that I suspected he was still out there somewhere.

I turned right on Seventh, then headed toward the National Mall, pushing a little harder. When I got to my building at Indiana Avenue, I eked out just enough wind to take the four flights up, two steps at a time.

My new office was a converted studio apartment, one large room with a small bath and alcove kitchen off to the side. Lots of natural light streamed in through a semicircle of windows in the turreted corner.

That's where I'd set up two comfortable chairs and a small couch for therapy sessions.

Just being here got me pretty excited. I'd put out my shingle, and I was ready to see my first patient.

Three stacks of case files were waiting on my desk, two from the Bureau and another sent over from DCPD. Most of the files represented possible consulting jobs. A few crimes to solve? An occasional dead body? I guess that was realistic.

The first file I looked at was a serial case in Georgia, someone the media had dubbed 'the Midnight Caller.' Three black men were dead already, with a successively shorter interval between each homicide. It was a decent case for me, except for the six hundred miles between DC and Atlanta.

I set the file aside.

The next case was closer to home. Two history professors at the University of Maryland, perhaps intimately involved, had been found dead in a classroom. The bodies had been hung from ceiling beams. Local police had a suspect but wanted to work up a profile before they went any further.

I put that file back on my desk with a yellow sticker attached.

Yellow, for *maybe.*

There was a knock on my door.

'It's open,' I called out, and immediately became suspicious, paranoid, whatever it is that I am most of the time.

What had Nana said when I'd left the house earlier? *Try not to get shot at.*

Chapter Forty-Seven

Old habits die hard. But it wasn't Kyle Craig, or some other psychotic nutcase from my past come to visit.

It was my first patient.

The visitor took up most of the doorway, where she now paused, as if scared to come in. Her face was turned down at the mouth, and her hand gripped the jamb while she tried to catch her breath, while keeping some dignity.

'You putting in an elevator anytime soon?' she asked between gasps.

'Sorry about all the stairs,' I said. 'You must be Kim Stafford. I'm Alex Cross. Please, come in. There's coffee, or I can get you water.'

The very first patient of my new practice finally

lumbered into my office. She was a heavyset woman, in her late twenties, I guessed, though she could have passed for forty. She was dressed very formally, in a dark skirt and white blouse that looked old but well made. A blue-and-lavender silk scarf was carefully tied under her chin.

'You said on the machine that Robert Hatfield referred you?' I asked. 'I used to work with Robert on the police force. Is he a friend of yours?'

'Not really.'

Okay, not a friend of Hatfield's. I waited for her to say more, but nothing came. She just stood in the middle of the office, seeming to quietly appraise everything in the room.

'We can sit over here,' I prompted. She waited for me to sit first, so I did.

Kim finally sat down herself, perched tentatively on the forward edge of the chair. One of her hands fluttered nervously around the knot in her scarf. The other was clenched into a fist.

'I just need some help trying to understand someone,' she began. 'Someone who gets angry sometimes.'

'Is this someone close to you?'

She stiffened. 'I'm not giving you his name.'

'No,' I said. 'The name isn't important. But is this a family member?'

'Fiancé.'

I nodded. 'How long have you two been engaged? Is that all right to ask?'

'Four years,' she said. 'He wants me to lose some weight before we get married.'

Maybe it was force of habit, but I was already working up a profile on the fiancé. Everything was her fault in the relationship; he took no account for his own actions; her weight was his escape hatch.

'Kim, when you say he gets angry a lot – can you tell me a little more about that?'

'Well, it's just . . .' She stopped to think, although I'm sure it was embarrassment and not a lack of clarity that held her back. Then tears pearled at the corners of her eyes.

'Has he been physically violent with you?' I asked.

'*No*,' she said, a little too quickly. 'Not violent. It's just . . . Well, yes. I guess so.'

With one shaky breath, she seemed to give up on words. Instead, she untied the scarf around her neck and let it float down into her lap.

I hated what I saw. The welts were easy enough to make out. They ran like blurred stripes around her throat.

I'd seen those kinds of striated markings before. Usually they were on dead bodies.

Chapter Forty-Eight

I had to remind myself – *the murders are behind you now; this is just a therapy session.*

'Kim, how did you get those marks on your neck? Tell me whatever you can.'

She winced as she tied the scarf back on. 'If my cell phone rings, I have to answer it. He thinks I'm at my mother's house,' she said.

A terrible look crossed her face, and I realized it was too early to ask her about specific instances of abuse.

Still not looking at me, she unbuttoned the sleeve of her blouse. I wasn't sure what she was doing until I saw the angry red sore above the wrist on her forearm. It was just beginning to heal.

'Is that a burn mark?' I asked.

'He smokes cigars,' she said.

I breathed in. She'd answered so matter-of-factly. 'Have you called the police?'

She laughed bitterly. 'No. I haven't.'

Her hand went up to her mouth, and she looked away again. This man had obviously scared her into protecting him, no matter what.

A cell phone chirped inside her purse.

Without a word to me, she took out the phone, looked at the number, and answered.

'Hey, baby. What's up?' Her voice was soft and easygoing, and totally convincing. 'No,' she said. 'Mom went out to get some milk. Of course I'm sure. I'll tell her you said hi.'

It was fascinating to watch Kim's face as she spoke. She wasn't just acting for him. She was playing this part for herself. That's how she was getting by, wasn't it?

When she finally hung up, she looked at me with the most incongruous smile, as though no conversation had taken place at all. It lasted less than a few seconds. Then she broke up, all at once. A low moan turned into a sob that racked her body; she rocked forward, clutching herself around the middle.

'Th-this is too hard,' she choked out. 'I'm sorry. I can't do it. I can't . . . *be here.*'

When the cell phone rang a second time, she jumped in her seat. These surveillance calls were the thing that made it hardest for her to be here – trying to juggle awareness and denial at the same time.

She wiped at her face as though her appearance mattered, then answered in the same soft voice as before.

'Hey, baby. No, I was washing my hands. Sorry, baby. It took me a second to get to the phone.'

I could hear him shouting about something as Kim nodded patiently and listened.

Eventually, she held up a finger to me and let herself out into the hall.

I used the time to go through a few of my provider directories and to calm down my own anger. When Kim came back in, I tried to give her the names of some shelters in the area, but she refused them.

'I've got to go,' she said suddenly. The second call had sealed her up tight. 'How much do I owe you?'

'Let's call this an initial consult. Pay me for the second appointment.'

'I don't want charity. I don't think I can come back anyway. How much?'

I answered reluctantly. 'It's one hundred an hour on a sliding scale. Fifty would be good.'

She counted it out for me, mostly fives and singles that she had probably stashed away over time. Then she left the office. My first session had ended.

Chapter Forty-Nine

Mistake. Bad one.

A New Jersey mob boss and former contract killer named Benny 'Goodman' Fontana was whistling a bouncy Sinatra tune as he strolled around to the passenger side of his dark-blue Lincoln; then he opened the door with a flourish and a one-hundred-kilowatt smile that would have made Ol' Blue Eyes proud.

A bosomy blonde woman got out of the sedan, stretching her long legs like she was auditioning for the Rockettes. She was a former Miss Universe contestant, twenty-six years old, with some of the best moving parts money could buy. She was also a little too classy and hot for the mobster to have snagged without some cash having changed hands. Benny was a tough little weasel, but he wasn't exactly a movie star, unless maybe you counted the guy who played Tony Soprano as one.

The Butcher watched, mildly amused, from his own car parked half a block down the street. He guessed that the blonde was setting Benny back five hundred or so an hour, maybe two grand for the night if Mrs Fontana happened to be out of town visiting their daughter, who was tucked away in school at Marymount Manhattan.

Michael Sullivan checked his watch.

Seven fifty-two. This was payback for Venice. The beginning of payback anyway. The first of several messages he was planning to send.

At eight fifteen, he took his briefcase from the backseat, got out, and crossed the street, staying in the soft shadows of maple and elm trees. It didn't take much waiting time for a blue-haired woman wrapped in a fur coat to come out of the apartment building. Sullivan held the door for her with a friendly smile and then let himself inside.

Everything was more or less the way he remembered it. Apartment 4C had been in the Family for years, ever since opportunities had started opening up in Washington for the mob. The place was a perk for anyone in town who needed some extra privacy, for whatever reason. The Butcher had used it himself once or twice when he was doing jobs for Benny Fontana. This was before John Maggione took over from his father, though, and began to shut the Butcher out.

Even the cheap Korean dead bolt on the front door was the same, or close enough. *Another mistake.* Sullivan jimmied it with a three-dollar awl from his workshop at home. He put the tool back into the briefcase and took out his gun and a surgical blade, a very special one.

The living room was mostly dark. Cones of light spilled in from two directions – the kitchen on his left, a bedroom on his right. Benny's insistent grunting told Sullivan it was somewhere past halftime. He swiftly padded across the living room rug to the bedroom door and looked inside. Miss Universe was on top – no surprise – with her slender back to him.

'That's it, baby. That's what I like,' Benny said, and then, 'I'm gonna put my finger—'

Sullivan's silencer popped softly, and just once. He shot the former Miss Universe contestant in the back of her hairdo, and the woman's blood and brains splattered all over Benny Fontana's chest and face. The mobster yelled out like he'd been shot himself.

He managed to roll himself out from under the

dead girl and then off the bed, away from the night-stand, also away from his own gun. The Butcher started to laugh. He didn't mean to disrespect the mob boss, or disrespect the dead, but Fontana had done just about everything wrong tonight. He was getting soft, which was why Sullivan had come after him first.

'Hi there, Benny. How you been?' the Butcher said as he flipped on the overhead light. 'We need to talk about Venice.'

He took out a scalpel that had a special edge for cutting muscle. 'Actually, I need you to send a message to Mr Maggione for me. Could you do that, Benny? Be a messenger boy? By the way, you ever hear of Syme's operation, Ben? It's a foot amputation.'

Chapter Fifty

Michael Sullivan couldn't go right home to his family in Maryland, not after what he'd just done to Benny Fontana and his girlfriend. He was too riled up inside, his blood boiling. He was hot-flashing scenes from his old man's shop in Brooklyn again – sawdust stored in a big cardboard barrel, the terracotta tile floor with white grout, handsaws, boning knives, meat hooks in the freezer room.

So he wandered around Georgetown for a while, looking for trouble if he could find the right kind. The thing was, he liked his ladies tucked in a little. He especially liked lawyers, MBAs, professor-librarian types – loved their glasses, the buttoned-down clothes, the conservative hairstyles. Always so in control of themselves.

He liked helping them lose some of that control, while blowing off a little steam of his own, relieving his stress, breaking all the rules of this dumbass society.

Georgetown was a good pickup place for him. Every other chippie he spotted on the street was a little too tightly wound. Not that there were so many to choose from, not at this time of night. But he didn't need that many choices, just one good one. And maybe he'd already spotted her. He thought so anyway.

She looked like she could be a trial attorney, dressed to impress in that smart tweed outfit of hers. The heels ticktocked a steady rhythm on the sidewalk – *this way, that way, this way, that way.*

In contrast, Sullivan's Nikes didn't make much noise at all. With a hooded sweatshirt, he was just another Bobo jogger out for a late-night run in the neighborhood. If someone peeked from their window, that's what they'd see.

But no one was looking, least of all Miss Tweedy. *Tweedy Bird,* he thought with a grin. *Mistake. Hers.*

She kept her stride city-fast, her leather purse and briefcase tucked like the key to the Da Vinci Code under one arm, and she stayed to the outside edge of the sidewalk – all smart moves for a woman alone on the street late at night. Her one mistake was not looking around enough, not taking in the surroundings. Not spotting the *jogger* who was *walking* behind her.

And mistakes could kill you, couldn't they?

Sullivan hung back in the shade as Tweedy passed under a streetlamp. Nice pipes and a great ass, he noted. No ring on the left hand.

The high heels kept their rhythm steady on the sidewalk for another half block; then she slowed in front of a redbrick townhouse. Nice place. Nineteenth-century. From the look of it, though, one of those buildings that had been butchered into condos on the inside.

She pulled a set of keys from her purse before she even got to the front door, and Sullivan began to time his approach. He reached into his own pocket and took out a slip of paper. A dry-cleaning ticket? It didn't really matter what it was.

As she put her key into the door, and before she pushed it open, he called out in a friendly voice. 'Excuse me, miss? Excuse me? Did you drop this?'

Chapter Fifty-One

No dummy, that Tweedy Bird – her momma didn't raise any foolish daughters. She knew she was in trouble immediately, but there was nothing much she could do about it in the next few seconds.

He hit the stoop fast, before she could close the glass door between them and let it lock her safely inside.

A faux gaslight on the foyer wall showed off the panic in her very pretty blue eyes.

It also illuminated the blade of the scalpel in his hand, extended out toward her face.

The Butcher wanted her to see the sharp edge so she'd be thinking about it, even more than about him. That's how it worked, and he knew it. Nearly 90 percent of people who were attacked remembered details about the weapon rather than the person wielding it.

An awkward stumble was about all Tweedy managed before he was inside the foyer door with her. Michael Sullivan positioned his back to the street, shielding her from view in case somebody happened to walk by outside. He kept the scalpel visible in one hand and snatched away her keys with the other.

'*Not one word,*' he said, with the blade up near his lips. 'And try to remember – I don't administer anesthesia with this. Don't even use topical Betadine. I just cut.'

She stood on her tiptoes as she backed up against an ornately carved newel post. 'Here.' She thrust her small designer purse at him. 'Please. It's yours. Go now.'

'Not going to happen. I don't want your money. Now, *listen* to me. Are you listening?'

'Yes.'

'You live alone?' he asked. It had the effect he wanted. Her pause gave him his answer.

'No.' She tried to cover herself too late.

There were three mailboxes on the wall. Only number two had a single name: L. Brandt.

'Let's go upstairs, Miss Brandt.'

'I'm not—'

'Yes you are. No reason to lie. Now move it, before you lose it.'

In less than twenty seconds, they were inside her second-floor condo. The living room, like L. Brandt herself, was neat and organized. Black-and-white photos of kissing scenes were up on the walls. Movie posters – *Sleepless in Seattle, An Officer and a Gentleman.* The girl was a romantic at heart. But in some ways, so was Sullivan – at least he thought so.

Her body went stiff as a two-by-four as he picked her up. She was a tiny thing; it took all of one arm to get her into the bedroom, then down on her bed, where she lay without moving.

'You're a very beautiful girl,' he said. 'Just lovely. Like an exquisite doll. Now, if you don't mind, I'd like to see the rest of the package.'

He used the scalpel to cut the buttons off that pricey tweed suit of hers. L. Brandt came undone right along with her clothes; she went from paralyzed to limp, but at least he didn't have to remind her to keep quiet.

He used his hands on her bra and panties, which were black and lacy. *On a weekday, too.* She didn't wear pantyhose, and her legs were just great, slender and lightly tanned. Toenails painted bright red. When she tried to squeeze her eyes shut, he slapped her just enough to get her full attention.

'Stay with me, L. Brandt.'

Something on her dresser caught his eye. Lipstick. 'You know what, put some of that on. And a nice perfume. You pick something out.' L. Brandt did as she was told. She knew she had no choice.

He held his cock in one hand, the scalpel in the other – a visual she would never, ever forget. Then he forced himself inside her. 'I want you to play along,' he said. 'Fake it if you have to. I'm sure you've done that before.' She did her best, arching her pelvis, moaning once or twice, just not looking at him.

'Now, *look* at me,' he commanded. 'Look at me. Look at me. *Look at me.* That's better.' Then it was over for him. For both of them.

'A quick chat before I go,' he said. 'And, believe it or not, I am planning to leave. I'm not going to hurt you. No more than I already have.'

He found her purse on the floor. Inside was what he was looking for – a driver's license and a black address book. He held the license under the bedside lamp.

'So it's *Lisa.* Very nice picture for government-issue. Of course, you're even prettier in real life. Now let me show you a few pictures of my own.'

He hadn't brought many, just four of them, but some of his personal favorites. He fanned them out in the palm of one hand. Lisa was back to frozen again. It was almost funny, like if she was still enough, he might not notice her there.

He held up the photos for her to see – one at a time. 'These are all people I've met *twice*. You and I, of course, have only met *once*. Whether or not we meet again is entirely up to you. Do you follow? Am I making myself clear?'

'Yes.'

He stood up and walked around to her side of the bed, gave her a few seconds to process what he was saying. She covered herself with a sheet. 'Do you understand me, Lisa? Truly? I know it can be a little hard to concentrate right now. I imagine it would be.'

'I won't say – anything,' she whispered. 'I promise.'

'Good, I believe you,' he said. 'Just in case, though, I'm going to take this, too.'

He held up the address book. Flipped it open to *B*. 'Here we go. Tom and Lois Brandt. Is that Mom and Dad? Vero Beach, Florida. Supposed to be very nice down there. The Treasure Coast.'

'Oh God, please,' she said.

'Entirely up to you, Lisa,' he said. 'Of course, if you ask me, it would be a shame after all this for you to end up like those others in the photographs. You know – in parts, sewn up. Whatever I was in the mood to do.'

He lifted up the sheet and looked her over one more time. 'They'd be pretty parts in your case, but *parts* all the same.'

And with those last words, he left Lisa Brandt alone with her memories of him.

Chapter Fifty-Two

'*This* is why I don't wear ties.'

John Sampson pulled at the constricting knot around his neck and ripped the damn thing off. He tossed it and what remained of his coffee into the trash. Immediately, he wished he hadn't thrown away the coffee. He and Billie had been up half the night with little Djakata and her flu. A truckload of caffeine was exactly what he needed right now.

When the phone on his desk rang, he was in no mood to talk to anybody about anything.'Yeah, what?'

A woman's voice came on the other end. 'Is this Detective Sampson's line?'

'Sampson here. What?'

'This is Detective Angela Susan Anton. I'm with the Sex Assault Unit, assigned to the Second District.'

'Okay.' He waited for her to connect some dots for him.

'I was hoping to pull you in on a disturbing case, Detective. We're running into some serious dead ends over here.'

Sampson fished in the wastebasket for the coffee container. All right! It had landed right-side up.

'What's the case?'

'A rape. Happened in Georgetown last night. The woman was treated at GUH, but all she'll say is that she was attacked. She won't ID the guy. Won't describe him at all. I was with her all morning and got nowhere. I've never seen anything quite like it, Detective. The level of fear the woman is exhibiting.'

Sampson crooked the phone to his ear and scribbled some notes on a tablet that said 'Dad Pad' at the top, a Father's Day knick-knack from Billie. 'Okay so far. But I'm curious why you're calling me, Detective.'

He sipped the bad coffee again, and suddenly it seemed not so bad.

Anton took a beat before answering. 'I understand that Alex Cross is a friend of yours.'

Sampson set down his pen and leaned back in his desk chair. 'Now I see.'

'I was hoping you could—'

'I hear you loud and clear, Detective Anton. You want me to pimp the deal for you?'

'No,' she said quickly. 'Rakeem Powell tells me you two are seriously good when you work serials together. I'd like to have you both in on this. Hey, I'm just being honest.'

Sampson stayed quiet, waiting to see if she'd get out of this one or hang herself some more.

'We left messages for Dr Cross last night and this morning, but I have to imagine everyone and their uncle want a piece of his time. Now that he's free-lancing.'

'Well, you're right about that, everybody wants a piece of him,' he said. 'But Alex is a big boy. He can take care of himself and make his own decisions. Why don't you keep trying his phone?'

'Detective Sampson, this perp is a particularly sick bastard. I don't have the luxury of wasting *anyone's* time on this case, including my own. So if I've stepped on your toes in any way, maybe you can get the hell over it, cut through the bullshit, and tell me if you'll help me or not.'

Sampson recognized the tone, and it made him smile. 'Well, since you put it that way – yeah, okay. I can't make any commitments for Alex. But I'll see what I can do.'

'Great. Thank you. I'll send over the files now. Unless you want to pick them up here.'

'Hold on. Files? Plural?'

'Am I going too fast for you, Detective Sampson? The whole reason I'm calling is your and Dr Cross's experience with *serial* cases.'

Sampson rubbed the telephone receiver against his temple. 'Yeah, I guess you are going too fast for me. Are we talking homicide here too?'

'Not serial murder,' Anton said tightly. 'Serial rape.'

Chapter Fifty-Three

'This isn't a consult,' I told Sampson. 'It's a *favor*. To you *personally*, John.'

Sampson raised his eyebrows knowingly. 'In other words, you promised Nana and the kids no more field-work.'

I waved him off. 'No, I didn't promise anybody anything. Just drive and try not to hit anyone on the way. At least no one that we like.'

We were in McLean, Virginia, to interview Lisa Brandt, who had left her Georgetown apartment to go stay with a friend in the country. I had her case file on my lap, along with three others, women who had been raped but wouldn't say anything to help the investigation and possibly stop the rapist. The *serial* rapist.

This was my first chance to look the papers over, but it hadn't taken me long to agree with the originating detective's conclusion. These attacks were all committed by one man, and the perp was definitely a psycho. The known survivors were of a type: white women in their twenties or early thirties, single, living alone in the Georgetown area. Each of them was a successful professional of some kind – a lawyer, an account executive. Lisa Brandt was an architect. These were all smart, ambitious women.

And not one of them was willing to say a word against or about the man who had attacked her.

Our perp was clearly a discerning and self-controlled animal who knew how to put the fear of God into his victims and then make it stick. And not just once, but four times. Or maybe more than four. Because chances were very good he had other victims, women too afraid to even report they had been attacked.

'Here we are,' Sampson said. 'This is where Lisa Brandt is hiding herself.'

Chapter Fifty-Four

I looked up from the heap of detective files on my lap as we pulled in through a giant hedgerow onto a long crescent-shaped driveway paved with broken seashells. The house was a stately Greek revival, with two-story white columns in front, and looked like a suburban fortress. I could see why Lisa Brandt might come here for refuge and safety.

Her friend Nancy Goodes answered the door and then stepped outside the house to speak with us in private. She was a slight blonde and looked to be about Ms Brandt's age, which the file put at twenty-nine.

'I don't have to tell you that Lisa has been through hell,' she said in a whisper that really wasn't necessary out here on the porch. 'Can you please keep this interview as brief as possible? I wish you could just leave. I don't understand why she has to talk to more police. Can either of you explain that to me?'

Lisa's friend clutched her elbows across her chest, obviously uncomfortable but also pushing herself to be a good advocate. Sampson and I respected that, but there were other considerations.

'We'll be as brief as we possibly can,' he said. 'But this rapist is still out there.'

'Don't you *dare* lay a guilt trip on her. Don't you dare.'

We followed Ms Goodes inside through a marble-tiled foyer. A sweeping staircase to our right echoed the curve of the chandelier dangling overhead. When I heard the chatter of children's voices off to the left, they seemed somewhat incongruous with the formality of the house. I began to wonder where these people kept their messes.

Ms Goodes sighed, then showed us into a side parlor where Lisa Brandt sat alone. She was tiny but pretty, even now, under these unfortunate circumstances. I had the sense that she was dressed for normality, in jeans and a striped oxford shirt, but it was her bent-over posture – and her eyes – that told more of the story. She obviously didn't know if the pain she was feeling now would ever go away.

Sampson and I introduced ourselves and were invited to sit down. Lisa even forced a polite smile before looking away again.

'Those are beautiful,' I said, pointing at a vase of fresh-cut rhododendrons on the coffee table between us. It was easy enough to say because it was true, and I honestly didn't know where else to start.

'Oh.' She looked at them absently. 'Nancy is amazing with all that. She's a real country girl now, a mom. She always wanted to be a mother.'

Sampson began gently. 'Lisa, I want you to know how sorry we are that this happened to you. I know you've spoken with a lot of people already. We'll try not to repeat the background detail too much. Okay so far?'

Lisa kept her eyes fixed on the corner of the room. 'Yes. Thank you.'

'Now, we understand you received the necessary prophylaxis but preferred not to provide any physical evidence in your exam at the hospital. Also, that you're choosing for the time being not to give any description of the man who committed the crime against you. Is that correct?'

'Not now, and *not ever*,' she said. Her head shook slightly back and forth, like a tiny *no* repeated over and over.

'You're not under any obligation to talk,' I assured her. 'And we're not here to get any information that you don't want to give.'

'With all that in mind,' Sampson went on, 'we have some assumptions that we're working with. First, that your attacker was *not* someone you knew. And second, that he threatened you in some way, to keep you from identifying him or talking about him. Lisa, are you comfortable telling us whether or not that's accurate?'

She went very still. I tried to gauge her face and body language but saw nothing. She didn't respond to Sampson's question, so I tried a different angle.

'Is there anything you've thought about since you spoke with the detectives earlier? Anything you'd like to add?'

'Even a small detail might aid in the investigation,' Sampson said, 'and catch this rapist.'

'I don't *want* any investigation of what happened to me,' she blurted. 'Isn't that my choice?'

'I'm afraid it's not,' Sampson said in the softest voice I'd ever heard out of him.

'Why not?' It came out of Lisa more as a desperate plea than a question.

I tried to choose my words carefully. 'We're fairly certain that what happened to you wasn't an isolated incident, Lisa. There have been other women—'

At that, she came undone. A choking sob escaped her, letting loose everything behind it. Then Lisa Brandt doubled over onto her lap, sobbing with her hands clutched tightly over her mouth.

'I'm sorry,' she said in a moan. 'I can't do this. I can't. I'm sorry, I'm sorry.'

Ms Goodes rushed back into the room then. She must have been listening just outside the door. She knelt in front of Lisa and put her arms around her friend, whispering reassurances.

'I'm sorry,' Lisa Brandt got out again.

'Nothing to be sorry for, sweetheart. Nothing at all. Just let it out, that's it,' said Nancy Goodes.

Sampson put a card on the coffee table. 'We'll show ourselves out,' he said.

Ms Goodes answered without turning away from her sobbing friend.

'Just go. Please don't come back here. Leave Lisa alone. Go.'

Chapter Fifty-Five

The Butcher was on a job – a hit, a six-figure one. Among other things, he was trying to keep his mind off of John Maggione and the pain he wanted to cause him. He was observing an older well-dressed man with a young girl draped on his arm. A 'bird,' as they had called them here in London at one time.

He was probably sixty; she could be twenty-five at most. Curious couple. *Eye-catching*, which could be a problem for him.

The Butcher watched them as they stood in front of the tony Claridges hotel waiting for the man's private car to pull up. It did so, just as it had the previous evening and then again around ten o'clock that morning.

No serious mistakes so far by the couple. Nothing for him to pounce on.

The driver of the private car was a bodyguard, and he was carrying. He was also decent enough at what he did.

There was only one problem for the bodyguard – the girl obviously didn't want him around. She'd tried, unsuccessfully, to have the older man ditch the driver the night before, when they had attended some kind of formal affair at the Saatchi Gallery.

Well, he would just have to see what developed today. The Butcher pulled out a few cars behind the gleaming black Mercedes CL65. The Merc was fast, more than six hundred horsepower, but a hell of a lot of good that would do them on the crowded streets of London.

He was a little paranoid about working again, and with pretty good reason, but he'd gotten the job through a solid contact in the Boston area. He trusted the guy, at least as far as he could throw him. And he needed the six-figure payday.

A possible break finally came on Long Acre near Covent Garden underground station. The girl jumped out of the car at a stoplight, started to walk off – and the older man got out as well.

Michael Sullivan pulled over to the curb immediately, and he simply abandoned his car. The rental could never be traced back to him anyway. The move was a classic in that most people wouldn't even think of doing it, but he couldn't have cared less about just leaving the car in the middle of London. The car was of no consequence.

He figured the driver-bodyguard wouldn't do the same with the two-hundred-thousand-dollar Mercedes, and that he had several minutes before the guy caught up with them again.

The streets around Covent Garden piazza were densely packed with pedestrians, and he could see the couple, their heads bobbing, laughing, probably about their escape from the bodyguard. He followed them down James Street. They continued to laugh and talk, with not a care in the world.

Big, big mistake.

He could see a glass-roof-covered market up ahead. And a crowd gathered around street performers dressed as white marble statues that moved only when someone threw them a coin.

Then, suddenly, he was on top of the couple, and it felt right, so he fired the silenced Beretta – two heart shots.

The girl went down like a throw rug had been pulled out from under her feet.

He had no idea who she was, who had wanted her dead or why, and he didn't care one way or the other.

'Heart attack! Someone had a heart attack!' he called out as he let the gun drop from his fingertips, turned, and disappeared into the thickening crowd. He headed up Neal Street past a couple of pubs with Victorian exteriors and found his abandoned car right where he left it. What a nice surprise.

It was safer to stay in London overnight, but then he was on a morning flight back to Washington.

Easy money – like always, or at least how it had been for him before the cockup in Venice, which he still had to deal with in a major way.

Chapter Fifty-Six

John and I met that night for a little light sparring at the Roxy Gym after my last therapy session. The practice was building steadily, and my days there made me happy and satisfied for the first time in a few years.

The quaint idea of *normality* was in my head a lot now, though I'm not sure what the word really meant.

'Get your elbows in,' Sampson said, 'before I knock your damn head off.'

I pulled them in. It didn't help much, though.

The big man caught me with a good right jab that stung like only a solid punch can. I swung and connected solidly with his open side, which seemed to hurt my hand more than it hurt him.

It went on like that for a while, but my mind never really got into the ring. After less than twenty minutes, I held up my gloves, feeling an ache in both shoulders.

'TKO,' I said through my mouthpiece. 'Let's go get a drink.'

Our 'drink' turned out to be bottles of red Gatorade on the sidewalk in front of the Roxy. Not what I'd had in mind, but it was just fine.

'So,' Sampson said, 'either I'm getting a whole lot better in there or you were out of it tonight. Which is it?'

'You aren't getting better,' I deadpanned.

'Still thinking about yesterday? What? Talk to me.'

We both had felt lousy about the tough interview with Lisa Brandt. It's one thing to push a witness like that and get somewhere; it's another to probe hard and get nothing out of it.

I nodded. 'Yesterday, yeah.'

Sampson slid down the wall to sit next to me on the sidewalk. 'Alex, you've got to get off the worry train.'

'Nice bumper sticker,' I told him.

'I thought things were going pretty good for you,' he said. 'Lately anyway.'

'They are,' I said. 'The work is good, even better than I thought it would be.'

'So what's the problem then? Too much of a good thing? What ails you, man?'

In my mind, there was the long answer and the short answer. I went for the short answer. 'Maria.'

He knew what I meant, knew why too. 'Yesterday reminded you of her?'

'Yeah. In a weird way, it did,' I said. 'I was thinking. You remember back around the time when she was killed? There was a serial rape going on then, too. Remember that?'

Sampson squinted into the air. 'Right, now that you mention it.'

I rubbed my sore knuckles together. 'Anyway, that's what I mean. It's all like two degrees of separation these days. Everything I think about reminds me of Maria. Everything I do brings me back to her murder case. I kind of feel like I'm living in purgatory, and I don't know what I'm supposed to do about that.'

Sampson waited for me to finish. He usually knows when his point has been made and when to shut up. He had nothing more to say at the moment. Finally, I took a deep breath, and we rose and started up the sidewalk.

'What do you hear about Maria's killer? Anything new?' I asked him. 'Or was Giametti just playing with us?'

'Alex, why don't you move on?'

'John, if I could move on, I would. Okay? Maybe this is how I do it.'

He stared at his shoes for half a block. When he finally answered, it was begrudgingly. 'If I find out something about her killer, you'll be the first to know.'

Chapter Fifty-Seven

Michael Sullivan had stopped taking shit from anybody when he was fourteen or fifteen years old. Everybody in his family knew that his grandpa James had a gun and that he kept it in the bottom drawer of the dresser in his bedroom. One afternoon in June, the week he got out of school, Sullivan broke in and stole the gun from his grandfather's apartment.

For the rest of the day, he moseyed around the neighborhood with the pistola stuck in his pants, concealed under a loose shirt. He didn't feel the need to show the weapon off to anybody, but he found that he liked having it, liked it a lot. The handgun changed everything for him. He went from a tough kid to an invincible one.

Sullivan hung out until around eight, then he made

his way along Quentin Road to his father's shop. He got there when he knew that the old man would be closing up.

A song he hated, Elton John's 'Crocodile Rock,' was on somebody's car radio down the block, and he was tempted to shoot whoever was playing that shit.

The butcher shop's front door was open, and when he waltzed in, his father didn't even look up – but he must have seen his son pass the window outside.

The usual stack of *Irish Echo* newspapers was by the door. Everything always in its goddamn place. Neat, tidy, and completely messed-up.

'Whattaya want?' his father growled. The broom he was using had a scraper blade to dislodge fat from the grout on the floor. It was the kind of scut work Sullivan hated.

'Have a talk with you?' he said to his father.

'Fuck off. I'm busy earning a living.'

'Oh. Is that right? Busy cleaning floors?' Then his arm swung out fast.

And that was the first time Sullivan hit his father – with the gun – in the temple over his right eye. He hit him again, in the nose, and the large man went down into the sawdust and meat shavings. He began to moan and spit out sawdust and gristle.

'You know how badly I can hurt you?' Michael Sullivan

asked his father, bending low to the floor. 'Remember that line, Kevin? I do. Never forget it as long as I live.'

'Don't call me Kevin, you punk.'

He hit his father again with the gun handle. Then he kicked him in the testicles, and his father groaned in pain.

Sullivan looked around the store with total contempt. Kicked over a stand of McNamara's soda bread, just to kick something. Then he put the gun to his old man's head and cocked it.

'Please,' his father gasped, and his eyes went wide with shock and fear and some kind of bizarre realization about who his son was. 'No. Don't do this. Don't, Michael.'

Sullivan pulled the trigger – and there was a loud *snap* of metal against metal.

But no deafening explosion. No brain-splattering gunshot. Then there was powerful silence, like in a church.

'Someday,' he told his father. 'Not today, but when you least expect it. One day when you don't want to die, I'm going to kill you. You're gonna have a hard death, too, Kevin. And not with a pop gun like this one.'

Then he walked out of the butcher shop, and *he* became the Butcher of Sligo. Three days before

Christmas of his eighteenth year, he came back and killed his father. As he'd promised, not with a gun. He used one of the old man's boning knives, and he took several Polaroid shots as a keepsake.

Chapter Fifty-Eight

Out in Maryland, where he lived nowadays, Michael Sullivan shouldered a baseball bat. Not just any bat, either, a vintage Louisville Slugger, a 1986 Yankees game bat, to be exact. Screw collector's items, though, this solid piece of ash was meant to be used.

'All right,' Sullivan called out to the pitcher's mound. 'Let's see what you can do, big man. I'm shaking in my boots here. Let's see what you got.'

It was hard to believe that Mike Junior was old enough to have a windup this fluid and good, but he did. And his changeup was a small masterpiece. Sullivan only recognized it coming because he'd taught the pitch to the boy himself.

Still, he wasn't handing his eldest son any charity. That would be an insult to the boy. He gave the pitch the extra fraction of a second it needed, then swung hard and connected with a satisfying crack of the bat. He pretended the ball was the head of John Maggione.

'And she's out of here!' he crowed. He ran the bases for show while Seamus, his youngest, scrambled over the ballpark's chain-link fence to retrieve the home-run ball. 'Good one, Dad!' he screamed, holding up the scuffed ball where it had landed.

'Dad, we should go.' His middle son, Jimmy, already had his catcher's mitt and face mask off. 'We've got to leave the house by six thirty. Remember, Dad?'

After Sullivan himself, Jimmy was the most excited about tonight. Sullivan had gotten them tickets to see U2's Vertigo tour at the 1st Mariner Arena in Balti-more. It was going to be a fine night, the kind of family activity he could tolerate.

On the ride to the concert, Sullivan sang along with the car stereo until his boys started to groan and make jokes in the backseat.

'You see, boys,' Caitlin said, 'your father thinks he's another Bono. But he sounds more like . . . Ringo Starr?'

'Your mother's just jealous,' Sullivan said, laughing. 'You kids and I have rich Irish blood running in our veins. She's got nothing but Sicilian.'

'Oh, right. One question: Which would you rather eat – Italian or Irish? Case closed.'

The boys howled and high-fived one for their mom.

'Hey, what's *this*, Mom?' Seamus asked.

Caitlin looked; then she pulled a small silver flip phone from under the front seat. Sullivan saw it, and his stomach heaved.

It was Benny Fontana's cell phone. Sullivan had taken it with him the night he'd visited Benny and had been looking for it ever since. Talk about mistakes.

And mistakes will kill you.

He kept his face in perfect control. 'I'll bet that's Steve Bowen's phone,' he lied.

'Who?' Caitlin asked.

'Steve Bowen. My client? I gave him a ride to the airport when he was in town.'

Caitlin looked puzzled. 'Why hasn't he tried to get it back?'

Because he doesn't exist.

'Probably because he's in London.' Sullivan kept improvising. 'Just stick it in the glove compartment.'

Now that he had the cell phone, though, he knew what he wanted to do with it. In fact, he couldn't wait. He drove the family as close to the arena as he could get then pulled over to the curb.

'Here you go – door-to-door service. Can't beat it. I'll park this buggy and meet you inside.'

It didn't take him long to find a parking garage with vacancies. He drove all the way to the top for some added privacy and a good signal. The number he wanted was right there in the phone's address book. He punched it in. *This should be good. Now just let the bastard scum be there.*

And let him have caller ID.

John Maggione answered himself. 'Who's this?' he asked, and sounded bent out of shape already.

Bingo! The man himself. They'd hated each other since Maggione's father had let Sullivan do some jobs for him.

'Take a guess, Junior.'

'I have no fucking idea. How'd you get this number? Whoever you are, you're a dead man.'

'Then I guess we've got something in common.'

Adrenaline raced through Sullivan's system. He felt unstoppable right now. He was the best around at this kind of thing: setting up a target, playing with a mark.

'That's right, Junior. The hunter becomes the hunted. It's Michael Sullivan. Remember me? And you know what? I'm coming for you next.'

'The Butcher? Is that you, punk? I was going to kill

you anyway, but now I'm going to make you pay for what you did to Benny. You piece of shit, I'm gonna hurt you so bad.'

'What I did to Benny is nothing compared to what I'm going to do to you. I'm going to cut you in two with a butcher saw, and send half to your mother, and the other half to your wife. I'll let Connie see it just before I fuck her in front of your kids. What do you think of that?'

Maggione exploded. 'You are *dead*! You are so *dead*! Everything you ever cared about is . . . *dead*. I'm coming after you, Sullivan.'

'Yeah, well take a number.'

He flipped the phone closed, then looked at his watch. That felt good – talking to Maggione like that. Seven fifty. He wouldn't even miss U2's opening number.

Chapter Fifty-Nine

I had just finished up with the day's final session and was looking through the old files on Maria's case again when an unexpected hard knock came against the office door. What now?

I opened it to find Sampson standing out in the hallway.

He had a twelve-pack of Corona stuffed under one arm, and the carton of beer looked ridiculously small in relation to his body. Something was up.

'Sorry,' I said. 'I don't allow drinking during sessions.'

'All right. I hear you. I guess me and my imaginary friends will just be on our way.'

'But seeing how much you obviously need therapy, I'll make an exception this one time.'

He handed me a cold beer as I let him in. Something was definitely going on. Sampson had never been to my office before.

'Looking good around here already,' he said. 'I still owe you a hanging plant or something.'

'Don't pick out any art for me. Spare me that.'

Thirty seconds later, the Commodores were on the CD player – Sampson's choice – and Sampson was flopped down on my couch. It looked like a love seat under him.

But before I could even begin to unwind, he blind-sided me. 'Do you know Kim Stafford?'

I took a swill of beer to cover my reaction. Kim had been my last patient of the day. It made sense that Sampson might have seen her leaving, but how he knew who she was, I had no idea.

'Why do you ask that?'

'Uh, I'm a *police detective* . . . I just saw her outside. The lady is kind of hard to miss. She's Jason Stemple's girlfriend.'

'Jason Stemple?' Sampson had said it like I should know who that was. And in a strange way, I did, just not by his name.

I was glad Kim had come back for more sessions, but she was firm about not identifying her fiancé, even as the abuse at home seemed to have gotten worse.

'He works Sixth District,' Sampson said. 'I guess he came on the force after you left.'

'Sixth District? As in, he's a cop?'

'Yeah. I don't envy him that beat, though. It's rough over there these days.'

My mind was reeling, and I felt a little sick to my stomach. *Jason Stemple was a cop?*

'How's the Georgetown case going?' I asked, probably to get Sampson off the track he was going down.

'Nothing new,' he said, sliding right over to the new subject. 'I've covered three out of the four known victims, and I'm *still* not out of the gate.'

'So no one's talking at all? After what happened to them? That's hard to believe. Don't you think so, John?'

'I do. A woman I spoke with today, army captain, she admitted the rapist made some kind of bad threat against her family. Even that was more than she wanted to say.'

We finished our beers in silence. My mind alternated between Sampson's case and Kim Stafford and her policeman fiancé.

Sampson downed the last of his Corona, then he sat up and handed me another. 'So listen,' he said. 'I've got one more interview to do – lawyer who was raped. One more chance to maybe crack this thing open.'

Uh-oh, here it comes.

'Monday afternoon?'

I swiveled in my chair to look at the appointment book on my desk. *Wide open.* 'Damn, I'm all booked up.'

I opened my second beer. A long slat of light came in through the wooden blinds, and I traced it with my eyes back over to where Sampson sat, looking at me with that heavy glare of his. Man Mountain, that was one of the names I had for him. Two-John was another.

'What time on Monday?' I finally asked.

'Three o'clock. I'll pick you up, sugar.' He reached over and clinked his beer bottle against mine. 'You know, you just cost me seven bucks.'

'How's that?'

'The twelve-pack,' he said. 'I would have gotten a six if I'd known you'd be this easy.'

Chapter Sixty

Monday, three o'clock. I shouldn't be here, but here I am anyway.

From what I could tell so far, the firm of Smith, Curtis and Brennan's legal specialty was old money. The expensive-looking wood-paneled reception area, with its issues of *Golf Digest*, *Town & Country*, and *Forbes* on the side tables, seemed to speak for itself: The clients of this firm sure didn't come from my neighborhood.

Mena Sunderland was a junior partner and also our third known rape victim, chronologically. She seemed to blend into the office, with a gray designer business suit and the kind of gracious reserve that sometimes comes from Southern breeding. She led us back to a small conference room and closed the vertical blinds on the glass wall before letting the conversation begin.

'I'm afraid this is a waste of your time,' she told us. 'I don't have anything new to say. I told that to the other detective. Several times.'

Sampson slid a piece of paper over to her. 'We were wondering if this might help.'

'What is it?'

'A draft press statement. If any information goes public, this will be it.'

She scanned the statement while he explained. 'It puts this investigation on an aggressive path and says that none of the known victims have been willing to identify the attacker or testify against him.'

'Is that actually true?' she asked, looking up from the paper.

Sampson started to respond, but a sudden gut reaction flashed through me, and I cut him off. I started to cough. It was kind of a sloppy move, but it worked fine.

'Could I trouble you for a glass of water?' I asked Mena Sunderland. 'I'm sorry.'

When she left the room, I turned to Sampson. 'I don't think she should know it's all down to her.'

'Okay. I guess I agree.' Sampson nodded and added, 'But if she asks—'

'Let me take this,' I said. 'I've got a feeling about her.' My famous 'feelings' were part of my reputation, but that didn't mean Sampson had to go along. If there had been more time for discussion, I would have worried about it, but Mena Sunderland came back a second later. She had two bottles of Fiji water and two glasses. She even braved a smile.

As I drank the water she gave me, I noticed Sampson sit back in his chair. That was my cue to take over.

'Mena,' I said, 'we'd like to try to find some kind of common ground with you. Between what you're comfortable talking about and what we need to know.'

'Meaning what?' she asked.

'Meaning, we don't necessarily need a *description* of this man to catch him.'

I took her silence as a green flag, however tentative.

'I'd like to ask you some questions. They're all yes or no. You can answer with one word or even just shake your head if you like. And if any question is too uncomfortable for you, it's fine to pass.'

A smile threatened the corners of her mouth. My technique was facile, and she knew it. But I wanted to keep this as nonthreatening as possible.

She tucked a long strand of blond hair behind her ear. 'Go ahead. For the moment.'

'On the night of the attack, did this man make specific threats to keep you from talking after he was gone?'

She nodded first, then verbalized her answer. 'Yes.'

Suddenly, I was hopeful. 'Did he make threats against other people you know? Family, friends, that sort of thing?'

'Yes.'

'Has he contacted you since that night? Or made his presence known in any other way?'

'No. I thought I saw him again on my street one time. It probably wasn't him.'

'Were his threats more than verbal? Was there anything else he did to make sure you wouldn't talk?'

'Yes.'

I'd hit on something, I could tell. Mena Sunderland looked down at her lap for a few seconds and then back up at me again. The tension on her face had given way to something more like resolve.

'Please, Mena. This is important.'

'He took my BlackBerry,' she said. She paused for a few seconds, then went on. 'It had all my personal information. Addresses, everything. My friends, my family back home in Westchester.'

'I see.'

And I did. It fit right in with my preliminary profile of this monster.

I started a silent ten count in my head. When I got to eight, Mena spoke again.

'There were pictures,' she said.

'I'm sorry? Pictures?'

'Photographs. Of people he killed. Or at least, said he killed. And' – she took a moment to muster the next part – '*mutilated.* He talked about using butcher saws, surgical scalpels.'

'Mena, can you tell me anything else about those photos he showed you?'

'He made me look at several, but I only really remember the first one. It was the worst thing I've ever seen in my life.' The sudden memory of it came into her eyes, and I saw it take hold. Pure horror. Her focus went soft.

After several seconds, she collected herself and spoke again. 'Her hands,' she said, then stopped herself.

'What about her hands, Mena?'

'He'd cut off both her hands. And in the picture – *she was still alive.* She was obviously screaming.' Her voice closed down to barely a whisper. We were at the danger line; I felt it right away. 'He called her Beverly. Like they were old friends.'

'Okay,' I said gently. 'We can stop here if you want.'

'I want to stop,' she said. 'But.'

'Go ahead, Mena.'

'That night . . . he had a scalpel. There was already somebody's blood on it.'

Chapter Sixty-One

This was huge, but it was also bad news. It could be anyway.

If Mena Sunderland's description was accurate – and why wouldn't it be? – we weren't just talking about serial rape anymore. It was a serial *murder* case. Suddenly, my mind flipped over to Maria's murder, the serial rape case back then. I tried to put Maria out of my mind for the moment. One case at a time.

I wrote down as much as I could remember right after the meeting with Mena, while Sampson gave me a ride home. He had taken his own notes during the interview, but getting these things from my mind onto paper helps me piece a case together sometimes.

My preliminary profile of the rapist was making more and more sense. Trusting first impressions, wasn't that what the best seller *Blink* was all about? The photos that Mena described – keepsakes of whatever kind – were fairly common in serial cases, of course. The photographs would help tide him over during his downtime. And in a grisly new twist, he had used the souvenirs to keep his living victims right where he wanted them – paralyzed with fear.

As we drove through Southeast, Sampson finally broke the silence in the car. 'Alex, I want you to come onto this case. *Officially,*' he said. 'Work with us. Work with *me* on this one. Consult. Whatever you want to call it.'

I looked over at him. 'I thought you might be ticked off at me about taking over a little back there.'

He shrugged. 'No way. I don't argue with results. Besides, you're already in this, right? You might as well be getting paid for it. You couldn't walk away from the case now if you tried.'

I shook my head and frowned, but only because he was right. I could feel a familiar buzz starting in my mind – my thoughts involuntarily locking onto the case. It's one of the things that makes me good at the job, but also the reason I find it impossible to be *kind of* involved in an investigation.

'What am I supposed to tell Nana?' I asked him, which I guess was my way of saying yes.

'Tell her the case needs you. Tell her Sampson needs you.' He took a right onto Fifth Street, and my house came into view. 'Better think of something fast, though. She'll smell it on you for sure. She'll see it in your eyes.'

'You want to come in?'

'Nice try.' He left the car running when he stopped at the curb.

'Here I go,' I said. 'Wish me luck with Nana.'

'Hey, man, no one said police work wasn't dangerous.'

Chapter Sixty-Two

I worked on the case that night in the attic office. It was late when I decided I'd had enough.

I went downstairs and grabbed my key – I was in the habit most nights of taking a spin in the new Mercedes, my crossover car. It drove like an absolute dream, and the seats were as comfy as anything in our living room. Just turn on the CD player, sit back, and relax. This was good stuff.

When I finally got to bed that night, my thoughts took me back to a place I still needed to visit now and then. A sanctuary. My honeymoon with Maria. Maybe the best ten days of my life. Everything was still vivid in my mind.

The sun drops just below the palms as it sinks toward a horizontal line of blue out beyond the balcony of our hotel. *The empty spot in the bed next to me is still warm where Maria was until a minute ago.*

Now she's standing at the mirror.

Beautiful.

She's wearing nothing but one of my dress shirts, open down the front, and getting ready for dinner.

She always says her legs are too skinny, but I find them long and lovely and get turned on just looking at them — at her in the mirror.

I watch as Maria sweeps her shiny black hair back into a clip. It shows off the long line of her neck. God, I adore her.

'Do that again,' I say.

She indulges me without a word.

When she tilts her head to put on an earring, her eye catches mine in the mirror.

'I love you, Alex.' She turns to face me. 'No one will ever love you the way I do.'

Her eyes hold mine, and I believe that I can see what she's feeling inside. The way we think is so unbelievably close. I stretch my hand out from the bed for her, and say—

Chapter Sixty-Three

Something heartfelt.

But I couldn't remember what it was now.

I sat up – all alone in my bed – jarred from the half-awake, half-asleep place I'd just been. My memory had stumbled onto a blank spot, like a hole in the ground that wasn't there before.

The details of our honeymoon in Barbados had always been so crystal clear in my mind. Why couldn't I remember what I'd said to Maria?

The clock next to me glowed: 2:15.

I was wide awake, though.

Please God, I thought, *these memories are what I have left. All I have. Don't take them away too.*

I switched on the light.

Staying in bed now wasn't an option. I wandered

out into the hall, thinking maybe I'd go down and play the piano.

At the top of the stairs, I stopped with my hand on the banister. The soft, rasping sound of Ali's breath held me where I was.

I stepped into his room and watched my little boy from the doorway.

He was just a small lump under the covers, and a bare foot sticking out; his breath sounded like a miniature snore.

The *Blues Clues* nightlight on the wall was just enough to show his face. Little Alex's eyebrows were knitted tightly, as though he was deep in thought, just the way I look sometimes.

When I crawled under the covers, he nuzzled up to my chest and pressed his head into the crook of my arm.

'Hi, Daddy,' he said, half-awake.

'Hey, pup,' I whispered. 'Go back to sleep.'

'Did you have a bad dream?'

I smiled. It was a question I'd asked him countless times in the past. Now the words came back to me like a piece of myself I'd let go.

He'd given me my words. I gave him Maria's. 'I love you, Ali. No one will ever love you the way I do.'

The boy was perfectly still, probably asleep already.

I lay there with my hand on his shoulder until his breathing went back to that same soft rhythm as before. And then somewhere in there, I went back to be with Maria.

Chapter Sixty-Four

The memories of his father were always the strongest when Michael Sullivan was with his sons. The bright-white butcher shop, the freezer in the back, the Bone Man who came once a week to pack up meat carcasses, the smells of Irish Carrigaline cheese, and of black-and-white pudding.

'Hey, batta, batta, batta,' Sullivan heard, and it brought him hurtling back to the present – to the ball-field near where he lived in Maryland.

Then he heard, 'This guy can't hit worth spit! This guy's nothin'! You own this mutt!'

Seamus and Jimmy were the trash-talkers for the family baseball games. Michael Jr was as focused as ever. Sullivan saw it in his oldest son's bright-blue eyes – a need to strike out the old man once and for all.

His son wound up and let fly. A sharp-breaking curveball, or maybe a hard slider. Sullivan exhaled as he swung – then heard the smack of the ball as it hit Jimmy's catcher's mitt behind him. Son of a bitch had brought some heat!

Something like pandemonium broke out on the otherwise deserted American Legion field where they practiced. Jimmy, the catcher, ran a circle around his father, holding the ball in the air.

Only Michael Jr stayed calm and cool. He allowed himself a slight grin but didn't leave the pitching mound, didn't celebrate with his brothers.

He just bad-eyed his old man, whom he had never struck out before.

He ducked his chin, ready to go into the windup – but then stopped.

'What's *that*?' he asked, looking at his father.

Sullivan looked down and saw something move onto his chest. *The red pinpoint of a laser sight.*

He dropped to the dirt beside home plate.

Chapter Sixty-Five

The vintage Louisville Slugger, still in his hand, splintered apart before it hit the ground. A loud metal *ping* sounded as a bullet ricocheted off the backstop. *Someone was shooting at him! Maggione's people? Who else?*

'Boys! Dugout – now! Run! Run!' he yelled.

The boys didn't have to be told twice. Michael Jr grabbed his youngest brother's arm. All three of them sprinted for cover, fast little bastards, running like they just stole somebody's wallet.

The Butcher ran for all he was worth in the opposite direction; he wanted to draw fire off of his boys.

And he needed the gun in his car!

The Humvee was parked at least sixty yards away, and he ran as straight a line as he dared to get there.

Another shot came so close that he heard it whiz by his chin.

The gunshots were coming from the woods to the left of the ballfield, away from the road. That much he knew. He didn't bother looking around, though. Not yet.

When he got to the Humvee, he threw open the passenger-side door and dove inside. An explosion of glass followed.

The Butcher stayed low, face pressed against the floor mat, and reached under the driver's seat.

The Beretta clipped there represented a broken promise to Caitlin. He drove the magazine home and finally took a look up top.

There were two of them, coming out of the woods now – two of Maggione's wiseguys for sure. They were here to put him down, weren't they? And maybe his kids too.

He unlatched the driver's door, then rolled outside onto gravel and dirt. Chancing a look under the car, he saw a pair of legs headed his way in a shuffling run.

No time for deep thought or any kind of planning. He fired twice under the chassis. Maggione's man yelped as a blossom of red opened above his ankle.

He went down hard, and the Butcher fired again,

right into the hood's twice-shocked face. The bastard never got off another shot, word, or thought. But that was the least of his worries now.

'Dad! Dad! Dad, help!'

It was Mike's voice – coming from all the way across the park, and it was hoarse with panic.

Sullivan jumped up and saw the other hit man headed for the dugout, maybe seventy-five yards away. He raised his gun but knew he'd be firing toward his boys, too.

He jumped in and slammed the Humvee into Drive.

Chapter Sixty-Six

He floored it as if his boys' lives depended on it. Probably they did. Maggione was the kind of coward who would kill your family. Then he held the Beretta out the window, looking for one clear shot. This was going to be close. No way to tell the outcome, either. Suspense city!

The hit man was sprinting across the infield, really moving now. Sullivan guessed the guy had been a decent athlete when he'd been younger. Not too long ago, either.

Michael Jr watched from the dugout steps. The kid was a cool head, but that wasn't necessarily helpful now. Sullivan screamed at him. 'Get down! Michael, down! Right now!'

The hit man knew Sullivan was coming up behind

him. Finally, he stopped and turned to make a shot of his own.

Mistake!

Possibly fatal.

His eyes went wide just before the Humvee's grille caught him in the chest, moving at fifty miles an hour plus. The vehicle didn't slow down until it had given the hitter a swift ride, then rammed him into the chain link of the backstop.

'You boys all right?' Sullivan yelled, keeping his eyes on the hit man, who wasn't moving and looked like he'd have to be peeled off the fence.

'We're okay,' Michael Jr said, sounding shaky but still in control of his emotions.

Sullivan walked around to look at the punk, what was left of him anyway. The only thing keeping him on his feet was the steel sandwich he was trapped in. His head lolled lazily to one side. He seemed to be looking around through the one eye not totally obscured by blood.

Sullivan went and picked up the remains of the Louisville Slugger from the dirt.

He swung once, twice, again, and again, punctuating each blow with a shout.

'Don't.

'Fuck.

'With.

'My.

'Family!

'Ever!

'Ever!

'Ever!'

The last swing went wild and missed; Sullivan put a huge crater in his hood. But it helped him remember where he was.

He got in the car and backed up to where his boys were watching like a crowd of zombies at somebody's funeral. When they climbed inside, none of them spoke, but nobody cried, either.

'It's okay now,' he told them. 'It's over, boys. I'm going to take care of this. Do you hear me? I promise. I promise you on my dead mother's eyes!'

And he would keep his word. They had come after him and his family, and the Butcher would come after them.

The mob.

John Maggione.

Chapter Sixty-Seven

I had another session with Kim Stafford, and when she came in, she was wearing dark sunglasses and looked like someone on the run. My stomach just about dropped to the ground floor of the brownstone. It struck me that my professional worlds were colliding on this case.

Now that I knew who Kim's fiancé was, it was harder for me to respect her wish to keep him out of this. I wanted to confront this piece of crap in the worst way.

'Kim,' I said at one point, not too far into the session, 'does Sam keep any weapons in the apartment?' *Sam* was the name we had agreed to use in our sessions; Sam was also the name of a bulldog that had bitten Kim when she was a little girl.

'A pistol in the nightstand,' she said.

I tried not to show the concern I was feeling, the alarm sounding loudly inside my head. 'Has he ever pointed the gun at you? Threatened to use it?'

'Just once,' she said, and picked at the fabric of her skirt. 'It was a while ago. If I'd thought he was serious, I would have left him.'

'Kim, I'd like to talk to you about a safety plan.'

'What do you mean?'

'Identifying some precautionary measures,' I said. 'Setting aside money; keeping a packed suitcase somewhere; finding somewhere you could go – if you needed to leave quickly.'

I'm not sure why she took off her sunglasses at that moment, but this is when she chose to show me her black eye. 'I can't, Dr Cross,' she said. 'If I make a plan, I'll use it. And then I think he truly would kill me.'

After my last session that day, I dialed into my voice mail before heading out. There was only one message. It was from Kayla.

'Hey, it's me. Well, hang onto your hat because Nana is letting me cook dinner for all of us tonight. *In her kitchen!* If I weren't scared silly, I'd say I can't wait. So, I've got a couple of house calls to make, and then I'm stopping at the store. Then I might shoot myself in the parking lot. If not, I'll see you at home around six. That's *your* house.'

It was already six when I got the message. I tried to put the troubling session with Kim Stafford out of my mind, but only partly succeeded. I hoped she was going to be okay, and I wasn't sure if I should try to interfere just yet. By the time I got to Fifth Street and hurried inside, Kayla was ensconced in the kitchen. She was wearing Nana's favorite apron and sliding a rib roast into the oven.

Nana sat erect at the kitchen table with an untouched glass of white wine in front of her. Now *this* was interesting stuff.

The kids were flitting around in the kitchen too, probably waiting to see how long Nana could sit still.

'How was your day, Daddy?' Jannie asked. 'What's the best thing that happened?' she said.

That brought a big smile from both of us. It was a question we liked to throw around the dinner table sometimes. We'd been doing it for years.

I thought about Kim Stafford, and then I thought about the Georgetown rape case and Nana's reaction to my working on it. Thinking about Nana brought me right back to the present, to my answer to Jannie's question.

'So far?' I said. 'This is it. Being here with you guys is the best thing.'

Chapter Sixty-Eight

Things were heating up now.

The Butcher hated the beach; he hated the sand, the smell of briny water, the bottlenecked traffic, everything about a visit to the crummy seashore. Caitlin and the boys, with their summertime trips to Cape May – they could have it, keep it, shove it.

So it was business, and business only, that brought him to the shore, much less all the way to South Jersey. It was revenge against John Maggione. The two of them had hated each other since Maggione's father had permitted this 'Irish crazy' to become his killer of choice. Then Sullivan had been ordered to take out one of Junior's buddies, and the Butcher had done the job with his usual enthusiasm. He'd cut Rico Marinacci into pieces.

John Maggione had been making himself scarce lately – *no surprise there* – so the Butcher's plan had changed a little, for now. If he couldn't cut off the head just yet, he'd start with some other body part.

The part, in this case, was named Dante Ricci. Dante was the youngest made man in the Maggione syndicate, a personal favorite of the don's. Like a son to him. The inside joke was that John Maggione didn't let an associate wipe his ass without checking with Dante.

Sullivan got to the shore town of Mantoloking, New Jersey, just before dusk. As he drove across Barnegat Bay, the ocean in the distance looked almost purple – beautiful, if you liked that kind of picture-postcard, Kodak-moment thing. Sullivan rolled up his windows against the salt air. He couldn't wait to do his business, then get the hell out of here.

The town itself lay on an expensive strip of land less than a mile across. Ricci's house, on Ocean Avenue, wasn't real hard to find. He drove past the front gate, parked up the road, and walked back about a fifth of a mile.

It looked like Ricci was doing pretty well for himself. The main house was a big honking Colonial: three stories, brown cedar shakes, all perfectly maintained, and right on the water. Four-bay garage, a guesthouse, hot tub up on the dune. Six million, easy. Just the kind of shiny object modern-day wiseguys dangled in front of their wives to distract them from the day-to-day stealing and killing they did for a living.

And Dante Ricci was a killer; that was what he did best. Hell, he was the new-and-improved Butcher.

Sullivan couldn't see too much of the layout from the front. He imagined most of the house was oriented to the water view in the back. But the beach would offer no good cover for him. He'd have to settle in where he was, and take his time.

That wasn't a problem for him. He had whatever it took to do the job, including patience. A snatch of Gaelic ran through his head, something his grand-father James used to say. *Coimhéad fearg fhear na foighde,* or some shit like that. *Beware the anger of a patient man.*

Just so, Michael Sullivan thought as he waited, perfectly still in the gathering dusk. Just so.

Chapter Sixty-Nine

It took a while for him to get a sense of the beach house and its immediate surroundings. There wasn't much movement inside, but enough to see that the family was home: Dante, two small kids, and – at least from this distance – what looked to be the hot young wife, a nice Italian blonde.

But no visitors, and no bodyguards out in plain sight. Specifically, no capital F: *Family*. That meant any firepower in the house would be limited to whatever Dante Ricci kept on hand. Whatever he had, it probably wasn't going to stack up against the 9mm machine-gun pistol Sullivan had holstered at his side. *Or his scalpel*.

Despite the chill in the air, he was perspiring under his jacket, and a patch of sweat had soaked through his T-shirt where the piece hugged his body. The ocean breeze did nothing to cool him down, either. Only his patience held him in check. His *professionalism*, he liked to think. Traits he had no doubt inherited from his father, the original Butcher, who, if nothing else, had been a patient bastard.

Finally, he moved in toward the beach house. He walked past a shiny black Jaguar sitting on the blond brick parking pad and entered into one of the open garage bays, where a white Jag made bookends with the black one.

Gee, Dante, ostentatious much?

It didn't take long to find something useful in the garage. The Butcher picked up a short-handled sledge-hammer from the workbench in the back. He hoisted it and felt its weight. Just about right. Very nice. Jeez, he liked tools. Just like his old man.

He'd have to swing lefty if he wanted to stay gun-ready, but his strike zone was as big as, well, a Jaguar's windshield.

He shouldered the hammer, paralleled his feet, and went all Mark McGwire on the glass.

A high-pitched car alarm started screaming at the first impact, just like he wanted it to.

Sullivan immediately hoofed it out to the front yard, about halfway back to the main road. He stepped just out of sight behind a mature red oak that seemed out of place here – like him. His finger was at the pistol's trigger, but no. No shooting yet. Let Dante think he was some shitbag Jersey Shore burglar. That should bring him running and cursing.

The front screen door flew open seconds later, smacked hard against the wall of the house. Two sets of floodlights flared.

Sullivan squinted against the light. But he could see ol' Dante on the porch – with a pistol in his hand. In swim shorts no less – and flip-flops. Well muscled and in good shape, but so what. What a cocky bastard this guy was.

Mistake.

'Who the hell's there?' the tough guy shouted into the darkness. 'I said, who's out there? You better start running!'

Sullivan smiled. *This* was Junior's enforcer? The new Butcher? This buffed punk at his beach house? In bathing trunks and plastic shoes?

'Hey, it's just Mike Sullivan!' he called back.

The Butcher stepped into plain view, took a little bow, then sprayed the front porch before Dante saw it coming. In truth, why would he? Who would have the balls to come after a made man at his house? Who could be that crazy?

'That's just for starters!' the Butcher roared as half a dozen shots struck Dante Ricci in the stomach and chest. The mobster dropped to his knees, glared out at Sullivan, then fell over face-first.

Sullivan kept his finger on the trigger and swept the two Jaguars in the garage and driveway. More glass shattered. Neat lines of holes opened along the expensive chassis. That felt pretty good.

When he stopped shooting, he could hear screams coming from inside the beach house. Women, children. He took out the porch floodlights with two quick, controlled bursts.

Then he approached the house, fingering the scalpel. As soon as he got to the body, he knew that Dante Ricci was dead as some bloated mackerel washed up on the beach. Still, he rolled the body and slashed the dead man's face a dozen times or so with the sharp blade. 'Nothing personal, Dante. But you're not the new me.'

Then he turned to go. Dante Ricci had gotten the message, and very, very soon, so would Junior Maggione.

Then he heard a voice coming from outside the house. A female.

'You killed him! You bastard! You killed my Dante!'

Sullivan turned back and saw Dante's wife standing

there with a gun in her hand. The woman was petite, a pretty bleached blonde, no more than five feet tall.

The wife fired blindly into the dark. She didn't know how to shoot, couldn't even hold a gun right. But she had some hot Maggione blood in her.

'Get back in the house!' Sullivan shouted. 'Or I'll blow your head off!'

'You killed him! You scumbag! You dirty son of a bitch!' She stepped off the porch, moving into the yard.

The woman was crying, blubbering, but coming to get him, the dumb bunny. 'I'm going to kill you, you fucker.' Her next shot exploded a concrete birdbath, only a yard or so to Sullivan's right.

Her crying had turned to a high-pitched wail. It sounded more like an injured animal than anything human.

Then something inside her snapped, and she charged across the driveway. She fired off one more shot before Sullivan put two into her chest. She dropped like she'd run into a wall, then lay there quivering pathetically. He cut her up too.

Once he got inside his car, he felt better, satisfied with himself. He even welcomed the long drive back. Riding along the turnpike, he opened the windows and cranked up the music, singing Bono's words at the top of his lungs as if they were his own.

Chapter Seventy

The next day would get filed under *What the Hell Was I Thinking?* I showed up at the Sixth District station house, where Jason Stemple was based, and I started asking around about him. I wasn't sure what I would do if I found him, but I was nervous enough for Kim Stafford that I had to try something, or thought I did.

I didn't carry creds or a badge anymore, but lots of DC cops knew who I was, who I *am*. Apparently not the desk sergeant, though.

He kept me waiting on the civilian side of the glass longer than I would have liked. That was okay, I guess, no big deal. I stood around, glancing over the Annual Crime Reduction Awards on the wall until he finally informed me that he had checked me out with his captain; then he buzzed me through.

Another uniformed officer was there waiting for me.

'Pulaski, take Mister' – the sergeant glanced down at the sign-in sheet – 'Cross back to the locker room please. He's looking for Stemple. I thought he'd be out by now.'

I followed him down a busy hallway, picking up strands of cop talk along the way. Pulaski pushed open a heavy swinging door into the locker room. The smell was familiar, sweat and various antiseptics.

'Stemple! You got a visitor.'

A young guy, late twenties, about my height but heavier, looked over. He was alone at a row of beat-up army-green lockers, and he was just pulling on a Washington Nationals road jersey. Another half-dozen or so off-duty cops were standing around, grousing and laughing about the state of the court system, which definitely was a joke these days.

I walked over to where Stemple was putting his watch on and still basically ignoring me.

'Could I talk to you for a minute?' I asked. I was trying to be polite, but it took an effort with this guy who liked to beat up on his girlfriend.

'About?' Stemple barely looked my way.

I lowered my voice. 'I want to talk to you . . . about Kim Stafford.'

All at once, the less-than-friendly welcome down-graded to pure animosity. Stemple rocked back on his heels and looked me up and down like I was a street person who'd just broken into his house.

'What are you doing in here anyway? You a cop?'

'I used to be a cop, but now I'm a therapist. I work with Kim.'

Stemple's eyes beaded and burned. He was getting the picture now, and he didn't like what he saw. Neither did I, because I was looking at a powerfully built male who beat up on women and sometimes burned them with lit objects.

'Yeah, well, I just pulled a double, and I'm out of here. You stay away from Kim if you know what's good for you. You hear me?'

Now that we'd met, I had a professional opinion of Stemple. He was a piece of shit. As he walked away, I said, 'You're beating her up, Stemple. You burned her with a cigar.'

The locker room grew still, but I noticed that no one hurried to get in my face on Stemple's behalf. The others just watched. A couple of them nodded, as though maybe they knew about Stemple and Kim already.

He slowly turned back to me and puffed himself up. 'What are you trying to start with me, asshole? Who the hell are you? She screwing you?'

'It's nothing like that. I told you, I just came here to talk. If you know what's good for you, you should listen.'

That's when Stemple threw the first punch. I stepped back, and he missed, but not by much. He was definitely hot-tempered, and strong.

It was all I needed, though, maybe all I wanted. I feinted to the left, then countered with an uppercut into his gut. Some of the air rushed out of him.

But then his powerful arms latched around my middle. Stemple drove me hard against a row of lockers. The metal boomed with the impact. Pain radiated through my upper and lower back. I hoped nothing was broken already.

As soon as I could get my footing again, I bull-dozed him back, and he stumbled, losing his grip. He swung again. This time, he connected hard with my jaw.

I returned the favor – a solid right to the chin – followed with a looping left hook that landed just over his eyebrow. One for me, one for Kim Stafford. Then I hit him with a right to the cheekbone.

Stemple spun halfway around; then he surprised me and went down to the locker room floor. His right eye was already starting to close.

My arms pulsed. I was ready for more of this punk,

this coward. The fight never should have started, but it had, and I was disappointed when he didn't get up again.

'Is that how it is with Kim? She pisses you off, you take a swing?'

He groaned but didn't say anything to me.

I said, 'Listen, Stemple. You want me to keep what I know to myself, not go any higher with this? Make sure it doesn't happen again. Ever. Keep your hands off her. And your cigars. Are we clear?'

He stayed where he was, and that told me what I needed to know. I was halfway to the door when one of the other cops caught my eye. 'Good for you,' he said.

Chapter Seventy-One

If Nana had been working the Georgetown case, in her own inimitable style, she'd have said it was 'simmering' about now. Sampson and I had tossed a bunch of interesting ingredients into the mix, and we'd turned the heat up high. Now it was time for some results.

I looked at the big man across a table full of crime reports spread out between us. 'I've never seen so much information lead to so little,' I said grumpily.

'Now you know what I've been dealing with on this,' he said, and squeezed and unsqueezed a rubber stress ball in his fist. I was surprised the thing hadn't burst into a million pieces by now.

'This guy is careful, seems smart enough, and he's cruel. Got a powerful angle too – using his souvenirs to threaten these women. Making it personal. In case you hadn't figured that out already,' I said. I was just talking it through out loud. Sometimes that helps.

My thing lately, my habit, was pacing. I'd probably covered about six miles of carpet in the past fourteen hours, all in the same Second District station conference room where we were holed up. My feet hurt some, but that's how I kept my brain going. That and sour-apple Altoids.

We'd started that morning by cross-referencing the last four years of Uniform Crime Reports, looking for potentially related cases – reaching for anything that could start to tie this thing together. Given what we now knew about our perp, we had looked at female missing persons, rape cases, and especially murder where mutilation was involved. First for Georgetown and then for the whole DC metro area.

To keep our mood as light as possible, we'd listened to 'Elliot in the Morning' on the radio, but even Elliot and Diane couldn't brighten our moods that day, good as they are at mood-brightening.

In order to cover all our bases, we made a second pass, checking unsolved murders in general. The result was a list of potential follow-ups that was just as large as it was unpromising.

One good thing had happened today. Mena

Sunderland had granted us another interview, where she went so far as to give a few descriptive details on her rapist. He was a white man, in his forties, she guessed. And from what we could glean from Mena, he was good-looking, which was difficult for her to admit. 'You know,' she'd told us, 'the way Kevin Costner is good-looking for an older guy?'

It was an important part of the profile for us to pin down, though. Attractive attackers had an edge that made them even more dangerous. My hope was that with a little time and the promise of a lot of protection, Mena would be willing to keep talking to us. What we had so far wasn't enough for a useful police sketch. As soon as we had a likeness that didn't match about twelve thousand other faces on the streets of Georgetown, Sampson and I wanted to go wide with it.

Sampson tilted his chair back and stretched his long legs. 'What do you think about getting some sleep and starting in on the rest of these in the morning? I'm cooked.'

Just then, Betsey Hall came whizzing in, looking a lot more awake than either of us did. Betsey was a newbie detective, eager, but the kind who knew how to be helpful without getting underfoot.

'You only looked at *female* victims in your cross-refs?' she said. 'That's right, isn't it?'

'Why?' Sampson asked.

'Ever heard of Benny Fontana?'

Neither of us had.

'Midlevel mob soldier, *underboss,* I guess is the term. *Was,* anyway,' Betsey said. 'He was killed two weeks ago. In an apartment in Kalorama Park. Actually, on the night that Lisa Brandt was raped in Georgetown.'

'And?' Sampson asked. I could hear the same tired impatience in his voice that I felt. 'So?'

'And so, *this.'*

Betsey flipped open a file and spread half a dozen black-and-white photographs out on the table. They showed a white man, maybe fifty years old, dead on his back in a living room somewhere. Both of his feet were completely – and freshly – severed at the ankle.

All of a sudden, I wasn't so tired anymore. Adrenaline was pumping through my system.

'Jesus,' Sampson muttered. We were both on our feet now, scanning from one grisly photo to another, repeating the process a couple of times.

'The ME's report says all the cutting on Mr Fontana was done antemortem,' Betsey added. 'Possibly with surgical tools. Maybe a scalpel and saw.' Her expression was hopeful, kind of sweetly naive. 'So you think this is the same perp?'

I answered, 'I think I want to know more. Can we get the keys to that apartment?'

She fished a set out of her pocket, jangling them proudly. 'Thought you might ask me that.'

Chapter Seventy-Two

'**S**hit, Alex. Multiple rapes, multiple murders. Now a mob connection?' Sampson punched the roof of the car. 'It can't all be coincidental. Can't be! *Cannot!*'

'Could definitely be something – *if* it's the same guy,' I reminded him. 'Let's see what happens here. Try not to get too far ahead of ourselves.'

Not that John was off base. Our suspect was looking more and more like a sadistic monster with a very bad, very distinctive habit. It wasn't that we'd been looking in the wrong place for him, just maybe not in *enough* places.

'But if this does pan out,' Sampson went on, 'no phone calls to your old pals tonight. All right? I want a little time with this before the Feds come on board.'

The FBI would already know about the Fontana

murder, assuming it was mob related. But the rapes were still DCPD. Local stuff.

'You don't know that they'll necessarily take over the case,' I said.

'Oh yeah.' Sampson snapped his fingers and pointed at me. 'I forgot. You had your memory wiped when you left the Bureau, like they do it in *Men in Black*. Well, let me remind you – *they'll take over this case.* They love cases like this one. We do all the work; the Feebies take all the credit.'

I stole a glance at him. 'When I was at the Bureau, you ever resent me coming in on a case? Did I do that?'

'If it happened, don't worry about it,' he said. 'If it was worth talking about then, I would have brought it up. Hell *no*, you never moved in on one of my cases!'

I pulled over in front of a tan brick apartment house across from Kalorama Park. It was a nice location; I'm sure the Fontana murder had rocked that building, if not the neighborhood. It was also less than two miles from the location where Lisa Brandt had been attacked not long after Benny Fontana died.

We spent the next hour inside, using crime-scene photos and the bloodstains still in the carpet to re-create what might have happened. It didn't give us any concrete connection to the other attacks, but it was a start.

When we left, we rode southwest into George-town, taking the most logical route to Lisa Brandt's neighborhood. By now, it was around midnight. Neither of us felt like stopping yet, so we did a full tour of the case, riding by each of the known rape sites in chronological order. They weren't that far apart.

At 2:30 a.m. we were in a booth at an all-night coffee shop. We had crime files spread out on the table and were reading them over, too revved-up to stop, too tired to go home.

This was my first chance to really get into the Benny Fontana file. I had read the police and ME's reports several times. Now I was looking over the list of items taken from the apartment. On my fourth or fifth time through, my eyes stopped on one item in particular: a torn-off corner of a white foil-lined envelope. It had been found under the sofa, only a few feet from Fontana's body. Speaking of *feet*, or a lack of them.

I sat up. These are the moments you hope for in an unsolved case.

'We have to go somewhere.'

'You're right. We have to go home,' Sampson said.

I called to the waitress, who was half-asleep at the

counter. 'Is there a twenty-four-hour drugstore some-where around here? It's important.'

Sampson was too tired to argue. He followed me out of the coffee shop and around the corner, up a few blocks to a brightly lit Walgreens. A quick scan of the aisles inside and I found what I was looking for.

'Mena Sunderland said the pictures she saw were Polaroids.' I ripped open a box of film.

'You have to pay for that first,' a clerk called from the front. I ignored him.

Sampson was shaking his head. 'Alex, what the hell are you doing?'

'The evidence list from the Fontana murder scene,' I said. 'There was a white foil-lined envelope. A piece of one anyway.'

I pulled the new envelope out of the box, tore off a corner, and held it up. 'Just like this.'

Sampson started to smile.

'He took pictures of Benny Fontana after he cut him up. *It's the same guy, John.*'

Chapter Seventy-Three

I worked a long, long day, but the next night, I was grounded.

Nana had a weekly reading class she was teaching at the First Baptist-run shelter on Fourth Street, and I stayed home with the kids. When I'm with them, there's nowhere I'd rather be. The problem, sometimes, is just getting me there.

I played chef for the night. I made my and the kids' favorite, white-bean soup, along with a chopped Cobb salad, and I'd brought home some nice fresh cheddar bread from the bakery next to my office. The soup tasted almost as good as Nana's. Sometimes I think she has *two* versions of every recipe – the one in her head and the one she shares with me, minus some key secret ingredient. It's her mystique; and I doubt it has changed much in the last half century.

Then the kids and I had a long-overdue session with the punching bag downstairs. Jannie and Damon took turns pummeling leather, while Ali ran his trucks around and around the basement floor, which he declared was I-95!

Afterward we migrated upstairs for a swimming lesson with little brother. Yes, *swimming*. It was Jannie's concoction, inspired by Ali's reluctance to get into the bathtub. Never mind that it was even harder to get him *out* of the bath once he got started. That distinction was lost on him, and he fussed every single time, as if he were allergic to cleanliness. I was skeptical about Jannie's idea until I saw how it worked.

'Breathe, Ali!' she coached him from the side. 'Let's see you breathe, puppy.'

Damon kept his hands under Ali's belly while Ali lay facedown on top of the water, mostly blowing bubbles and splashing around. It was hilarious, but I didn't dare laugh, for Jannie's sake. I sat at a safe – as in dry – distance, watching from the toilet seat.

'Pick him up for a second,' Jannie said.

Damon stood the big boy up in the claw-foot tub.

Ali blinked and sprayed out a mouthful of water, his eyes gleaming from the game.

'I'm swimming!' he declared.

'Not yet you're not,' Jannie said, all business. 'But you're definitely getting there, little bro.'

She and Damon were practically as soaked as he was, but no one seemed to care. It was a blast. Jannie was kneeling right in a puddle, while Damon stood up and gave me a conspiratorial oldest-child look that said, *Aren't they crazy?*

When the phone rang, they both sprang for the door. 'I'll get it!' they chorused.

'*I'll* get it,' I said, cutting them off at the pass. 'You're both sopping wet. No swimming until I get back.'

'Come on, Ali,' I heard as I started out of the bathroom. 'Let's wash your hair.'

The girl was a genius.

I trotted down the hall to catch the phone before the machine picked up. 'Cross family YMCA,' I said, loud enough for the kids' benefit.

Chapter Seventy-Four

'Is this Alex Cross?'

'Yes?' I said. I didn't recognize the voice on the line though. Just that it was a woman.

'It's Annie Falk.'

'Annie,' I said, embarrassed now. 'Hi, how are you?'

We were acquaintances, not quite friends. Her son was one or maybe two grades ahead of Damon. Annie was an ER doc at St Anthony's.

'Alex, I'm at the hospital—'

I suddenly made a connection, and my heart skipped the next beat. 'Is Nana there?'

'It's not Nana,' she said. 'I didn't know who else to call. Kayla Coles was just admitted to St Anthony's. She's here in the ER.'

'Kayla?' I said, my voice rising. 'What's going on? Is she okay?'

'I don't know, Alex. We don't know enough yet. It's not a good situation though.'

That wasn't the answer I expected, or the one I wanted to hear.

'Annie, what happened? Can you tell me that much?'

'It's hard to know exactly. What's certain is that someone attacked Kayla.'

'Who?' I practically shouted into the phone, feeling horrible, as though I already knew the answer to my own question.

Damon stepped halfway into the hall and stared at me, his eyes wide and scared. It was a look I'd seen far too many times in our house.

'All I can tell you is that she was stabbed with a knife. Twice, Alex. She's alive.'

Stabbed? My mind screamed the word, but I held it in. I swallowed hard. *But she's alive.*

'Alex, I'm not supposed to talk about this over the phone. You should get down here to the hospital as soon as you can. Can you come right now?'

'I'm on my way.'

Chapter Seventy-Five

Nana was still at her class, but it only took a couple of minutes for me to get Naomi Harris from next door over to stay with the kids. I jumped into my car and ran the siren the whole way.

The drive to the hospital was *fast*; that's all I really remember about it, and that Kayla was on my mind the whole way. When I pulled up outside the emergency room, her car was parked under the canopy by the entrance.

The driver's door hung open, and as I ran past and looked inside, I saw blood on the front seat. Jesus, she drove herself here! Somehow she got away from him.

The waiting room was crowded; as it always is at St Anthony's. There was a line of forlorn, raggedy-looking people at the front desk. The walking wounded and their friends and relations. *Maria had been pronounced dead here.*

'Sir, you can't—'

But I was already sliding through the doors to the treatment area before they could close. Once inside, I saw it was another very busy night at St Tony's. Paramedics were wheeling gurneys; doctors, nurses, and patients crisscrossed every which way around me.

A young male lay on a cot with a gash in his hairline, leaking blood onto his forehead. 'Am I gonna die?' he kept asking everybody who passed.

'No, you'll be fine,' I told him, since nobody else was stopping to talk to him. 'You're all right, son.'

Where was Kayla, though? Everything was moving way too fast. I couldn't find anyone to ask about her. Then I heard a voice call out my name.

'Alex, over here!'

Annie was waving to me from down the hall. When I reached her, she took my arm and ushered me into a trauma room – a bay with two beds partitioned by a green plastic curtain.

Several medical personnel stood in a horseshoe around the bed. Their hands were moving quickly, many of them in bloodstained gloves.

Other hospital people came and went, pushing past me as if I weren't even there.

That meant Kayla was alive. I assumed that the goal here would be to stabilize her if possible, then get her to the operating room.

I craned my neck to see as much as I could, and then I saw Kayla. She had a mask over her mouth and nose. Someone was just lifting a red-soaked compress from her belly where they had already cut her shirt away.

The head physician, a woman in her thirties, said, '*Stab wound, abdomen, questionable spleen injury.*'

Other voices in the room blended together, and I tried to make sense of them as best I could, but everything was turning foggy on me.

'BP seventy, pulse one twenty. Respiration thirty-forty.'

'Give me some suction here, please.'

'Is she okay?' I blurted out. I felt like I was in a nightmare where no one could hear me.

'Alex—' Annie's hand was on my shoulder. 'You need to give them some room. We don't know very much yet. As soon as we do, I'll tell you.'

I realized I'd been pushing forward to get closer to the bed, to Kayla. My God, I ached for her and was finding it hard to breathe.

'Call the seventh floor, tell them we're ready,' said the woman doctor who seemed in charge of everyone else in the room. 'She has a surgical belly.'

Annie whispered to me, 'That means the stomach's hard, no digestion going on.'

'Let's go. Hurry up, people.'

I was being pushed from behind, and not with any kindness. 'Move, sir. You have to move out of the way. This patient is in trouble. She could die.'

I stepped sideways to make room as they wheeled her gurney into the corridor. Kayla's eyes were still closed. Did she know I was there? Or who had done this to her? I followed the procession as near as I could get. Then just as quickly as they had done everything else, they loaded her onto an elevator, and the metal doors slid shut between us.

Annie was right there at my side. She gestured toward another elevator bank. 'I can take you to the waiting room upstairs if you want. Believe me, everybody's doing the best they can. They know Kayla's a doctor. And everybody knows she's a saint.'

Chapter Seventy-Six

This patient is in trouble. She could die . . . Everybody knows she's a saint.

I spent the next three hours in the waiting room, alone and without any further word about Kayla. My head was filled with disturbing ironies. Two of my kids had been born at St Anthony's. Maria had been pronounced dead here. And now Kayla.

Then Annie Falk was with me again, down on one knee, speaking in a quiet, respectful voice that scared me like nothing else could right then.

'Come with me, Alex. Come, please. Hurry. I'll take you to her. She's out of the OR.'

At first I thought Kayla was still asleep in the recovery room, but she stirred when I came near. Her eyes opened, and she saw me – recognized me an instant later.

'Alex?' she whispered.

'Hey there, you,' I whispered back, and gently took her hand in both of mine.

She looked very confused and lost for a moment; then she squeezed her eyes shut. Tears rolled down her cheeks, and I almost started up myself, but I thought if Kayla saw me that way it might scare her.

'It's okay,' I said. 'It's over now. You're in recovery.'

'I was . . . so scared,' she said, sounding like a young girl, an endearing part of Kayla I had never seen before.

'I'll bet you were,' I said, and I pulled over a chair without letting go of her hand. 'Did you really drive yourself here?'

She actually smiled, though her eyes stayed slightly unfocused. 'I know how long it can take to get an ambulance in this neighborhood.'

'Who did this to you?' I asked then. 'Do you know who it was, Kayla?'

In response to the question, she shut her eyes again. My free hand tightened into a fist. Did she know who attacked her, and was she afraid to say? Had Kayla been warned not to talk?

We sat quietly for a moment – until she felt ready to say more. I wouldn't push her on this, the way I had pushed poor Mena Sunderland.

'I was on a house call,' she finally said, eyes still closed. 'This guy's sister called. He's a junkie. He was trying to detox at home. When I got there, he was just about out of his mind. I don't know who he thought I was. He stabbed me . . .'

Her voice trailed off. I smoothed her hair and put the back of my hand against her cheek. I've seen how fragile life can be, but it's not something you ever get used to, and it's different when it's somebody you care for, when it sticks this close to home.

'Will you stay with me, Alex? Until I fall asleep? Don't go.'

It was her young girl's voice again. Kayla had never seemed as vulnerable to me as she did right then, in that fleeting moment in the recovery room. My heart broke for her and what had happened when she was trying to do some good out there.

'Of course,' I said. 'I'll be right here. I'm not going anywhere.'

Chapter Seventy-Seven

'I've been depressed for a while, as you know. You of all people know this.'

'More than ten years. That's a while, I guess, Alex.'

I sat across from my favorite doctor, my personal shrink, Adele Finaly. Adele is also my mentor from time to time. She's the one who encouraged me to start up my practice again, and she even got me a couple of patients. 'Guinea pigs,' she likes to call them.

'I need to tell you a few things that are bothering me a lot, Adele. This may require several hours.'

'No problem.' She shrugged. Adele has light-brown hair and is in her early forties, but she doesn't seem to have aged since we met. She isn't married right now, and every so often I think about the two of us together, but then I push it out of my mind. Way too dumb, too *crazy*.

'As long as you can fit several hours of your bull-shit into fifty minutes,' she continued, ever the wise girl, which is exactly the right tone to take with me.

'I can do that.'

She nodded. 'Better get going then. I have the clock on you. It's ticking.'

I started by telling her what had happened to Kayla and how I felt about it, including the fact that she had gone to her parents' home in North Carolina to recuperate. 'I don't think it's my fault. So I'm not feeling guilty about the attack on Kayla . . . not directly anyway.'

Adele couldn't help it, good as she is – her eyebrows rose and betrayed her inner thoughts. 'And indirectly?'

My head moved up and down. 'I do feel this gener-alized guilt – like I could have done something to stop the attack from happening.'

'For instance?'

I smiled. Then so did Adele.

'Just to use one example, eliminating all of the crime in the DC area,' I said.

'You're hiding behind your sense of humor again.'

'Sure I am, and here's the really bad part. Rational as I make myself out to be, I *am* feeling some guilt over the fact that I could have protected Kayla somehow. And yes, I know how ridiculous that is, Adele. To *think.* And to say it out loud. But there it is anyway.'

'Tell me more about this "protection" you could have afforded to Kayla Coles somehow. I need to hear this, Alex.'

'Don't rub it in. And I don't think I used the word *protection.*'

'Actually, you did. Anyway, talk it out for me, please. You said you wanted to tell me everything. This is probably more important than you think.'

'I couldn't have done a damn thing to help Kayla. Happy now?'

'I'm getting there,' Adele said – then she waited for more from me.

'It all goes back to that night with Maria, of course. I *was* there. I watched her die in my arms. I couldn't do anything to save the woman I loved. I didn't do anything. I never even caught the son of a bitch who killed her.'

Adele still said nothing.

'You know the worst thing? I'll always wonder if that bullet was meant for me. Maria turned into my arms . . . *then* she was hit.'

We sat in silence for a long time then, even for us,

and we're pretty good at enduring silences. I had never admitted that last part to Adele until now, never said it out loud to anybody.

'Adele, I'm going to change my life somehow.'

She didn't say anything to that, either. Smart and tough, the way I like my shrinks, and what I aspire to be myself someday, when I grow the hell up.

'Don't you believe me?' I asked.

She finally spoke. 'I want to believe you, Alex. Of course I do.' Then she added, 'Do *you* believe yourself? Do you think any of us can really change? Can you?'

'Yes,' I told Adele. 'I do believe I can change. But I get fooled a lot.'

She laughed. We both did.

'I can't believe I pay for this shit,' I finally said.

'Me neither,' said Adele. 'But your time is up.'

Chapter Seventy-Eight

Later that afternoon I found myself in St Anthony's Church – St Tony's, as I've called it since I was a kid growing up nearby in Nana's equally revered house. The church is about a block from the hospital where Maria died. I'd moved my spiritual care from head doctor to head of the universe, and I hoped it was an upgrade but figured it might not be.

I knelt in front of the altar and let the overly sweet smell of incense and the familiar scenes of the nativity and the crucifixion wash over me and do their dirty work. The most striking thing about beautiful churches, to me, is that they were mostly designed by people who were inspired by a belief in something larger and more important than themselves, and this is how I try to lead my own life. I gazed up at the altar, and a sigh escaped my lips. As far as God goes, I believe. It's as simple as that and always has been. I guess I feel it's a little odd, or presumptuous, to imagine that God thinks as we do; or that God has a big, kind human face; or that God is white, brown, black, yellow, green, whatever; or that God listens to our prayers at all times of the day or night, or anytime at all.

But I said a few prayers for Kayla in the front row of St Tony's – asking not just that she would survive her wounds but that she would mend in other important ways. People react differently to life-threatening attacks on their persons, on their family members, on their homes. I know about that firsthand. And now, unfortunately, so did Kayla.

While I was in a prayerful mood, I said some private words for Maria, who had been in my thoughts so much lately.

I even talked to Maria, whatever that means. I hoped she liked the way I was raising the kids – a frequent subject between us. Then I said a prayer for Nana Mama and her fragile health; prayers for the kids; and even a few words for Rosie the cat, who had been suffering from a severe cold, which I was afraid might be pneumonia. *Don't let our cat die. Not now. Rosie is good people too.*

Chapter Seventy-Nine

The Butcher was in Georgetown to let off a little pent-up steam – otherwise things might not go so well when he got back to Caitlin and the kiddies, to his life on the straight and narrow. Actually, he had learned a long time ago that he enjoyed living a double life. Who the hell wouldn't?

Maybe another game of Red Light, Green Light was in order today. Why not? His war with Junior Maggione was creating a lot of stress for him.

The 3000 block of Q Street, where he walked briskly now, was nicely tree-lined and dominated by attractive townhouses and even larger manorlike homes. It was mostly an upscale residential area, and the parked cars spoke to the social status and tastes of those who lived here: several Mercedes, a Range

Rover, a BMW, an Aston Martin, a shiny new Bentley or two.

For the most part, pedestrian traffic was limited to those entering and leaving their homes. Good deal for his purposes today. He had on earphones and was listening to a band from Scotland that he liked, Franz Ferdinand. Finally, though, he turned off the music and got serious.

At the redbrick home on the corner of Thirty-first and Q, some kind of elaborate dinner party was apparently being prepared for that evening. Assorted over-priced goodies were being transported from a stretch van marked 'Georgetown Valet,' and the faux gas lamps in front of the house were being tested by the yardmen. The lights seemed to work just fine. *Twinkle, twinkle.*

Then the Butcher heard the *click-clack* of a woman's high heels. The inviting, even intoxicating sound came from up ahead of him on the sidewalk, which was brick rather than pavement and wound through the neighborhood like a necklace laid out flat on a table.

Finally, he saw the woman from behind – a fine, shapely thing, with long black hair hanging halfway to her waist. An Irisher like himself? A pretty lassie? No way to tell for certain from the back view. But the chase was on. Soon he'd know as much as he wanted to about her. He felt he was already in control of her fate, that she belonged to him, to the Butcher, his powerful alter ego, or perhaps the *real* him. Who could say?

He was getting closer and closer to the raven-haired woman, checking out the narrow alleyways that ran behind some of the larger houses, the patches of woods, looking for a good spot – when he saw a store coming up ahead. What was this? The only place of business he'd encountered for blocks. It almost seemed misplaced in the neighborhood.

SARAH'S MARKET, said the sign out front.

And then the dark-haired beauty turned inside. 'Curses – foiled,' the Butcher whispered, and grinned and imagined twisting a villain's mustache. He loved this kind of game, this dangerous and provocative cat-and-mouse sort of thing in which he made up all the rules. But his smile instantly faded away – because he saw something else at this Sarah's Market, and that something else was not to his liking.

Newspapers were on display – copies of the *Washington Post*. And you know what? He suddenly remembered that Mr Bob Woodward himself lived somewhere in the area – but that wasn't the sticky part.

His *face* was the problem, an approximation anyhow, a line drawing of the Butcher that wasn't half-bad. It was situated above the fold of the daily news, right where it shouldn't be.

'My God, I'm famous.'

Chapter Eighty

This was no laughing matter, though, and Michael Sullivan quickly made his way back to where he'd parked on Q Street. Actually, what had happened was just about the worst development he could imagine. Nothing much seemed to be going his way lately.

He sat and calmly pondered the unfortunate situation in the front seat of his Cadillac.

He thought about the likely suspect, about the woman who must have told tales out of school about him. Possibly given the police a description. He considered that he was being attacked from a couple of sides at once, by the Washington police and the Mafia. *What to do, what to do?*

When a partial solution came, it was satisfying and

even exhilarating, because it felt like a new game to him. Another twist of the dial.

The DC police thought that they knew what he looked like, which could be serious trouble but might also make them sloppy and even overconfident.

Mistake.

Theirs.

Especially if he made the proper countermoves right now, which he definitely planned to do. But what, exactly, were those defensive actions he needed to take?

The first step took him to Wisconsin Avenue, near Blues Alley – right where he remembered the small shop to be. A barber named Rudy had a chair open for him in midafternoon, so Sullivan settled in for a haircut and shave.

It was relaxing and mildly enjoyable actually, wondering what he'd look like afterward, whether he'd like the new him.

Another ten to twelve minutes and the deed was done. *Take off the bandages, Dr Frankenstein.* The smallish, rotund barber seemed pleased with himself.

If you messed up, you're dead. I'm not kidding, Rudy, the Butcher thought to himself. *I'll cut you to ribbons with your own straight razor. See what the* Washington Post *has to say about that!*

But, hey! 'Not so bad. I sort of like it. Think I look a little like Bono.'

'Sonny and Cher – that Bono?' asked Rudy the Dense. 'I don't know about that, mister. I think you better lookin' than Sonny Bono. He's dead, you know?'

'Whatever,' said Sullivan, and paid his tab, gave the barber a tip, and got the hell out of there.

Next he drove over to the Capitol Hill neighborhood in DC.

He'd always liked the area, found it a turn-on. Most people's image of the Capitol was the graceful steps and terraces of the west facade. But on the *east* side, behind the Capitol and the Supreme Court and Library of Congress buildings, was a bustling residential neighborhood that he knew fairly well. *I've passed this way before.*

The Butcher walked through Lincoln Park, which had an exceptional view of the Capitol dome now that the leaves were falling away.

He smoked a cigarette and reviewed his plan in front of the somewhat bizarre Emancipation Memorial, which featured a slave breaking out of chains while Lincoln read the Emancipation Proclamation.

Lincoln, a good man by most accounts. Myself, a very bad man. Wonder how that happens? he thought.

A few minutes later, he was breaking in to a house

on C Street. He just knew this was the bitch who had talked about him. He felt it in his bones, in his blood. And soon he'd know for sure.

He found Mena Sunderland tucked away in her adorable little kitchen. She was dressed in jeans, an immaculate white tee, scuffed-up clogs, making pasta for one while she sipped a glass of red wine. Cute as a button he thought to himself.

'Did you miss me, Mena? I missed you. And you know what? I almost forgot how pretty you are.'

But I won't forget you again, darling girl. I brought a camera to take your picture this time. You're going to be in my prize photo collection after all. Oh, yes you are!

And he gave her the first cut with his scalpel.

Chapter Eighty-One

I was still inside the church when my cell phone went off, and it was trouble near the Capitol. I said a quick prayer for whoever was in jeopardy, and a prayer that we would catch the killer-rapist soon. Then I left St Anthony's on the run.

Sampson and I rushed to the neighborhood behind the Capitol building in his car with the siren blaring, lights flashing on the rooftop. Yellow crime-scene tape was strung up everywhere by the time we arrived. The scene, the backdrop of important government buildings, couldn't have been more dramatic, I thought, as Sampson and I hurried up the four stone front steps of a brownstone.

Is he putting on a show for us? Is he doing it on purpose? Or did it just happen this way?

I heard a car alarm whining and glanced back toward the street. What a strange, curious sight: police, news reporters, a growing crowd of looky-loos.

Fear was plainly stamped on many of the faces, and I couldn't help thinking that this was a familiar tableau of the age, this look of fear, this terrible state of fear that the whole country seemed to be caught up in – maybe the entire world was afraid right now.

Unfortunately, it was even worse inside the brownstone. The crime scene was already being tightly controlled by somber-faced homicide detectives and techies, but Sampson was let inside. He overrode a sergeant's objections and brought me along.

Into the kitchen we went.

The unthinkable murder scene.

The killer's workshop.

I saw poor Mena Sunderland where she lay on the reddish-brown tile floor. Her eyes were rolled back to the whites, and they seemed pinned to a point on the ceiling. But Mena's eyes weren't the first thing I noticed. Oh, what a bastard this killer was.

A carving knife was stuck in her throat, poised like a deadly stake. There were multiple wounds on the face, deep, unnecessarily vicious cuts. Her top, a white tee, had been torn away. Her jeans and panties had been pulled down around the ankles but hadn't been stripped off. One of her shoes was on, one off, a pale-blue clog lying on its side in blood.

Sampson looked at me. 'Alex, what are you getting? Tell me.'

'Not much. Not so far. I don't think he bothered to rape her,' I said.

'Why? He pulled down her pants.'

I knelt over Mena's body. 'Nature of the wounds. All this blood. The disfigurement. He was too angry at her. He told her not to talk to us, and she disobeyed him. That's what this is about. I think so. We might have gotten her killed, John.'

Sampson reacted angrily. 'Alex, we told her not to come back here yet. We offered her surveillance, protection. What more could we do?'

I shook my head. 'Left her alone maybe. Caught the killer before he got to her. Something else, John – anything but this.'

Chapter Eighty-Two

So now we were investigating the case for Mena Sunderland, too, in her memory – at least that was what I told myself, that was my rationalization. This was for Maria Cross, and Mena Sunderland, and all the others.

For the next three days I worked closely with Sampson during the day and then went out on the street with him at night. Our night shift usually took place from ten until around two. We were part of the task force patrolling Georgetown and Foggy Bottom, areas where the rapist-killer had struck before. Emotions were running high, but no one wanted him more than I did.

Still, I was trying my best to keep the very tense investigation in some kind of perspective and control.

Almost every night, I managed to have dinner with Nana and the kids. I checked in with Kayla Coles in North Carolina, and she sounded better. I also conducted half a dozen sessions with my patients, including Kim Stafford, who was coming to see me twice a week and maybe even making some progress. Her fiancé had never mentioned our 'talk' to her.

My morning ritual included grabbing a coffee at the Starbucks which was right in my building, or at the Au Bon Pain on the corner of Indiana and Sixth. The problem with Au Bon Pain was that I liked their pastries too much, so I had to stay clear of the place as much as I could.

Kim was my favorite patient. Therapists usually have favorites, no matter how much they rationalize that they don't.'Remember, I told you that *Jason* wasn't such a bad guy?' she said about fifteen minutes into our session one morning. I remembered, and I also recalled cleaning his clock pretty good at the station house where he worked.

'Well, he was pure, unadulterated garbage, Dr Cross. I've figured that much out. Took me a lot longer than it should have.'

I nodded and waited for more to come. I knew exactly what I wanted to hear from her next.

'I moved out on him. I waited until he went to

work, then I left. The truth? I'm scared to death. But I did what I had to do.'

She got up and went to the window, which looked out onto Judiciary Square. You could also see the US District Court House from my place.

'How long have you been married?' she asked, glancing at the ring I still wore on my left hand.

'I was married. I'm not anymore.' I told her a little about Maria, about what had happened more than ten years before – the abridged version, the unsentimental one.

'I'm sorry,' she said when I was through. There were tears in her eyes, the last thing I'd wanted. That morning, we got through a couple of rough patches, made some progress. Then a strange thing happened – she shook my hand before she left. 'You're a good person,' she said. 'Good-bye, Dr Cross.'

And I thought that I might have just lost a patient – my first – because I'd done a good job.

Chapter Eighty-Three

What happened that night blew my mind. Actually, everything had been really good about the night, until it went bad. I had treated Nana and the kids to a special dinner at Kinkead's, near the White House on Pennsylvania Avenue, our favorite restaurant in Washington. The great jazzman Hilton Fenton came over to our table and told us a funny story about the actor Morgan Freeman. Back at home, I climbed the steep wooden stairs to my office in the attic, cursing the steps under my breath, one by one.

I put on some Sam Cooke, starting with a popular favorite, 'You Send Me.' Then I pored over old DC police files from the time of Maria's murder – hundreds of pages.

I was looking for unsolved rape cases from back

then, particularly ones that had occurred in Southeast or nearby. I worked intently and listened to the music, and was surprised when I looked at my watch and saw that it was ten past three. Some interesting things had surfaced in the files from the serial case I'd remembered was going on around the same time Maria died. In fact, the rapes had started a few weeks before Maria was shot and ended just after the murder. They never started up again. Which meant what – that the rapist might have been a visitor to Washington?

Even more interesting to me, there were no IDs of the rapist from any of the victimized women. They had received medical attention but refused to talk to the police about what had happened to them. It didn't substantiate anything, but it kept me flipping through more pages.

I went over several more transcripts and still found no IDs from the victims.

Could it be a coincidence? I doubted it. I kept reading.

Then I was stopped cold by a page in the police notes. A name and more information jumped out at me.

Maria Cross.

Social worker at Potomac Gardens.

A Detective Alvin Hightower, whom I had vaguely known back then – I was pretty sure he was dead now – had written a workup on the rape of a college girl from George Washington University. The attack took place inside a bar on M Street.

As I continued to read, I was having a hard time breathing. I was remembering a conversation I'd had with Maria a couple of days before she died. It was about a case she was working on, about a girl who'd been raped.

According to the detective's report, the coed had given some kind of description of the rapist to a social worker – *Maria Cross.* He was a white male, a little over six foot, possibly from New York. When he had finished with the girl he had taken a little bow.

My fingers shaking, I turned the page and checked the date of the initial report. And there it was – *the day before Maria was murdered.*

And the rapist?

The mob killer we'd been tracking. I remembered his rooftop bow, his unexplainable visit to my house.

The Butcher.

I would bet my life on it.

PART FOUR

DRAGON SLAYER

Chapter Eighty-Four

Nana picked up the phone in the kitchen, where the family had gathered to fix supper that night. We all had a task for the meal, from peeling potatoes to making a Caesar salad and setting the table with the good silver. I tensed whenever the phone rang though. Now what? Had Sampson found something on the Butcher?

Nana spoke into the receiver. 'Hello, sweetheart, how are you? How are you feeling? Oh, that's good, that's so good to hear. Let me get him. Alex is right here chopping vegetables like he works at Benihana. Oh, yeah, he's doing pretty good. He'll be lots better when he hears your voice.'

I knew it had to be Kayla, so I took the call out in the living room. Even as I did, I wondered when we had evolved into a family with telephones in just about every room, not to mention the cell phones that Damon and Jannie carried to school these days.

'So, how *are* you, sweetheart?' I picked up and tried to imitate Nana's dulcet tones. 'I've got it. You can hang up in the kitchen,' I added for the peanut gallery listening in, cackling and giggling out there.

'Hi, Kayla! Bye, Kayla!' chorused the kids.

'Bye, Kayla,' added Nana. 'We love you. Get better real soon.'

She and I heard a *click*, and then Kayla said, 'I'm doing just fine. The patient is doing beautifully. Almost healed and ready to kick some butt again.'

I smiled and felt the warmth flow through me just hearing her voice, even long distance like this. 'Well, it's good to listen to your butt-kicking voice again.'

'Yours too, Alex. And the kids and Nana. I'm sorry I didn't call last week. My father has been under the weather, but he's coming around now too. And you know me. I've been doing some pro bono work in the neighborhood. I just *hate* to get paid, you know.'

There was a brief pause, but then I filled the space with inane questions about Kayla's folks and life in North Carolina, where both of us had been born. By this time, I had calmed down some about the unexpected call from Kayla, and I was more myself.

'So how *are* you?' I asked her. 'You really okay? Almost recovered?'

'I am. I'm clearer on certain things than I've been in a while. Had some time to process and reflect for a change. Alex, I've been thinking that . . . I might not be coming back to Washington. I wanted to talk to you about it before I told anyone else.'

My stomach dropped like a runaway elevator in a skyscraper. I had suspected something like this might be coming, but I still buckled from the blow.

Kayla continued to talk. 'There's so much to do down here. Lots of sick people, of course. And I'd forgotten how nice, how *sane*, this place is. I'm sorry, I'm not putting this . . . saying it very well.'

I snuck in a light thought. 'You're not real verbal. That's a problem with you scientists.'

Kayla sighed deeply. 'Alex, do you think I'm wrong about this? You know what I'm saying? Of course you do.'

I wanted to tell Kayla she was dead wrong, that she should rush back here to DC, but I couldn't bring myself to say it. *Why was that?* 'All right, here's the only answer I can give, Kayla. You know what's right for yourself. I would never try to influence you at all. I know that I couldn't if I wanted to. I'm not sure that came out exactly right.'

'Oh, I think it did. You're just being honest,' she said. 'I do have to figure out what's best for me. It's my nature, isn't it? It's both of our natures.'

We went on talking for a while, but when we finally hung up I had this terrible feeling about what had just happened. *I lost her, didn't I? What is wrong with me? Why didn't I tell Kayla I needed her? Why didn't I tell her to come back to Washington as soon as she could? Why didn't I tell her I loved her?*

After dinner, I went upstairs to the attic, my retreat, my escape hatch, and I tried to lose myself in the remainder of the old files from the time of Maria's death. I didn't think too much about Kayla. I just kept thinking about Maria, missing her more than I had in years, wondering what our life could have been like if she hadn't died.

Around one in the morning, I finally tiptoed downstairs. I slipped into Ali's room again. Quiet as a church mouse, I lay down beside my sweet, dreaming boy.

I held little Alex's hand with my pinkie, and I silently mouthed the words, *Help me, pup.*

Chapter Eighty-Five

Things were happening fast now . . . for better or worse. Michael Sullivan hadn't been this wired and full of tension in years, and actually he kind of liked the revved-up feeling just fine. He was back, wasn't he? Hell yes, he was in his prime, too. He'd never been angrier or more focused. The only real problem was that he was finding he needed more action, any kind would do. He couldn't sit still in that motel anymore, couldn't watch old episodes of *Law & Order* or play any more soccer or baseball with the boys.

He needed to hunt; needed to keep moving; needed his adrenaline fixes in closer proximity.

Mistake.

So he found himself back in DC – where he

shouldn't be – not even with his new short haircut and wearing a Georgetown Hoyas silver-and-blue hoodie that made him look like some kind of lame Yuppie wannabe who deserved to be punched in the face and kicked in the head while he was down.

But damn it all, he did like the women here, the tight-assed professional types best of all. He'd just finished reading John Updike's *Villages* and wondered if old man Updike was half as horny as some of the characters he wrote about. Hadn't that horned toad written *Couples* too? Plus, Updike was like seventy-something and still scribbling about sex like he was a teenager on the farm in Pennsylvania, screwing anything with two, three, or four legs. But hell, maybe he was missing the point of the book. Or maybe Updike was. Was that possible? That a writer didn't really get what he was writing about himself?

Anyway, he did fancy the fancy-pants women of Georgetown. They smelled so good, looked really good, talked good. *The Women of Georgetown,* now that would be a good book for somebody to write, maybe even Johnny U.

Jeez, he was amusing to himself anyway. On the car ride in from Maryland he'd been listening to U2, and Bono had been wailing about wanting to spend some time *inside* the head of his lover, and Sullivan wondered – all cornball Irish romanticism aside – if that was really such a capital idea. Did Caitlin need to be inside his head? Definitely not. Did he need to be inside hers? No. Because he didn't really like a lot of empty space.

So where the hell was he?

Ah, Thirty-first Street. Coming up on Blues Alley, which was fairly deserted at this time of day – as opposed to nighttime, when the clubs were open around these parts of Washington and the crowds came calling. He was listening to James McMurtry and the Heartless Bastards now. He liked the CD well enough to stay in his parked car an extra few minutes.

Finally he climbed out, stretched his legs, and took a breath of moderately foul city air.

Ready or not here I come. He decided to cut through to Wisconsin Avenue and check out the ladies there, maybe lure one back into the alley somehow. Then what? Hell, whatever he damn well felt like. He was Michael Sullivan, the Butcher of Sligo, a real crazy bastard if ever there was one on this spinning ball of gas and rock. What was that old line he liked? *Three out of four voices inside my head say go for it.*

The Thirty-first Street entrance to the alley was bathed in this faded yellow glow from the lights at a spaghetti joint called Ristorante Piccolo. A lot of the hot spots on M Street, which ran parallel to the alley, had their service entrances back here.

He passed the back entrance of a steakhouse, then a French bistro, and some kind of greasy burger joint spewing smoke.

He noticed another guy entering the alley – then two guys – coming his way, too.

What the hell was this?

What was going down here now?

But he thought he knew what it was, didn't he? This was the end of the road. Somebody had finally gotten a step ahead of him instead of the other way around. Leather car coats. Squared-off, bulky types. Definitely not Georgetown students taking a shortcut to get a bite of cow at the Steak & Brew.

He turned back toward Thirty-first – and saw two more guys.

Mistake.

Big one.

His.

He had underestimated John Maggione.

Chapter Eighty-Six

'Mr Maggione sent us,' called one of the toughs who was headed Michael Sullivan's way, walking with plenty of strut and attitude from the entrance into the alley on Wisconsin. The hoods were moving fast now, and they had him penned in. So much for mystery and intrigue, not to mention that a couple of the goons had their guns out already, hanging loosely at their sides, and the Butcher wasn't armed except for the surgeon's scalpel in his boot.

No way in hell he could take out four of them, not with a blade. Probably not even if he had a gun on him. So what could he do? Take their picture with his camera?

'I misspoke, Butcherman. Mr Maggione doesn't want to *see* you,' said an older guy. 'He just wants you to disappear. The sooner the better. Like today. Think you could do that for Mr Maggione? I'll bet you can. Then we'll find your wife and three kids and make them disappear too.'

Michael Sullivan's brain was reeling through all the permutations and possibilities now.

Maybe he could take the one guy out, the loud-mouth; then it wouldn't be a total loss anyway. Shut his ugly hole once and for all. Cut him bad, too.

But what about the other three?

Maybe he could get two of them, if he was good and lucky. If he could get them close enough to use his blade, which wouldn't happen. They were probably stupid, but not that stupid. So how could he make something happen? He didn't want to go down without a fight.

'You man enough to take me out yourself?' he called to the bigmouth. 'Ay, *babbo*?' He used the mob term for idiot, for some useless underling. He was trying to get under his skin if he could. Hell, he'd try anything right now. He was going to die in the next minute or so, and he just wasn't ready to go yet.

The killer's mouth twisted into a grim smile. 'No doubt about it. I could take you out myself. But guess what, guess who's the *babbo* today? Give you a hint. You probably wiped his ass this morning.'

The Butcher reached into the pocket of his sweat-shirt, and he kept his hand there.

The bigmouthed hood immediately had second thoughts and put his free hand up. The others stopped walking. They all had their guns out, but they weren't coming any closer to the legendary Butcher.

The big talker gestured for the men behind Sullivan to move to the right, while he and the fourth man moved left. That gave everybody a clear line of fire. Smart thinking.

'You stupid Mick. Messed up this time, didn't you? Question for you: you ever think it'd end like this?'

Sullivan had to laugh at that one. 'You know what? I never thought it would end. Never occurred to me. Still hasn't actually.'

'Oh, it's gonna end all right. Right here, right now. Just keep watching the movie until the houselights go out for you!'

Which was obviously the truth, no doubt about it – but then the Butcher heard something that was hard for him to believe.

It came from behind, so he had to turn around to check it out, to see if it was real or some cruel joke being played on him.

Somebody was shouting at the far end of the alley

– this had to be some kind of seriously messed-up *miracle*.

Or it was the luckiest day of his life.

Maybe both.

The cavalry had arrived!

Look who was here to save the day.

Chapter Eighty-Seven

'**D**C police! Everybody put the guns down. Do it now! We're police officers. Guns down on the ground.'

Sullivan saw the cops, and they looked like detectives, two buff-looking black guys in street clothes.

They were coming up behind the Mafia hoods who were standing near Thirty-first Street and trying to figure out what the hell to do next, their next move.

So was he.

What a sight the two cops were, though, and Sullivan wondered, could they be part of the task force put into Georgetown to catch the rapist, to catch him?

Hell, he'd bet a bundle that's what they were, and if it was true, he was the only one in the alleyway who had figured it out so far.

One of the cops was already calling in for help. Then the two mob guys near Wisconsin just turned around – *and they walked away.*

The detectives had their guns out, but what were they going to do? Realistically, what could they do?

Sullivan almost began to laugh as he turned slowly and walked toward Wisconsin too.

Then he began to run, a full-out sprint toward the busy street. Madman that he was, he started laughing his ass off. He'd decided to brazen it out, just run. Like in the old days back in Brooklyn when he was a kid making his bones in the game.

Run, Mikey, run. Run for your life.

What could the DC metro cops do? Shoot him in the back? For what? Running? Being the potential victim of four armed men in an alleyway?

The cops were yelling, threatening him, but all they could do was watch him get away. Funniest thing he'd seen in years, maybe ever. The cavalry had come to the rescue – *his.*

Huge mistake.

Theirs.

Chapter Eighty-Eight

Half a dozen uniforms were moving in and out of the station house on Wisconsin when Sampson and I got there that afternoon. A detective named Michael Wright had finally made the connection that he and his partner might have just missed capturing the Georgetown rapist, that he'd maybe missed the biggest deal of his career. Still, they were holding two men in the cage who might know what was going on. They needed a closer look.

Sampson and I passed inside a ten-foot-high bulletproof partition and headed for the interrogation rooms, which were beyond the detectives' cubicle area. The work space looked familiar – scarred, badly littered desks, old computers and phones from another era, overhead storage bins filled to overflowing.

Before we entered the interrogation room, Wright told us that the two men in there hadn't said a word so far, but they'd been armed with Berettas, and he was sure they were killers. 'Have fun,' Wright said; then John and I walked inside.

Sampson spoke up first. 'I'm Detective John Sampson. This is Dr Alex Cross. Dr Cross is a forensic psychologist involved in the investigation of a series of rapes in the Georgetown area. I'm a detective on the case.'

Neither of the men said a word, not even a wise-crack, to break the ice. Both of them looked to be in their early thirties, bodybuilder types, with permanent smirks on their faces.

Sampson asked a couple more questions; then we just sat there in silence across the table from the two men.

Eventually an administrative assistant knocked on the door and entered. She handed Sampson a couple of faxes, hot from the machine.

He read the pages – then handed them to me.

'I didn't think the Mafia was active in the DC area,' Sampson said. 'Guess I was wrong. You're both soldiers in the mob. Either of you have anything to say about what was going down in that alley?'

They didn't, and they were annoyingly smug about

not answering our questions and pretending we weren't even there.

'Dr Cross, maybe we can work this out without their help. What do you think?' Sampson asked me.

'We can try. It says here that John "Digger" Antonelli and Joseph "Blade" Lanugello work for John Maggione out of New York City. That would be John Maggione. Maggione Sr was the one who hired a man named Michael Sullivan, also known as the Butcher, to do a hit in DC several years back. You remember that one, John?'

'I do. Took out a Chinese drug dealer. Your wife, Maria, was also murdered right around that time. Mr Sullivan is now a suspect in this case.'

'This same Michael "the Butcher" Sullivan is also a suspect in a series of rapes in Georgetown, and at least one murder connected to the rapes. Was Sullivan the man you had cornered in Blues Alley?' I asked the Mafia hitters.

Not a word came from either of them. Nothing at all. Real tough guys.

Sampson finally stood up, rubbing his chin. 'So I guess we don't need Digger and Blade anymore. Well, what should we do with them? Wait, I have an idea. You'll like this one, Alex,' Sampson said, and chuckled to himself.

He motioned for the Mafia soldiers to get up.'We're finished here. You can come with me, gentlemen.'

'Where?' Lanugello finally broke his silence. 'You ain't charged us yet.'

'Let's go. Got a surprise for you.' Sampson walked in front of the two of them, and I walked behind. They didn't seem to like having me at the rear. Maybe they thought I might still be harboring a grudge about what had happened to Maria. Well, maybe I was.

Sampson signaled a guard at the end of the hall, and he used his keys to open a cell door. The holding area was already filled with several prisoners awaiting arraignment. All but one of them was black. John led the way inside.

'You'll be staying here. If you change your mind and want to talk to us,' Sampson said to the Mafia guys, 'give a holler. That is if Dr Cross and I are still in the building. If not, we'll check in on you in the morning. If that's the case, have a nice night.'

Sampson tapped his shield a few times against the bars of the holding pen. 'These two men are suspects in a series of rapes,' he announced to the other prisoners. 'Rapes of black women in Southeast. Be careful, though, these are tough guys. *From New York.*'

We left, and the lockup guard slammed the cell door behind us.

Chapter Eighty-Nine

Four o'clock on a cold, rainy morning, and his two younger boys were crying their eyes out in the backseat of the car. So was Caitlin up in front. Sullivan blamed Junior Maggione and La Cosa Nostra for everything, the huge, ugly mess that was happening now. Somehow Maggione was going to pay for this, and he looked forward to the day of retribution.

So did his scalpel and his butcher's saw.

At two thirty in the morning he had piled his family into the car and snuck away from a house six miles outside Wheeling, West Virginia. It was their second move in as many weeks, but he had no choice in the matter. He'd promised the boys they would return to Maryland one day, but he knew that wasn't true. They wouldn't ever go back to Maryland. Sullivan already had an offer on the house there. He needed the cash for their escape plan.

So now he and the family were running for their lives. As they left their 'Wild West Virginny Home,' as he called it, he had a feeling that the mob would find them again – that they could be right around the next bend in the road.

But he rounded the next curve, and the curve after that, and made it out of town safe and sound and in one piece. Soon they were singing Rolling Stones and ZZ Top tunes, including a twenty-minute version of 'Legs,' until his wife put her foot down about the nonstop high-testosterone noise. They stopped at Denny's for breakfast, at Micky D's for a second bathroom break, and by three in the afternoon they were somewhere they had never been before.

Hopefully, Sullivan had left no trail to be followed by a crew of mob killers. No bread crumbs like in 'Hansel and Gretel'. The good thing was, neither he nor his family had ever been in this area before. It was virgin territory, with no roots or connections.

He pulled into the driveway of a shingle-style Victorian house with a steep roof, a couple of turrets, even a stained-glass window.

'I love this house!' Sullivan crowed, and he was all

fake smiles and hyperenthusiasm.'Welcome to *Florida,* kiddos,' he said.

'Very funny, Dad. *Not,*' said Mike Jr from the back-seat, where all three boys were looking grim and depressed.

They were in Florida, *Massachusetts,* and Caitlin and the kids groaned at another of his dumb jokes. Florida was a small community of less than a thou-sand, situated high in the Berkshires. It had stunning mountain views, if nothing else. And there were no Mafia hit men waiting in the driveway. What more could they ask for?

'Just perfect. What could be better than this?' Sullivan kept telling the kids as they started to unpack again.

So why was Caitlin crying as he showed her their new living room with the sweeping views of big bad Mount Greylock and the river? Why was he lying to her when he said, 'Everything is going to be all right, my queen, light of my life'?

Maybe because he knew it wasn't true, and prob-ably, so did she. He and his family were going to be murdered one day, maybe in this very house.

Unless he did something dramatic to stop it. And fast. But what could that be? How could he stop the Mafia from coming after him?

How could you kill the mob?

Chapter Ninety

Two nights later, the Butcher was on the move again. *Just him. One man.*

He had a plan now and was traveling south to New York City. He was uptight and nervous but singing along with Springsteen, Dylan, the Band, Pink Floyd. Nothing but Oldies and Greaties for the four-hour ride south. He didn't particularly want to leave Caitlin and the boys at the house in Massachusetts, but he figured they'd probably be safe there for now. If not, he had done the best he could for them. Better than his father ever did for him, or for his mother and brothers.

He finally pulled off the West Side Highway at around midnight; then he went straightaway to the Morningside Apartments on West 107th. He'd stayed there before and knew it was just out of the way enough to suit his purposes. Convenient too, with four different subway lines going through the two nearby stations.

No air-conditioning in the rooms, he remembered, but that didn't matter in November. He slept like a baby safe in a mother's womb. When Sullivan woke at seven, covered in a light sheen of his own sweat, his mind was focused on a single idea: *payback against Junior Maggione.* Or maybe an even better idea: *survival of the fittest and the toughest.*

Around nine that morning he took a subway ride to check out a couple of possible locations for murders he wanted to commit in the near future. He had a 'wish list' with several different targets and wondered if any of these men, and two women, had an idea that they were as good as dead, that it was up to him who lived and died, and when, and where.

In the evening, around nine, he drove over to Brooklyn, his old stomping grounds. Right into Junior Maggione's neighborhood, his turf in Carroll Gardens.

He was thinking about his old buddy Jimmy Hats, and missing him some, figuring that Maggione's father had probably popped Jimmy. Somebody had, and then made the body disappear, as if Jimmy had never been born. He'd always suspected it had been Maggione Sr, so that was another score for the Butcher to settle.

It was building up inside him, this terrible rage. About something. Maybe about his father – the original Butcher of Sligo, that piece of Irish scum who had ruined his life before he was ten years old.

He turned on to Maggione's street, and he had to smile to himself. The powerful don still lived like a mildly successful plumber or maybe a local electrician, in a yellow-brick two-family house. More surprising – he didn't spot any guards posted on the street.

So either Junior was seriously underestimating him, or his people were damn good at hiding themselves in plain sight. Hell, maybe somebody had a sniper rifle sight pinned on his forehead right now. *Maybe he had a couple of seconds to live.*

The suspense was killing him. He had to see what was going on here. So he hit his car horn once, twice, three times, and not a goddamn thing happened.

Nobody shot him through the skull. And for the first time, the Butcher let himself think, *I might win this fight after all.*

He'd figured out the first mystery: Junior Maggione had moved his family out of the house. Maggione was running too.

Then he stopped that train of thought with just one word – *mistake*.

He couldn't make any – not one misstep from now until this was all over. If he did, he was dead.

Simple as that.

End of story.

Chapter Ninety-One

It was late, and I decided to go for a drive in the R350. I was loving the car. The kids felt the same way. Even Nana did, praise the Lord. I found myself thinking about Maria again. The long investigation into her murder I had conducted and *failed* at. I was messing with my own mind, trying to picture her face, trying to hear the exact sound of her voice.

Later that night, back at home, I tried to get to sleep but couldn't. It got so bad that I went downstairs and watched *Diary of a Mad Black Woman* again. Actually, I found myself cheering like a crazy person at the flickering TV screen. Tyler Perry's movie matched up perfectly with my frame of mind.

I called up Tony Woods at the director's office around nine the next morning. Then I swallowed my pride and asked Tony for some help on the rape and murder case. I needed to find out if the Bureau had anything on the contract killer called the Butcher, anything that might be helpful to Sampson and me – maybe something classified.

'We knew you'd call one of these days, Alex. Director Burns is eager to work with you again. You up for some consulting? Just light stuff. It's your call what and where, especially now that you're taking on cases again.'

'Who said I'm taking on cases? This is a special situation,' I told Tony. 'The Butcher probably murdered my wife years ago. It's the one case I can't leave unsolved.'

'I understand. I do understand. We'll try to help if we can. I'll get you what you need.'

Tony arranged for me to use the office of an agent who was out of town, and he said it was okay if I wanted to start a dialogue with an FBI researcher-analyst named Monnie Donnelley.

'I already talked to Monnie,' I told him.

'We know you did. Monnie told us. We cleared it for her now. *Officially.*'

The next couple of days, I pretty much lived in the FBI building. Turned out the Bureau had quite a lot on Michael Sullivan, the Butcher. His file included dozens of photographs. One problem was that the photos were five to seven years old, and there didn't seem to have been any contact with Sullivan recently. Where had he disappeared to? I did learn that Sullivan grew up in a part of Brooklyn known as the Flatlands. His father had been a real butcher there. I even got the names of some old contacts and friends of Sullivan's from his days in New York.

What I read of Sullivan's backstory was curious. He'd attended parochial schools through tenth grade, and he'd been a good student, even though he never seemed to work at it.

Then Sullivan dropped out of school. He took up with the Mafia and was one of the few non-Italians to break in. He wasn't a 'made man,' but he was well paid. Sullivan earned in the six figures when he was in his early twenties and became Dominic Maggione's go-to hit man. His son, the current don, had never approved of Sullivan.

Then something strange and disturbing to all concerned started to happen. There were reports of Michael Sullivan torturing and mutilating the bodies of victims; murdering a priest and a layman accused of misconduct with boys at his old grade school; a couple of other vigilante hits; a rumor that Sullivan might have murdered his own father, who disappeared from his shop one night and whose body had never been found to this day.

Then Sullivan seemed to completely disappear off the Bureau's radar screen. Monnie Donnelley agreed with my assessment: that Sullivan might have become somebody's informer in the Bureau. It was possible that the FBI, or the New York police, was protecting him. Even that Sullivan might be in Witness Protection. Was that what had happened to Maria's killer?

Was he somebody's snitch?

Was the FBI protecting the Butcher?

Chapter Ninety-Two

John Maggione was a proud man, too showy at times, too cocksure, but he wasn't stupid, and he wasn't usually careless. He was aware of the current situation involving the mad-dog hit man his father had used back in the day – *the Butcher*, an Irishman, of all things. But even his crazy old man had tried to eliminate Michael Sullivan once he found out how dangerous and unpredictable he was. Now the job would be done, and it had to be done right away.

Sullivan was still on the loose, Maggione knew. As an extra safeguard against him, he'd moved his family out of the house in South Brooklyn. They were living at the compound in Glen Cove on Long Island. He was there with them now.

The house was a brick Colonial, waterfront, on a

quiet cul-de-sac. It had its own dock on the channel and a speedboat, *Cecilia Theresa*, named after his first child.

Although the compound's location was well known, the gates around the place were secure, and Maggione had doubled his bodyguards. He felt good about the safety of his family. The Butcher was only one guy, after all. Realistically, how much damage could he do? How much *more* damage?

Junior had plans to go in to work later in the morning, then make his regular stop at the social club in Brooklyn. It was important for him to keep up appearances. Besides, he was sure he had things under control now. He had assurances from his people: Sullivan would be dead soon, and so would his family.

At eleven in the morning, Maggione was swimming in the indoor pool at the compound. He'd already done thirty laps and planned to do fifty more.

His cell phone began to ring on the chaise longue.

Nobody else was around, so finally he climbed out of the pool and answered it himself. 'Yeah? What?'

'Maggione.' He heard a male voice on the line.

'Who the hell is this?' he asked, even though he knew who it was.

'This happens to be Michael Sullivan, chief. The nerve of the cheeky bastard, huh?'

Maggione was quietly stunned that the madman was actually calling him again. 'I think we better talk,' he said to the hit man.

'We *are* talking. Know how come? You sent killers after me. First in Italy. Then they came near my house in Maryland. They shot at my kids. Then they showed up in Washington looking for me. Because *I'm* supposed to be a loose cannon? *You're* the loose cannon, Junior! You're the one who needs to be put down!'

'Listen, Sullivan—'

'No, you listen, you asshole punk bastard. You listen to me, Junior! There's a package arriving at your fortress right about now. Check it out, chief. *I'm coming after you!* You can't stop me. Nothing can stop me; nobody can. I'm crazy, right? You try and remember that. I'm the craziest bastard you ever met, or even heard of. And we *will* meet again.'

Then the Butcher hung up on him.

Junior Maggione put on a robe; then he walked out to the front of the house. He couldn't believe it – *FedEx was making a delivery!*

That meant that the crazy bastard Sullivan might be watching the house right now. Was that possible? Could it be happening, just like he said it would?

'Vincent! Mario! Get your asses out here!' he called

to his bodyguards, who came running from the kitchen holding sandwiches.

He had one of his men open the delivery box – out in the pool house.

After a couple of nervous moments, the guy called out, 'It's *pictures*, Mr Maggione. Not exactly Kodak moments.'

Chapter Ninety-Three

'**W**e might have found him, sugar.'

A woman named Emily Corro had just finished her morning therapy session with me, and she'd gone off to her teaching job, hopefully with a slightly better self-image. Now Sampson was on my cell phone. Big John didn't usually get excited, so this had to be something good.

Turned out, it was.

Late that afternoon, the Big Man and I arrived in the Flatlands section of Brooklyn. We proceeded to locate a neighborhood tavern called Tommy McGoey's.

The neat-and-clean gin mill was nearly empty when we walked inside. Just a tough-looking Irish bartender and a smallish, well-built guy, probably midforties, sitting at the far end of a well-polished mahogany bar. His name was Anthony Mullino, and he was a graphic artist in Manhattan who'd once been best pals with Michael Sullivan.

We sat down on either side of Mullino, pinning him in.

'Cozy,' he said, and smiled. 'Hey, I'm not going to run out on you guys. I came here of my own free recollection. Try not to forget it. Hell, two of my uncles are cops here in Crooklyn. Check it out if you want.'

'We already did,' Sampson said. 'One's retired, living in Myrtle Beach; one's on suspension.'

'Hey, so I'm batting five hundred. That's not so awful. Keep you in the Big Leagues.'

Sampson and I introduced ourselves, and at first Mullino was sure he knew John from somewhere, but couldn't place where it might be. He said he'd followed the case of the Russian Mafia head called the Wolf, an investigation I'd worked on while I was at the Bureau, and which had played out right here in New York.

'I read about you in some magazine too,' he said. 'What magazine was that?'

'I didn't read the story,' I said. 'In *Esquire*.'

Mullino got the joke and laughed in a way that was like speeded-up coughing. 'So how did you find out about me and Sully? That's kind of a stretch nowadays. Ancient history.'

Sampson told him a little bit of what we knew – that the FBI had done audio surveillance on a social club frequented by John Maggione. We knew that Maggione had ordered a hit on Sullivan, probably because of the Butcher's unorthodox methods, and that the Butcher had retaliated. 'The Bureau asked around on Bay Parkway. Your name came up.'

Mullino didn't even wait for Sampson to finish. I noticed that when he talked his hands were in constant motion. 'Right, the social club over in Benson-hurst. You been there? Old Italian neighborhood. Mostly two-story buildings, storefronts, y'know. Seen better days, but still pretty nice. Sully and I grew up not far from there.

'So how do I fit in again? I'm a little confused about that part. I haven't seen Mike in years.'

'FBI files,' I said. 'You're his friend, right?'

Mullino shook his head. 'When we were kids, we were kind of close. That was a long time ago, guys.'

'You were friends into your twenties. And he still keeps in touch,' I said. 'That's the information we were given.'

'Aw, *Christmas cards*,' Mullino said, and laughed. 'Go figure that one out. Sully's a complicated guy, totally unpredictable. He sends a holiday card now and then. What else is going on here? Am I in trouble? I'm not, am I?'

'We know that you have no association with the mob, Mr Mullino,' Sampson said.

'That's good to hear, because I don't, never did. Actually I'm a little tired of all the bullshit slurring against us Italians. *Bada bing*, all that crap. Sure some guys talk like that. Know why? Because it's on the TV.'

'So tell us about Michael Sullivan,' I said. 'We need to hear whatever you know about him. Even things from the old days.'

Anthony Mullino ordered another drink – seltzer water – from Tommy McGoey himself. Then he began to talk to us, and it came easily for him, the words anyway.

'I'll tell you a funny thing, a story. I used to be Mikey's protector in grammar school. Immaculate Conception, this was. Irish Christian Brothers. In our neighborhood, you had to develop a pretty good sense of humor to keep out of fights every other day. Back then, Sullivan didn't have much of one – a sense of humor. He also had this mortal fear about having his front teeth knocked out. Thought he might be a movie star or somethin' one day. I swear to God that's true. *Verdad*, right? His old man and his mom both slept with their store-boughts in a glass of water by the bed.'

Mullino said that Sullivan changed when they were in high school. 'He got tough, and mean as a snake. But he developed a pretty good sense of humor, for an Irish guy anyway.'

He leaned in close to the bar and lowered his voice. 'He killed a guy in ninth grade. Name of Nick Fratello. Fratello worked at the newspaper store, with the bookies. He used to hassle Mikey all the time, break his balls strenuously. No reason. So Sully just killed him with a box cutter! That got the attention of the Mafia, of Dominic Maggione in particular. Dominic Maggione *Senior* I'm talking about.

'That's when Sully started to hang around the social club in Bensonhurst. Nobody knew what he was doing exactly. Not even me. But suddenly he had money in his pockets. Seventeen, maybe eighteen years old, he bought a Grand Am, a Pontiac Grand Am. Very hot wheels at that time. Maggione Jr always hated Mike because he'd gotten the old man's respect.'

Mullino looked from Sampson's face to mine, and he made a gesture like *What else can I tell you? Can I go now?*

'When was the last time you saw Michael Sullivan?' Sampson asked him.

'Last time?' Mullino sat back and made a big show of trying to remember. Then his hands started flapping around again. 'I would say it was Kate Gargan's wedding in Bay Ridge. Six, seven years ago. That's my last recollection anyway. Of course, you guys probably have my life on audio and video, right?'

'Could be, Mr Mullino. So where is Michael Sullivan now? The Christmas cards? Where were they sent from?'

Mullino shrugged and threw up his hands, as if he was getting a little exasperated with the conversation. 'There were only a couple of cards. I think, postmarked in New York. Manhattan? No return address, guys. So you tell me – where is Sully these days?'

'He's right here in Brooklyn, Mr Mullino,' I said. 'You saw him two nights ago at the Chesterfield Lounge on Flatbush Avenue.' Then I showed him his picture – with Michael Sullivan.

Mullino shrugged and smiled. No big deal – we'd caught him in a lie. 'He used to be my friend. He called, wanted to talk. What could I do, blow him off? Not a good idea. So why didn't you grab him then?'

'Bad luck,' I said. 'The agents on surveillance had no idea what he looks like now – the baldie haircut, the seventies punk look. So now I have to ask you again – where is Sully these days?'

Chapter Ninety-Four

Michael Sullivan was breaking the time-honored customs and unwritten rules of the Family, and he knew it. And he understood the consequences all too well. But they had started this foolishness, hadn't they? They'd come after him, and they'd done it in front of his kids.

Now he was going to finish it, or maybe he would die trying. Either way, it had been a helluva ride for him, helluva ride.

Ten thirty on a Saturday morning and he was driving a UPS truck that he'd hijacked less than twenty minutes earlier. First FedEx, now UPS, so at least he was an equal opportunity jacker. The driver was in the back, trying his best to recover from a slit throat.

There was a picture of his girlfriend, or wife or

whatever she was, on the dash, and the lady was almost as ugly as the dying driver. The Butcher couldn't have cared less about the incidental murder. He felt nothing for the stranger, and truthfully, everyone was a stranger to him, even his own family most of the time.

'Hey, you okay back there?' he called over the rumbling, rattling noise of the truck.

No answer, nothing from the back.

'I thought so, buddy. Don't worry about it – the mail and whatnot must go through. Rain, snow, sleet, death, whatever.'

He pulled the big brown delivery truck up in front of a medium-size ranch house in Roslyn. Then he grabbed a couple of bulky delivery boxes off the metal shelf behind the driver's seat. He headed to the front door, walking fast, hurrying like the Boys in Brown always do on TV, even whistling a happy tune.

The Butcher pressed the doorbell. Waited. Still whistling. Playing the part perfectly, he thought.

A man's voice came over the intercom. 'What? Who's there? Who is it?'

'UPS. Package.'

'Just leave it.'

'Need a signature, sir.'

'I said leave it, okay. Signature's not a problem. Leave the package. Bye, bye.'

'Sorry, sir, I can't do that. Real sorry. Just doing my job here.'

Then nothing more over the intercom. Thirty seconds went by, forty-five. Might need a plan B here.

Finally, a very large man in a black Nike sweatsuit came to the door. He was physically impressive, which made sense since he'd once played football for the New York Jets and Miami Dolphins.

'Are you hard of hearing?' he asked. 'I told you to leave the package on the porch. Capisce?'

'No, sir, I'm Irish American actually. I just can't leave these valuable packages without a signature.'

The Butcher handed over the electronic pad, and the big ex-footballer angrily scrawled a name with the marker.

The Butcher checked it – *Paul Mosconi*, who just happened to be a mob soldier married to John Maggione's little sister. This was *so* against the rules, but you know what, were there really any rules anymore? In the mob, government, churches, the whole messed-up society?

'Nothing against you personally,' said the Butcher.

Pop.

Pop.

Pop.

'You're dead, Paul Mosconi. And the big boss is

going to be really pissed at me. By the way, I used to be a Jets fan. Now I go for New England.'

Then the Butcher stooped down and slashed the dead man's face over and over again with his scalpel. Then he cut his throat, crisscross, right on the Adam's apple.

A woman popped her head into the living room, dark hair still in curlers, and she started to scream. 'Pauli! Pauli, oh my God! Oh, Pauli, oh, Pauli! No, no, no!'

The Butcher did his best little bow for the distraught widow.

'Say hello to your brother for me. *He* did this to you. Your big brother killed Pauli, not me.' He started to turn away, then spun around. 'Hey, sorry for your loss.'

And he took another little bow.

Chapter Ninety-Five

This could be it. The end of a long and winding road after Maria's murder.

Sampson and I took the Long Island Expressway to the Northern State, then headed all the way out to the tip of Long Island. We followed Route 27 and finally found the village of Montauk, which until that moment was just a name I'd heard and occasionally read about. But this was where Michael Sullivan and his family were hiding out according to Anthony Mullino. Supposedly they had just moved here today.

We found the house after twenty minutes of searching unfamiliar back roads. When we arrived at the address we'd been given, two boys were tossing a bloated-looking football on a small patch of front lawn. Blond, Irish-looking kids. Pretty good athletes, especially the littlest guy. The presence of kids could make this a lot more complicated for us, though.

'You think he's staying out here?' Sampson asked as he turned off the engine. We were at least a hundred yards away from the house, and pretty much out of sight now, playing it safe.

'Mullino says he's been moving around a lot. Says he's here now for sure. The kids are the right age. There's an older boy too, Michael Jr.'

I squinted to see better. 'Car in the driveway has Maryland plates.'

'Probably not a coincidence there. Sullivan was supposed to be living somewhere in Maryland before he and his family made their latest run. Makes sense that he was close to DC. Explains the rapes there. The pieces are starting to fall together.'

'His kids haven't seen us yet. Hopefully Sullivan hasn't, either. Let's keep it that way, John.'

We moved, and Sampson parked two streets away; then we got shotguns and pistols out of the trunk. We hiked into the woods behind a row of modest homes, though still with a view of the ocean. The place where the Sullivans were staying was dark inside, and we hadn't spotted anybody else so far.

No Caitlin Sullivan, no Michael Sullivan, or if they were in the house, they were staying back from the windows. That made sense. Plus, I knew that Sullivan was a good shot with a rifle.

I sat down with my back against a tree, huddled against the cold with a rifle in my lap. I started thinking through the problem of taking down Sullivan without harming his family. For one thing, could it be done? After a while, I began to think about Maria again. Was I finally close to clearing her murder? I didn't know for sure, but it felt like it. Or was that just wishful thinking?

I took out my wallet and slid an old picture from a plastic sleeve. I still missed her every day. Maria would always be thirty years old in my mind, wouldn't she? Such a waste of a life.

But now she'd brought me here, hadn't she? Why else would Sampson and I have come alone to get the Butcher?

Because we didn't want anybody to know what we were going to do with him.

Chapter Ninety-Six

The Butcher was seeing red, and that usually wasn't good for the world's population numbers. In fact, he was getting more pissed off by the minute. Make that by the second. Damn it, he hated John Maggione.

Distractions helped some. The old neighborhood wasn't much like Sullivan remembered it. He hadn't liked it then, and he cared for it even less now. Feeling a little bit of déjà vu, he followed Avenue P, then took a left onto Bay Parkway.

As far as he knew, this general area was still the main shopping hub of Bensonhurst. Block after block of redbrick buildings, with stores on the ground level: greaseball restaurants, bakeries, delis, greaseball everything. Some things never changed.

He was flashing images of his father's shop again

– everything always gleaming white; the freezer with its white enameled door; inside the freezer, hooks with hanging quarters of beef; bulbs in metal cages along the ceiling; knives, cleavers, and saws everywhere. His father standing there with his hand under his apron – waiting for his son to blow him.

He made a right at Eighty-first Street. And there it was. Not the old butcher shop – something even better. Revenge, a dish best served steaming, piping hot!

He spotted Maggione's Lincoln parked in the rear lot of the social club. License – ACF3069. He was pretty sure it was Junior's car anyway.

Mistake?

But whose mistake? he wondered as he continued up Eighty-first Street. Was Junior such an arrogant bastard that he could just come and go when he liked? Was it possible that he had no fear of the Butcher? No respect? Not even now?

Or had he set a trap for him?

Maybe it was a little of both. Arrogance and deception. Hallmarks of the world we live in.

Sullivan stopped at a Dunkin' Donuts at the intersection of New Utrecht and Eighty-sixth. He had some black coffee and a sesame bagel that was too doughy and bland. Maybe this kind of shit food played somewhere in Middle America, but a half-assed bagel had no place being sold in Brooklyn. Anyway, he sat at a table, watching the car lights pass back and forth out on New Utrecht, and he was thinking that he wanted to walk into the club on Eighty-first Street and start blasting. But that wasn't any kind of plan – it was just a nice, violent fantasy for the moment.

Of course, he had a real plan in mind.

Junior Maggione was a dead man now, and probably worse than that. Sullivan smiled at the thought, then checked to make sure that nobody was watching, thinking he was a crazy person. They weren't. He *was*. Good deal.

He took another sip. Actually, the Dunkin' coffee wasn't half-bad. But the bagel was the worst.

Chapter Ninety-Seven

Twenty minutes later, he was in position. Now here was the funny thing: he'd done this same kind of commando raid when he was just a kid. He and Jimmy Hats and Tony Mullino had climbed a rickety fire escape on Seventy-eighth, then sprinted over the tar-papered rooftops to a building near the social club. In broad daylight. No fear.

They were 'dropping in' on a girl Tony knew in the building attached to the social club. The chick's name was Annette Bucci. Annette was a hot little Italian number who used to put out for her boyfriends when they were all of thirteen, fourteen years old. They'd watch *Happy Days* and *Laverne & Shirley,* like the idiots they were, smoke cigarettes and weed, drink her father's vodka, screw their little brains out. Nobody had to use a rubber because Annette said she couldn't have babies, which made the three boys the luckiest bastards in the neighborhood that summer.

Anyway, this present escapade was a lot more serious – he wasn't here to screw Annette Bucci.

No, he had very serious business with Junior Maggione, unfinished business that probably went all the way back to Maggione Sr, who had bumped off his pal Jimmy Hats. What else could have happened to Hats? So this was about revenge, which was going to be so sweet that the Butcher could almost taste it. He could *see* Junior Maggione dying.

If the plan worked out tonight, they'd be talking about it in the neighborhood for years.

And, of course, there were going to be pictures!

He was pumped as he hurried across the old rooftops, hoping that nobody on the top floors could hear him and maybe come up for a look, or even call the cops. Finally, he made it to the brownstone attached to the social club building.

Nobody seemed to know he was up there. So he hunkered down on the roof and caught his breath. He let his heartbeat slow down, but he didn't lose his anger. At Maggione? At his father? What the hell difference did it make?

As he sat there, Sullivan wondered if maybe he

was suicidal at this point in his life. On some level anyway. He had a theory that people who smoked had to be, and assholes who drank and drove too fast, and anybody who got on a motorcycle. Or killed his own father and fed him to the fish in Sheepshead Bay. Secretly suicidal, right?

Like John Maggione. He'd been a punk all his life. He'd come after the Butcher. And now look what was going to happen to him.

If the plan worked.

Chapter Ninety-Eight

Surveillance. Waiting. Twiddling our thumbs. It was just like the old days again, and it only half-sucked this time.

As Sampson and I sat less than a hundred yards from the house in Montauk, along the South Fork of Long Island, I was growing more and more enthusiastic about the possibility of taking the Butcher down soon. At the same time, I couldn't help thinking that something wasn't right.

Maybe I even knew what was wrong. This killer hadn't been caught before. As far as I knew, no one had come close. So why did I think we could bring him down now?

Because I was the Dragon Slayer and had succeeded with other killers? Because I *used* to be the Dragon

Slayer? Because in the end life was fair, and killers ought to be caught, especially the one who had murdered my wife? Well, hell no, life wasn't fair. I'd known that from the moment Maria collapsed, then died in my arms.

'You don't think he's going to come back here?' Sampson asked. 'Is that what you're thinking about, sugar? You think he's on the run again? Long gone?'

'No, that's not it exactly. This isn't about Sullivan coming here or not. I think maybe he will. I don't know exactly what's bothering me, John. I just feel . . . it's like we're being set up somehow.'

Sampson screwed up his face.

'Set up by who? Set up why?'

'Don't know the answer, unfortunately. To either of those reasonable questions.'

It was a strange gut feeling at this point. Just a feeling, though. One of my famous feelings. Which were often right, but not always, not every time.

As the sun began to go down and it got colder, I watched a couple of insane surf casters down near the ocean. We could see the water from the woods. The fishermen were dressed in neoprene waders up to their chests, and they were probably going for stripers at this time of year. Their lure bags and gaffs were attached to their waists, and one of them had a crazy-looking miner's lamp strapped on to his Red Sox ball cap. It was very windy, and the windier it got, the better the fishing – or so I've been told.

I had the idea that Sampson and I were fishing too, always fishing for whatever cockamamy evil lurked deep beneath the surface. And as I watched the seemingly innocent activity down at the shoreline, one of the fishermen slipped under a wave and then scrambled to recover some of his dignity. That water had to be damn cold.

I hoped that didn't happen to Sampson and me tonight.

We shouldn't be here like this – but we were.

And we were exposed, weren't we?

And this killer was one of the best we had ever faced. Maybe the Butcher *was* the best.

Chapter Ninety-Nine

Simple stuff really, the basic ingredients of a professional murder, committed by a professional. This time out it was a jug of high-octane gasoline, propane, a stick of dynamite for ignition. Nothing too hard about the prep. But would the plan actually work? That was always the $64,000 question.

In a way, it almost seemed like a prank to the Butcher – some stunt that he and Tony Mullino and Jimmy Hats would have tried to pull off in the old days, back in the neighborhood. Get a few crazy yuks out of it. Maybe put some chump's eye out with a cherry bomb. Most of life had seemed like that to him – pranks, stunts, getting revenge for past wrongs.

That was what happened with his father, how he came to kill the sick bastard. He didn't like to think about it too much, so he didn't, just closed off the compartment. But one night, long ago in Brooklyn, he'd cut the original Butcher of Sligo, Kevin Sullivan, into little pieces, then fed him to the fish in the bay. The rumors were all true. Jimmy Hats had been out on the boat with him, and so had Tony Mullino. The guys he trusted.

Tonight wasn't that different in one respect – it was all about getting revenge. Hell, he'd hated Junior Maggione for twenty years.

He took a fire escape down from the roof of the building next to the social club. Once he was at street level he could hear gruff men's voices coming from inside the club. A ball game was playing – Jets and Pittsburgh on ESPN. Maybe the game was why everybody was preoccupied on this cold, overcast Sunday night. *Bollinger drops back! Bollinger stays in the pocket!*

Well, he was in the pocket too, the Butcher was thinking to himself. Perfect protection for the play, all the time he needed to execute it. And he hated these bastards inside the club. Always had. They'd never really let him inside their little society, not to this day. He'd always been on the outside.

He set his highly combustible bomb next to a wooden wall in an alleyway that looked out to the street. Through the alley, he spotted a couple of

Maggione's soldiers posted across the way. They were leaning against the hood of a black Escalade.

He could see them, but they couldn't see him in the darkened alley.

He backed away into the alley and took shelter behind a Dempsey Dumpster that stank like rotting fish.

An American Airlines jet roared overhead, heading into LaGuardia, making a noise like thunder shaking the sky. The timing was excellent for what came next.

The roar of the plane was nothing compared to the earsplitting explosion against the rear wall of the social club; then came the screams and cursing of men inside.

And fire! Jesus! The flames were dancing out of control in a hurry.

The rear door burst open, and two soldiers, Maggione's personal bodyguards, had the boss in their grasp like he was the president of the United States and they were the Secret Service, hurrying him to safety. The bodyguards were bleeding, coughing from the smoke, but they were moving forward, heading toward the boss's Lincoln. They tried to clear smoke from their eyes with their shirtsleeves.

Sullivan stepped out from behind the Dumpster and said, 'Hey there, assholes! You guys suck.' He fired four shots. The bodyguards fell to the pavement, side by side, dead before they hit the cement. The check-ered sports jacket of one of them was still on fire.

Then he ran up to Junior Maggione, whose face was cut and burned. He stuck his gun barrel up against Maggione's cheek.

'I remember you when you were just a little kid, Junior. Uptight, spoiled little fuck back then. Nothing's changed, huh? Get in the car or I'll shoot you dead right here in the back alley. Shoot you between the eyes, then cut them out, stick 'em in your ears. Get in the car before I lose it!'

And that's when he showed Junior Maggione the scalpel.

'Get in, before I use it.'

Chapter One Hundred

Sullivan drove the mob boss along the familiar streets of Brooklyn – New Utrecht Avenue, then Eighty-sixth Street – riding in the Don's own car, loving every minute of this.

'Trip down memory lane for me.' He gave a running commentary as he proceeded. 'Who says you can't go home again? Know who said that, Junior? Ever read any books? You should have. Too late now.'

He pulled into the Dunkin' Donuts on Eighty-sixth and transferred Maggione into the rented Ford Taurus, which was basically a piece of shit, but at least it wouldn't be noticed on the street. Then he put hand-cuffs on Junior. Tight ones, police-issue.

'What the hell do you think you're doing?' Maggione snarled as the cuffs bit into his wrists.

Sullivan wasn't sure what Junior meant – the changing of the cars, the fire-bombing, the next half hour or so? What?

'You came after me, remember? You started this whole thing. Tell you what, I'm here to finish it. I should have done this when we were both kids.'

The Don got red-faced and looked ready to have a major coronary in the car. 'You're *crazy*! You're a *lunatic*!' he screamed as they pulled out of the lot.

Sullivan almost stopped the car in the middle of the street. Was Junior really screaming at him like he was hired help?

'Hey, I'm not going to argue with you about the state of my mental health. I'm a contract killer, so presumably I'm a little crazy. I'm supposed to be crazy, right? I killed fifty-eight people so far.'

'You chop people up into little pieces,' said Maggione. 'You're a loose cannon, a madman. You killed a friend of mine. Remember that?'

'I fulfill my contracts on time, every time. Maybe I'm a little too high-profile for some tastes. But hold that thought – about chopping bodies into little pieces.'

'What the hell are you talking about? You're not that crazy. Nobody's that crazy.'

Amazing to see how Maggione's mind worked, or

didn't work. Still, Junior *was* a stone-cold killer, so he had to be careful. *No mistakes now.*

'Just so I'm clear on this part,' Michael Sullivan said, 'we're headed to a pier I know on the Hudson River. Once we get there, I'm going to take some art photos for all your goombah pals to see. I'm going to give them a clear warning I hope they'll understand about leaving me and my family alone.'

Then Sullivan put his finger to his lips. 'Don't talk anymore,' he said. 'I'm almost starting to feel a little sorry for you, Junior, and I don't want to feel like that.'

'What do I care what you feel like, *ahhh*,' said Maggione, on account of Sullivan had stuck him in the belly with a switchblade knife, stuck it in to the hilt, then pulled it out slowly.

'Just for starters,' he said in a weird, whispery voice. 'I'm just getting warmed up.'

Then the Butcher took a little half bow. 'I am *that* crazy.'

Chapter One Hundred and One

S ampson and I were back inside his car waiting for the Butcher to return to the house in Montauk. We were down to counting the minutes. Sooner or later he had to come back; only it hadn't happened yet, and Sampson and I were tired, cold, and, frankly, disappointed.

A pizza delivery guy from Papa John's showed up at around seven thirty. But no Sullivan, no Butcher, no relief in sight, and no pizza for us, either.

'Let's talk about something,' said Sampson. 'Keep our minds off food. And the cold.'

'Been thinking about Maria again while I'm sitting here freezing my ass off,' I said as we watched the long-haired pizza guy come and go. The thought had crossed my mind that Sullivan might use a delivery like this to get his wife a message. Had that just happened? Nothing we could do about it. *But had it just happened?*

'Not surprising, sugar,' said Sampson.

'What has happened over the last couple of months has dredged up a lot of the past for me. I figured I'd grieved enough. Maybe not, though. Therapist seems to think *not*.'

'You had two babies to take care of back then. Maybe you were a little too busy to mourn as much as you needed. I remember I used to come over the house some nights. You never seemed to sleep. Working homicide cases. Trying to be a daddy. Remember the Bell's palsy?'

'Now that you mention it.'

I'd had a disconcerting facial twitch for a while after Maria died. A neurologist at Johns Hopkins told me that it might go away or go on for years. It lasted a little more than two weeks, and it was kind of an effective tool on the job. Scared the hell out of perps I had to question in the cage.

'At the time, you wanted to catch Maria's killer so bad, Alex. Then you started obsessing over other murder cases. That's when you became a really good detective. In my opinion anyway. It's when you became focused. How you got to be the Dragon Slayer.'

I felt like I was in the confessional. John Sampson was my priest. So what was new?

'I didn't want to think about her all the time, so I guess I had to throw myself into something else. There were the kids, and there was work.'

'So did you grieve enough, Alex? This time? Is it over? Close to being over?'

'Honestly? I don't know, John. I'm trying to figure that out now.'

'What if we don't catch Sullivan this time? What if he gets away on us? What if he already has?'

'I think I'll be better about Maria. She's been gone a long time.' I stopped, took a breath. 'I don't think it was my fault. I couldn't have done anything differently when she was shot.'

'Ahh,' said Sampson.

'Ahh,' I said.

'But you're not completely sure, are you? You're still not convinced.'

'Not a hundred percent.' Then I laughed. 'Maybe if we do catch him tonight. Maybe if I blow his brains out. Then we'll definitely be even.'

'That's why we're out here, sugar? To blow his brains out?'

There was a knock against the car's side window, and I went for my gun.

Chapter One Hundred and Two

'What the hell is *he* doing here?' Sampson asked. None other than Tony Mullino was standing next to the car – on my side. What the hell *was* he doing out here in Montauk?

I slowly lowered the window, hoping to find out, to get an answer, maybe a whole bunch of answers.

'I could have been Sully,' he said, with his head cocked to one side. 'You'd both be dead if I was.'

'No, *you'd* be dead,' Sampson said. He gave Mullino a slow smile and showed off his Glock. 'I saw you coming up from behind about two minutes ago. So did Alex.'

I hadn't, but it was good to know that Sampson still had my back, that somebody did, because maybe

I was starting to lose my focus a little – and that could get you shot. Or worse.

Mullino was rubbing his hands together. 'Cold as shit out here tonight.' He waited, then repeated himself. 'I said it's fricking frigid, *freezing* cold out here.'

'Hop in,' I told him. 'C'mon inside.'

'You promise not to shoot us in the back?' Sampson said.

Mullino raised both hands and looked either puzzled or alarmed. Sometimes it was hard to tell with him. 'I don't even carry a weapon, fellas. Never did in my life.'

'Maybe you ought to, the friends you keep,' Sampson said. 'Something to think about, brother.'

'Okay, *brother*,' said Mullino, with a mean little laugh that made me rethink who he was.

He opened the car door and slid down into the backseat. The question was still on the table: Why had he shown up here and what did he want?

'He's not coming?' I said, once he'd shut the rear door on the cold. 'Is that right?'

'Nah, he's not coming,' said Mullino. 'Never was.'

'You warn him?' I asked. I was watching Mullino in the rearview mirror. His eyes narrowed and showed extreme nervousness, something uncomfortable, something not right.

'I didn't have to warn him. Sully's self-reliant, takes care of himself just fine.' His voice was low, almost a whisper.

'I'll bet,' I said.

'So what happened, Anthony?' asked Sampson. 'Where's your boy now? Why are you here?'

Mullino's voice sounded like it was coming from underwater. I didn't quite catch what he said this time.

Neither did Sampson. 'You have to speak up,' he said, turning around. 'You hear me? See how it works? You have to get your voice up to a certain volume.'

'He killed John Maggione tonight,' said Mullino. 'Kidnapped him, then carved him up. *That* has been a long time coming.'

There was complete silence in the car. I doubt there was anything he could have said that would have surprised me more. I'd felt earlier that maybe we'd been set up, and we had been.

'How did you hear about it?' I finally asked.

'I live in the neighborhood. Brooklyn's like being in a small town sometimes. Always been that way. Besides, Sully called me when it was done. He wanted to *share.*'

Sampson shifted all the way around to face him. 'So Sullivan's not coming here to collect his family. Isn't he afraid for them?'

I was still watching Tony Mullino in the rearview. I thought maybe I knew what he was going to say next.

'This isn't his family,' he said. 'He doesn't even know who they are.'

'Who's in the house then?'

'I don't know who they are. Central casting. A family that might look like Sully's.'

'You work for him?' I asked Mullino.

'No. But he's been a good friend. I was the one afraid of getting my face messed up in school, not him. Sully always protected me. So I helped him. I'd do it again. Hell, I helped him kill his crazy old man.'

'Why'd you come out here?' I asked him next.

'That one's easy. He told me to.'

'Why?' I asked.

'You'll have to ask him. Maybe because he likes to take a bow after a job well done. He does that, y'know. Takes a bow. You don't want to see it.'

'I already have,' I told him.

Mullino opened the back door of the car, nodded his head to us, and then he was gone into the night.

And so, I knew, was the Butcher.

Chapter One Hundred
and Three

What's that old line, new line, whatever it is –
*life is what happens when you're busy making
other plans?*

I went back to Washington that night because I
wanted to see the kids, and because of Nana Mama,
and because I had patients who depended on me and
were scheduled for the next day. Nana has always
preached that it's important for me to be helping
people; she calls it my curse. She's probably right.

I could clearly see Michael Sullivan's face, his little
bow, and it killed me that he was still out there somewhere. According to the FBI, the mob had already put
a million-dollar price tag on his head, and another
million on his family. I still had a suspicion that he

might be an FBI or police informant, and that one or the other was helping to protect him, but I didn't know that for sure, and maybe I never would.

On one of the nights after Sullivan escaped, a school night for the kids, I sat out on the sunporch and played rock and roll on the piano for Jannie and Damon. I played until it was almost ten. Then I talked to the kids about their mother. It was time.

Chapter One Hundred
and Four

I'm not sure why I needed to tell them about Maria
now, but I wanted the kids to have some more of
the truth about her.

Maybe I wanted them to have the closure that I
couldn't get myself. I had never lied about Maria to
the kids, but I had held back, and . . . no, I had lied
about one thing. I'd told Damon and Jannie that I
wasn't with Maria when she was shot, but that I got
to St Anthony's before she died, and we'd had a few
last words. The reason was that I didn't want to have
to tell them details that I could never get out of my
own head: the sound of the gunshots that felled Maria;
the sharp intake of her breath the instant she was hit;
the way she slid from my arms to the sidewalk. Then

the unforgettable sight of blood pouring from Maria's chest, and my realization that the wounds were fatal. I still could remember it with nightmare clarity more than ten years later.

'I've been thinking about your mom lately,' I said that night on the porch. 'I've been thinking about her a lot. You guys probably know that already.'

The kids were gathered around close, suspecting this wasn't one of our usual talks. 'She was a special person in so many ways. So many ways, Damon and Jannie. Her eyes were alive and always honest. She was a listener. And that's usually a sign of a good person. I think it is anyway. She loved to smile and to make other people smile if she possibly could. She used to say, "Here's a cup of sadness, and here's a cup of joy, which do you choose?" She almost always chose the cup of joy.'

'Almost always?' asked Jannie.

'Almost always. Think about it, Janelle. You're smart. She chose me, didn't she? All the cute boys she could have had, she chose this puss, this dour personality.'

Janelle and Damon smiled; then Damon said, 'This is because the one who killed her is back? Why we're talking about our mother now?'

'That's part of it, Day. But lately I realized I had

unfinished business with her. And with the two of you. *That's* why we're talking, okay?'

Damon and Janelle listened in silence, and I talked for a long while. Eventually, I choked up. I think it was the first time I'd let them see me cry about Maria. 'I loved her so much, loved your mother like she was a physical part of me. I still do, I guess. Still do, I *know*.'

'Because of us?' Damon asked. 'It's partly our fault, isn't it?'

'What do you mean, sweetheart? I'm not sure that I follow you,' I said to Damon.

'We remind you of her, don't we? We remind you of Mom every day; every morning when you see us, you remember that she's not here. Isn't that right?'

I shook my head. 'Maybe there's some little bit of truth in that. But you remind me in a good way, the best way. Trust me on that. It's all good.'

They waited for me to talk some more, and they didn't take their eyes off me, as if I might suddenly run away on them.

'Lots of changes are happening in our lives,' I said. 'We have Ali here now. Nana's getting older. I'm seeing patients again.'

'You like it?' Damon asked. 'Being a psychologist?'

'I do. So far.'

'*So far.* That's so *you*, Daddy,' said Jannie.

I snorted out a laugh, but I didn't go fishing for a compliment about what Jannie had said. Not that I was completely averse to compliments, but there was a time for everything, and this wasn't it. I remember that when I'd read Bill Clinton's autobiography, I couldn't help thinking that when he was confessing to the hurt he'd caused his wife and daughter, he couldn't seem to resist looking for forgiveness too, and even hugs from the reader. He just couldn't resist – maybe because his need for love is so great. And maybe that's where his empathy and compassion come from.

Then I finally did the hardest thing – I told Jannie and Damon what had happened to Maria. I told my children the truth as I knew it. I shared most of the details of Maria's death, her murder, and I told them that I had seen it happen, been with her when she died, felt her last breath on this earth, heard her last words.

When I was done, when I couldn't talk anymore, Jannie whispered, 'Watch the river, how it flows, Daddy. The river is truth.'

That had been my mantra for the kids when they were little and Maria wasn't around. I'd walk them by the Anacostia River or the Potomac and make them look at it, the water, and say, 'Watch the river . . . the river is truth.'

Or at least as close as we'll ever get to it.

Chapter One Hundred and Five

I was feeling strangely emotional and vulnerable, and I guess, maybe, alive these days.

It was both a good and a bad thing.

I had breakfast with Nana Mama at around five thirty or so almost every morning. Then I jogged to my office, changed clothes, and started my sessions as early as six thirty.

Kim Stafford was my first patient on Mondays and Thursdays. It was always a hard thing to keep personal feelings out of the sessions, at least for me, or maybe I was just out of practice. On the other hand, some of my colleagues had always struck me as too clinical, too reserved and distant. What was any patient, any human being, supposed to make of that? *Oh, it's okay if I have the effect of a turnip; I'm a therapist.*

I needed to do this my way, with warmth at times, with lots of feeling and compassion rather than empathy; I needed to break the rules, to be unorthodox. Like confronting Jason Stemple at his station house and trying to punch that scum's lights out. That's what I call *professional*.

I had a break in my schedule until noon, so I decided to check in with Monnie Donnelley at Quantico. She was doing some research on a theory of mine about the Butcher. I hadn't said much more than hello, when Monnie interrupted. 'I have something for you, Alex. I think you're going to like this. It's your idea anyway, your theory.'

Monnie then told me that she'd used my notes and tracked down news about Sullivan's wife through a mob soldier who was in the Witness Protection Program and now living in Myrtle Beach, South Carolina.

'I followed the trail you set up, and you were right on. It led me to a guy who was at Sullivan's wedding, which was small, as you might expect. The pal from Brooklyn you told me about, Anthony Mullino, he was there. Apparently, Sullivan didn't want many people to know about his private life. His own mother wasn't invited, and his father was dead, as you know.'

'Yeah, killed by his son and a couple of pals. What did you find out about Sullivan's wife?'

'Well, it's interesting stuff, not what you'd expect, either. She's originally from Colts Neck, New Jersey, and she was a first-grade teacher before she met Sullivan. How about that? Salvatore Pistelli, the Witness Protection guy, said she was a sweet girl. Said Sullivan was looking for a good mother for his kids. Touching, huh, Alex? Our psycho hit man has a soft spot. The wife's name was Caitlin Haney. Her family's still living in Colts Neck.'

That same day, we had a tap set up on the phones of Caitlin Sullivan's parents' place. Also on a sister who lived in Toms River, New Jersey, and a brother who was a dentist in Ridgewood.

I had some hope again. Maybe we could close this case after all and bring down the Butcher.

Maybe I would see him again and take a little bow myself.

Chapter One Hundred and Six

Michael Sullivan had been using the name Michael Morrissey since he'd been living in Massachusetts, Morrissey being a punk he'd more or less drawn and quartered in his early days as a hit man. Caitlin and the boys kept their first names but went under the surname Morrissey now too. The story they had learned by heart was that they had been living in Dublin for the past few years, where their father was a consultant to several Irish companies with business connections to America.

Now he was doing 'consultant' work in Boston.

The latter part happened to be true, since the Butcher had just gotten a job through an old contact in South Boston. A job – a hit, a murder for hire.

He left the house overlooking the river that morning at a very civilized nine o'clock. Then he headed down to the Massachusetts Turnpike in his new Lexus. He had his work tools in the trunk – guns, a butcher saw, a nail gun.

He didn't play any music on the first part of the trip, preferring to travel down memory lane instead. Lately, he'd been thinking a lot about his early kills: about his father, of course; a couple of jobs for Maggione Sr; and a Catholic priest named Francis X Conley. Father Frank X had been messing around with boys in the parish for years. The rumors were all around the neighborhood, the stories laced with plenty of kinky, slimy detail. Sullivan couldn't believe that some of the parents knew what was going on and hadn't stepped up to do something to stop it.

When he was nineteen and already working for Maggione, he happened to spot the priest down at the docks, where Conley kept a little outboard for his fishing trips. Sometimes he would take one of the altar boys for an afternoon. A reward. A little sweet treat.

On this particular day in the spring, the good father had come down to the dock to prepare his boat for the season. He was working over the engine when Sullivan and Jimmy Hats stepped on board.

'Hey, Father Frankie,' Jimmy said, and beamed a crooked smile. 'How 'bout we take a little boat trip today? Do some fishin'?'

The priest squinted up at the two young hoods, frowning when he recognized who it was. 'I don't think so, boys. Boat's not ready for action yet.'

That brought a laugh from Hats, who repeated, '*Ready for action* – yeah, I get you.'

Then Sullivan stepped forward. 'Yeah, it is ready, *Fodder*. We're goin' on a sea cruise. You know that song? Frankie Ford's "Sea Cruise"? That's where we're goin'. Just the three of us.'

So they cruised on out of the boatyard, and Father Frank X was never seen or heard from again. 'God rest his immoral soul in hell,' Jimmy Hats joked on the way back.

And that morning, as he drove out on his latest job, Sullivan remembered the old Frankie Ford song – and he remembered how the pathetic priest had begged for his life, and then for his death, before he got cut up into shark food. But most of all, he remembered wondering whether he had just done a *good deed* with Father Frank, and whether or not it was possible that he could.

Could he do anything good in his life?

Or was he just all bad?

Chapter One Hundred and Seven

He finally arrived in Stockbridge, near the Massachusetts–New York border, and used his GPS to find the right house. He was ready to do his worst, to be the Butcher again, to earn his day's wage.

To hell with good deeds and good thoughts, whatever they were supposed to prove. He located the house, which was very 'country' and, he thought, very tasteful. It sat on a tranquil pond in the middle of acres of maples and elms and pines. A black Porsche Targa was parked like a modern sculpture in the driveway.

The Butcher had been told that a forty-one-year-old woman named Melinda Steiner was at the house

– but that *she drove a spiffy red Mercedes convertible*.
So who did the black Porsche belong to?

Sullivan parked off the main road behind a copse
of pines, and he watched the house for about twenty
minutes. One of the things he noticed was that the
garage door was closed. And maybe there was a fine
red Mercedes convertible in the garage.

So – once again – who owned the black Porsche?

Careful to stay under the cover of thick branches,
he put a pair of German binoculars to his eyes. Then
he slowly scanned the east and south windows of the
house, each and every one of them.

No one seemed to be in the kitchen – which was
all darkened windows, no one moving about.

Or in the living room, either, which was also dark
and looked deserted.

But somebody was in the house, right?

He finally found them in a corner bedroom on the
second floor. Probably the master suite.

Melinda, or Mel, Steiner was up there.

And some blond dude. Probably in his early forties,
presumably the owner of the Porsche.

Too many mistakes to calculate, he was thinking to
himself. *A real cluster-fuck of errors.*

What he could also calculate was that his
seventy-five-thousand-dollar fee for this job had

just doubled, because he never did two for the price of one.

The Butcher started to walk toward the country house, gun in one hand, toolbox in the other, and he was feeling pretty good about this job, this day, this life he had for himself.

Chapter One Hundred and Eight

There was very little in life that could beat the feeling of having confidence in your ability to do a job well. Michael Sullivan was thinking about the truth in that statement as he neared the house.

He was conscious of the amount of land surrounding the white Colonial house, three or four acres of secluded woods and fields. Off in the back he saw a tennis court that looked like green clay. Maybe it was Har-Tru, which the tennis buffs back in Maryland seemed to favor.

But mostly he was focused on his work, on the job to be done, on its two working parts.

Kill someone named Melinda Steiner – and her lover, since he was definitely in the way now.

Don't get killed yourself.

No mistakes.

He slowly opened the wooden front door of the house, which wasn't locked. People did that a lot out in the country, didn't they? *Mistake.* And he was pretty sure he wasn't going to get much resistance once he got upstairs, either.

Still, you never know, so don't get cocky, don't get sloppy, don't get overly cute, Mikey.

He remembered the fiasco in Venice, Italy, what had happened there. The mess, and how he could have gotten tagged. La Cosa Nostra would be looking all over for him now, and one day they'd find him.

So why not today? Why not right here?

His contact for the job was an old friend, but the mob could have easily gotten to him. And then set the Butcher up.

He just didn't think so.

Not today.

The front door hadn't been locked. They would have locked it, especially if this was a trap and they wanted it to look good.

The couple he'd spotted in the bedroom had looked too natural, too much in the moment, and he didn't believe anybody – except maybe himself – was slick enough to create that kind of setup and honey trap.

That couple was upstairs humping their brains and vital fluids out; there was very little doubt about it in his mind.

As he climbed the front stairs, he could hear the pleasing sounds of their screwing drifting down to him. Bedsprings coiling and releasing, the headboard hitting the bedroom wall.

Of course, it could be a recording.

But the Butcher doubted it, and his instincts were usually very, very good. They had certainly kept him alive so far, and they'd made a lot of other people dead.

Chapter One Hundred
and Nine

As he reached the second floor, his heart was beating a lot faster, the moans and assorted bed noises had gotten louder, and he started to smile in spite of himself.

Peculiar thought. He was remembering a scene in this movie called *Sideways* that had completely cracked him up at the time. The shorter character, who was basically a drunk, had to retrieve the other schmuck's wallet, and he needed to sneak into a bedroom where a couple of tubby lowlifes were rutting like pigs in a trough. The scene was pretty great – hilarious, totally unexpected too. Just like this was going to be. For him anyway.

So he turned a corner and peered into the

bedroom, and he thought to himself, *Surprise, you're both dead.*

The man and woman were in pretty good shape. Well toned and athletic, nice tight asses. Kind of sexy together. Smiles on their faces.

They seemed to like each other, which made it good for them. Maybe they were in love. They definitely appeared to like the sex, which was a good, sweaty workout. The blond guy was going deep, and Melinda seemed to like it that way just fine. The whole thing was kind of a turn-on. Melinda had on white kneesocks, which Sullivan got a kick out of. Did she do it for him or for herself? he wondered.

After a minute or so of watching, he cleared his throat. *Ahem, ahem. Order in the fuck-room.*

The coupling couple jumped apart, which was no easy trick given the corkscrew position they'd been locked in a couple of milliseconds before.

'Wow – you two!' he said, and smiled pleasantly, as if he was here doing a survey on extramarital affairs or something. 'Really going at it. I'm impressed.'

He kind of liked the two of them actually, especially this Mel. No doubt about it, she was a looker for her age. Nice body and face – sweet face, he was thinking.

He even liked the way she didn't cover up and

stared right back at him, like *What the hell do you think you're doing here? This is my house, my affair, none of your goddamn business, whoever the hell you are. So get lost!*

'You're Melinda Steiner, right?' he asked, pointing the gun at her, but not in a threatening way. What was the point of threats, of scaring them any worse than he had to? He didn't have it in for these two. They weren't the Mafia; they hadn't come gunning for him or his family.

'Yes. I'm Melinda Steiner. Who are you? What do you want here?'

She was definitely kind of feisty but not being totally obnoxious about it. Hell, this *was* her house, and she had a right to know what he was doing here.

He took a few quick strides into the room and—

Pop!

Pop!

He shot the blond male in the throat and forehead, and he dropped off the bed onto the Indian-style area rug on the floor. So much for keeping in good shape so that you live longer.

Melinda put both hands to her mouth and gasped out loud. 'Oh my God.' But she didn't scream, which meant this was mostly about the sex. They were screwing, but the two of them weren't in love, not even close. Watching her face now, he didn't even think she liked Blondie all that much.

'Good girl, Melinda. You're thinking on your feet. He didn't feel a thing. No pain, I promise.'

'He was my architect,' she said, then quickly added, 'I don't know why I told you that.'

'You're just nervous. Who wouldn't be? You've probably already figured out that I'm here to kill you, not your former lover.'

He was standing about three feet from the woman, and his gun was pointed in the general direction of her heart. She seemed in pretty good control of herself, though – very impressive to him. Sullivan's kind of girl. Maybe *she* should be the head of the mob. Maybe he would put her name up for the job.

He definitely liked her, and he had the sudden thought that he didn't much like her husband. He sat down on the bed with the gun still on her – well, on her left tit actually.

'Mel, here's the thing. Your husband sent me here to kill you. He paid seventy-five thousand dollars,' he said. 'I'm improvising here, but do you have access to your own money? Maybe we could work out some kind of a deal. Is that an option?'

'Yes,' she said. 'It is.' That was all.

A deal was struck a couple of minutes later, and

his fee quadrupled. Lot of crazy people out there in the world – no wonder *Desperate Housewives* was so popular, he couldn't help thinking.

Chapter One Hundred and Ten

Sampson and I hadn't been to Massachusetts in a few years, not since we'd chased a madman killer named 'Mr Smith' in a case code-named Cat and Mouse. Mr Smith had probably been the most cunning of all the psychopaths we had tracked to that point. He almost murdered me. So not a lot of happy memories for us as we rode in Sampson's car from DC toward the Berkshires.

On the way, we stopped off for an out-of-this-world dinner and some congenial bullshit at my cousin Jimmy Parker's restaurant, the Red Hat, in Irvington, New York. Mmm, mmm, good. Otherwise, this trip was all business. We went alone, with no backup. I still wasn't sure what I planned to do if I found the

Butcher. *If* we found him; if he hadn't already fled.

We listened to some old Lauryn Hill and Erykah Badu tapes on the road and didn't discuss Michael Sullivan much, not until we crossed over into Massachusetts on I-91.

'So what are we doing here, John?' I finally broke the ice on the subject.

'Chasing the bad guy, same as always,' he said. 'Nothing's changed, has it? Guy's a killer, a rapist. You're the Dragon Slayer. I'm along for the ride.'

'Just me and you, huh? No call to the local police? No FBI in on this? You know, we just crossed a state line.'

Sampson nodded. 'I figure this time it's personal. Am I wrong about that? Plus, he deserves to die, if it comes to that, which it just might. Probably will.'

'It's personal all right. It's never been more personal. This has been bubbling over for a long time. It needs to end. But—'

'No *buts*, Alex. We need to put an end to him.'

We rode along in silence for another few miles. But I had to talk this out a little more with Sampson. We had to set some kind of rules of engagement.

'I'm not going to just take him out – if he's up here. I'm not a vigilante, John.'

'I know that,' said Sampson. 'I know who you are,

Alex. If anybody does. Let's see how it plays. Maybe he's not even here.'

We arrived in the town of Florida, Massachusetts, at around two that afternoon; then we went looking for the house where we hoped to find Michael Sullivan once and for all. I could feel the tension really building inside me now. It took us another half hour to locate the place, which was built on the side of a mountain overlooking a river. We watched the house, and nobody seemed to be there. Had someone tipped Sullivan off again?

If it had happened, who would have done it? The FBI? Was he in Witness Protection after all? Was the FBI watching his back? Were they the ones who told him we might be coming for him?

We drove into the town center and had lunch at a Denny's. Sampson and I didn't talk much over our eggs and potatoes, which was unusual for us.

'You all right?' he finally asked, once the coffee had arrived.

'If we get him, I'll be better. This has to end, though. You're right about that.'

'Then let's go do it.'

We went back to the house, and at a little past five a station wagon turned into the drive and parked right in front of the porch. *Was this him? Finally, the Butcher?*

Three boys piled out of the back; then a pretty, dark-haired woman got out of the driver's side. It was obvious that she and the boys got along well. They rough-housed on the front lawn; then they trooped inside the house.

I had a picture of Caitlin Sullivan with me, but I didn't need to look at it. 'That's definitely her,' I told Sampson. 'We're in the right place this time. That's Caitlin and the Butcher's boys.'

'He'll spot us if we stay here,' Sampson said. 'This isn't *Cops*, and he's no dumb crackhead waiting to be caught.'

'Yeah, I'm counting on it,' I said.

Chapter One Hundred
and Eleven

Michael Sullivan wasn't anywhere near the house in Western Massachusetts. At seven thirty that night, he entered a ten-bedroom home in Wellesley, a wealthy suburb outside Boston.

He was a few steps behind Melinda Steiner, who had long legs and a sweet little tush to watch. Melinda knew it, too. She also understood how to be subtle and, at the same time, nicely provocative with her wiggle-walk.

A light was on in one of the rooms off the wide front hallway – which had three chandeliers in a courtly procession, courtesy of Melinda or her decorator, no doubt.

'Sweetie, I'm home!' Melinda called out as she

dropped her travel bag loudly on the highly polished floor.

Not a hint of anything wrong in her voice. No alarm or warning, no edge, nothing but wifely bonhomie.

She's pretty damn good, Sullivan couldn't help thinking to himself. *Glad I'm not married to her.*

No greeting came back from the room where the TV was on. Not a peep.

'Honey?' she called again. 'You in there? Honey? I'm home from the country. Jerry?'

This ought to surprise the bastard for sure. *Honey, I'm home! Honey, I'm still alive!*

A fatigued-looking man in a wrinkled pinstriped dress shirt, boxer shorts, and electric-blue flip-flops finally appeared in the doorway.

Now – he's a pretty good actor too. Like nothing in the whole wide world could be wrong.

Until right about now, when he sees the Butcher walking stride for stride behind his beloved wife, whom he's just tried to murder at their country house.

'Hey, you. Who is this, Mel? What's going on?' Jerry asked as he saw Sullivan standing there in the hallway.

The Butcher already had his gun out, and it was

pointed at the guy in his underwear, aimed at his balls, but then Sullivan moved it up to the heart, if the conniving bastard had one. Murder your wife? What kind of cold, cold shit was that?

'Change of plans,' Sullivan said. 'What can I tell you? It happens.'

The husband, Jerry, put his hands up in the air without being asked. He was also coming wide awake – in kind of a big hurry.

'What are you talking about? What is this, Mel? Why is this man in our house? Who the hell is he?'

A classic line and a dynamite delivery.

Now it was Melinda's turn to say her piece, and she decided to shout her answer.

'He's the one who was supposed to kill me, Jerry! You paid to have me murdered, you miserable piece of shit! You are total worthless garbage, and you're a coward too. So I paid him *more* to have *you* hit. That's what this is, honey. I guess you could call him a switch-hitter,' she said, and laughed at her own joke.

Nobody else did – not Jerry and not Sullivan. It was kind of funny actually, but not laugh-out-loud funny. Or maybe her delivery was wrong, a touch too harsh, a little too much of the truth in it.

The husband jumped back into the TV room and

tried to pull shut the door, but it wasn't even a contest.

The Butcher was quick and had a foot, a work boot, wedged in the doorway. Then he put his shoulder to it and followed Jerry right inside.

Jerry, the original contractor, was a tall, potbellied CEO- or CFO-type dude who was balding up top. The den smelled of his body odor and a cigar smoldering in an ashtray by the couch. A two-ball putter and a couple of Titleist spheroids lay on the rug. A man's man, this guy who had paid to have his wife killed and now was practicing his putting to show he didn't have the yips.

'I'll pay you more than she can!' Jerry squealed. 'Whatever that bitch paid, I'll double it! I swear to God! The money's there. It's yours.'

Wow – this is getting better and better, thought Sullivan. It brought new meaning to a game like *Jeopardy!* – or *Let's Make a Deal.*

'You total piece of crap!' Melinda snarled at her husband from the doorway. Then she ran in and smacked him in the chops. Sullivan still thought that she was a cool lady in a lot of ways, though not some others.

He looked at the husband again. Then he looked at Melinda. Interesting couple, to be sure.

'I agree with Melinda,' said the Butcher. 'But Jerry does have a point, Mel. Maybe we should have a little auction here. You think? Let's talk this out like adults. No more hitting or name-calling.'

Chapter One Hundred
and Twelve

Two hours later, the auction was complete, and Michael Sullivan was driving on the Massachusetts Turnpike in his Lexus. The car could move reasonably well, and the ride was smooth as a baby's ass, or maybe he was just feeling good.

There were a few loose details to work out, but the job was done. Let's Make a Deal had netted him three hundred and fifty thousand, all of it wired into an account at the Union Bank of Switzerland. Truth be told, he hadn't felt this financially secure in a while, though he'd probably burned his Boston contact for the job. Maybe he'd have to move the family again too. Or maybe it was time for him to break free and set off on his own, something he'd been thinking about a lot.

It was probably worth it – three hundred fifty grand for a day's work. Jerry Steiner had been the winning bidder, but then he tapped the dumb, obnoxious bastard anyway. Melinda was a different story. He liked her, didn't want to hurt her. But what choice did he have? Leave her around to talk? So he made it pain-less – one to the back of Mel's head. Then a couple of pictures to memorialize her pretty face for his collection.

Anyway, he was singing a Stones ballad that he'd always liked, 'Wild Horses,' when he came around the bend in the road. There was his house on the hill, right where he'd left it.

And – what the hell was this?

Mistake?

But whose mistake?

He shut off his headlights around the next little crook in the road. Then he eased into a cul-de-sac, where he had a better view of his house and the grounds.

Man, he couldn't catch a break lately. Couldn't outrun his past no matter how far away he went.

He'd spotted them right away, in a dark-blue car, maybe a Dodge, with the grille pointed toward the house like a gun. Two men inside that he could see. Waiting for him, no doubt about that.

Mistake.

Theirs!

But who the hell were these two guys he had to kill now?

Chapter One Hundred and Thirteen

W ell, it didn't much matter. They were two dead men – dead over nothing, dead because they were miserable screwups at their jobs. Dead men watching his house, come to kill him and his family.

Sullivan had a three-year-old Winchester in the trunk of the car, which he kept cleaned, oiled, and ready to go. He popped the trunk, took out the long gun. Then he loaded it up with hollow-points.

He didn't quite have the skills to be an army sniper, but he was plenty good enough for this kind of bush-whacking.

He set up in the woods between a couple of tall, fluffy evergreens that provided a canopy of extra cover. Then he took a quick look through the nightscope. It had a bull's-eye rather than a site post, which was the way he liked it. Actually, it was Jimmy Hats who had taught him to be a long-distance marksman. Jimmy had been trained at Fort Bragg in North Carolina, before his dishonorable discharge.

He let the bull's-eye rest right on the driver's head, and he lightly touched the trigger with his finger. This was going to be easy, not a problem for him.

Then he shifted his aim to the head of the guy in the passenger seat. Whoever these two were, they were definitely DOA.

As soon as it was over, he'd have to gather up the family and boogie on out of here. No contact again with their past. That was the mistake, wasn't it? Somebody from ancient history they had kept in contact with? Maybe Caitlin's family in New Jersey. Somebody had probably tracked a phone call. He'd bet anything that's what had happened.

Mistake, mistake, mistake.

And Caitlin would keep making them, wouldn't she? Which meant Caitlin had to go. He didn't want to think too much about it but Caitlin was a goner too. Unless he just took off by himself.

Lots of decisions to make. Not much time to make them.

He set the bull's-eye back on the driver's head. He

was ready for two shots, and both men in the car were dead. They just didn't know it yet.

He slowly let out a breath until his body was calm and still and ready to do this.

He had a sense of his own heartbeat – slow, steady, confident; slow, steady, confident.

Then he pulled the trigger – and heard a sharp, satisfying *crack* in the night air.

An instant later, he pulled the rifle's trigger a second time.

Then a third and a fourth time.

That should do it.

The killing was done, and he had to get the hell out of here, pronto. With or without Caitlin and the boys.

But first he needed to know who he'd just killed and maybe take some pictures of the deceased.

Chapter One Hundred and Fourteen

S ampson and I watched the Butcher approach the car. He was being stealthy all right, but maybe he wasn't as good as he thought he was. He moved in quickly, bent low in a shooting crouch, ready for resistance if it came.

He was about to find out that he'd shot a pile of propped-up clothes and throw pillows from the local Wal-Mart. Sampson and I were crouched in the woods less than thirty yards behind the car he'd just ambushed. So who was better at this game? The Butcher or us?

'Your call, Alex, how it goes from here,' Sampson whispered out of the side of his mouth.

'Don't kill him, John,' I said, and touched Sampson's arm. 'Unless we have to. Just take him down.'

'Your call,' Sampson repeated.

Then everything went a little crazy, to put it mildly.

Suddenly the Butcher whirled around – but not in our direction! The opposite way!

What the hell was this? What was happening now?

Sullivan was facing the thick row of woods to the east – not where Sampson and I were coming from. He was paying no attention to us now.

He fired off two quick shots – and I heard somebody grunt in the distance.

A man dressed in black appeared for an instant; then he fell to the ground. Who was it? Then five more men came running out of the woods to the north. They had handguns, Bull Pups, one Uzi that I could make out.

Who were these guys?

As if to answer the question, one of them shouted, 'FBI. Drop your weapon! FBI!'

I didn't buy it.

'Mob!' I said to Sampson.

'You sure?'

'Yeah.'

Then everybody started blasting at everybody else, as if we were in the streets of Baghdad rather than somewhere in rural Massachusetts.

Chapter One Hundred and Fifteen

The mob hitters, if that's who they were, fired on us too. Sampson and I shot back at them. And so did the Butcher.

I hit a guy in a leather trench coat – the one with the Uzi, my first target.

The gunman spun around and dropped to the dirt, but then he raised the Uzi to fire again. He got hit square in the chest with a round, and the force knocked him flat. I wasn't the one who shot him though. Maybe Sampson?

Or was it Sullivan who'd shot him?

The darkness was a serious hazard to everybody. Bullets were flying everywhere, slugs of lead slamming into trees, ricocheting off rocks. It was total chaos and bedlam, hair-raising, death-defying madness being played out in the dark.

The Mafia thugs were fanning out, trying to create space between themselves, which would be even more trouble for us.

Sullivan had run to his left and was using the trees and shadows for some cover.

Sampson and I tried to hide ourselves as best we could behind skinny evergreens.

I was afraid we would die here; it felt like it could happen. Too many shots were being fired in too tight an area. This was a kill zone. It was like being heavily armed but up against a firing squad.

A Mafia hitter emptied his Bull Pup at the Butcher. I wasn't sure, but I didn't think he got his target.

He didn't, because Sullivan popped right up and shot the mob guy as he scurried back toward the safety of the woods. The shooter let out a scream, and then he was quiet. I thought that three of the mob soldiers had been shot so far. Sampson and I weren't hit, but we hadn't been primary targets.

Now what? Who would make the next move? Sullivan? John or me?

Then something strange – I heard a boy's voice. A tiny voice called out, 'Dad! Dad! Where are you, Dad?'

Chapter One Hundred and Sixteen

I swiveled my neck hard and peered in the direction of the house on the hill. I saw two of the Sullivan boys running down the front steps. They were dressed in their pajamas and had bare feet.

'Get back!' Sullivan screamed at them. 'Get inside the house, you two! Get inside!'

Then Caitlin Sullivan rushed out of the house in a bathrobe, trying to hold back her youngest son, then picking him up in her arms. She was screaming bloody murder at the two other boys to come back inside.

Meanwhile, gunshots were happening everywhere, loud blasts that echoed in the night. Bursts of light illuminated trees, boulders, fallen bodies on the grass.

Sullivan kept yelling – 'Get back in the house! Get back! Caitlin, get them inside!'

The boys didn't listen; they just kept coming across the lawn toward their father.

One of the hit men turned his gun on the running figures, and I shot him in the side of the neck. He spun around, fell, and stayed down. I thought, *I just saved the lives of Sullivan's boys.* What did it mean? That we were even for the time he came to my house and didn't kill anybody? Was I supposed to shoot Caitlin Sullivan now as payback for Maria?

Nothing made much sense to me on this dark, bloodstained lawn.

Another hit man zigzagged in a fast retreat until he reached the woods. Then he dove headfirst into the brush. One final hit man stood out in the open. He and Sullivan faced off and fired on each other. The soldier spun and went down, blood rushing from a gaping wound in his face. Sullivan was left standing.

He turned to Sampson and me.

Chapter One Hundred and Seventeen

Stalemate – at least for the moment. A couple of seconds? And then what happens?

I realized that Sampson's car wasn't a shield between Sullivan and me anymore. His sons had finally stopped running toward him. Caitlin Sullivan had the two smaller ones wrapped in her arms. The oldest boy stood beside her, looking protective, looking a lot like his father. I prayed the boy didn't get into this now too.

'I'm Alex Cross,' I told Sullivan. 'You came to my house once. Then you killed my wife. A long time ago, Washington, DC.'

'I know who you are,' Sullivan called back. 'I didn't kill your wife. I know who I killed.'

Then the Butcher took off on a dead run for the woods. I aimed at the square of his back – this was it – but I didn't pull the trigger. I couldn't do it.

Not in the back. Not with his wife and kids here, not under any circumstances.

'Dad!' one of the boys screamed again as Sampson and I took off after his father. 'Keep running! Keep running!'

'He's a killer, Alex,' Sampson said as we ran over uneven ground covered with high grass, jutting rocks, tree roots. 'We need to put him down. You know we do. Don't show mercy to the devil.'

I didn't need a reminder; I wasn't going to get careless.

But I hadn't taken the shot when I had it. I hadn't brought down Michael Sullivan when I had the chance.

The woods were dark, but there was enough moonlight to make out shapes and some finer detail. Maybe we'd be able to see Sullivan, but he'd see us too.

The stalemate continued. But one of us was going to die tonight. I knew it and hoped it wouldn't be me. But this had to be finished now. It had been building to this for so long.

I wondered where he was running – if he had an escape plan or if an ambush was coming.

We hadn't seen Sullivan since he'd gotten to the tree line. Maybe he was fast, or maybe he'd taken a sharp turn in another direction. How well did he know the woods?

Was he watching us right now? Getting ready to fire? To spring from behind a tree?

Finally, I saw movement – someone running fast up ahead. It had to be Sullivan! Unless it was the remaining mob guy.

Whoever it was, I didn't have a shot. Too many tree trunks, branches, and limbs in the way.

My breath was coming in short, harsh gasps. I wasn't out of shape, so it had to be the stress of everything going on. I was chasing down the son of a bitch who had killed Maria. I'd hated him for more than ten years, and I'd wanted this day to come. I'd even prayed for it.

But I hadn't taken the shot when I had it.

'Where is he?' Sampson was there at my side. Neither of us could see the Butcher. We couldn't hear him running now, either.

Then I heard an engine roar – in the woods! An engine? What kind of engine?

Headlights shone suddenly – two blazing eyes aimed right at us.

A car coming fast, Sullivan or somebody else

crouched at the wheel, down a track the driver knew well.

'Take the shot!' Sampson yelled. 'Alex, take the shot!'

Chapter One Hundred and Eighteen

Sullivan had stashed a car in the woods, probably for an emergency escape like this one. I held my ground, and put *one, two, three* shots into the driver's side of the windshield.

But the Butcher kept coming!

The car was a dark-colored sedan. Suddenly it slowed. Had I hit him?

I ran forward, stumbled over a rock, cursed loudly. I wasn't thinking about what to do, what not to do, just that this had to end.

Then I saw Sullivan sit up tall inside the car – and he saw me coming for him. I thought I could see his mouth curl into a sneer as he raised his handgun. I ducked just as he shot. He fired again, but I was out of his sight line by inches.

The car started to move again, its engine revving loudly. I let him slide by me; then I dove onto the car's trunk. I grabbed onto the sides and held tight, my face pressed against cold metal.

'Alex!' I heard Sampson yell behind me. 'Get off!'

I wouldn't – couldn't do it.

Sullivan accelerated, but there were too many trees and boulders for him to go very fast. The car hit a rock and bucked high; both front tires left the ground. I was almost thrown off the back, but I held on somehow.

Then Sullivan braked. Hard! I looked up.

He spun around in the front seat. For a fraction of a second we stared at each other, five feet apart, no more than that. I could see blood smeared on the side of his face. He'd been hit, maybe one of my shots through the windshield.

Up came his gun again, and he fired as I jumped off the car's rear end. I landed on the hard ground and kept rolling.

I scrambled to my knees. Aimed my gun at the car.

I shot twice through the side window. I was screaming at Sullivan – at the Butcher – whoever the hell he was. I wanted him dead, and I wanted to be the one to do it.

This has to end.
Right here, right now.
Somebody dies.
Somebody lives.

Chapter One Hundred and Nineteen

I fired again at the monster who had killed my wife and so many others, usually in unthinkable ways, with butcher hammers, saws, carving knives. *Michael 'the Butcher' Sullivan, die. Just die, you bastard. You deserve to die if anyone does on this earth.*

He was climbing out of the car now.

What was happening? What was he doing?

He started to hobble in the direction of his wife and three sons. Blood was running down his shirt, seeping through, dripping onto his pants and shoes. Then Sullivan plopped down on the lawn beside his family. He hugged them to his sides.

Sampson and I moved forward at a slow run, puzzled by what was happening, unsure what to do next.

I could see streaks of blood on the boys, and all over Caitlin Sullivan. It was their father's blood, the Butcher's. When I got closer, I saw that he looked dazed, as if he might pass out or even die. Then he spoke to me. 'She's a good person. She didn't know what I do, still doesn't. These are good boys. Get them away from here, from the Mafia.'

I still wanted to kill him, and I was afraid he might live, but I lowered my gun. I couldn't point it at his wife and his kids.

Sullivan laughed, and he suddenly raised his gun to his wife's head. He yanked her up from the ground. 'Put down the guns or I'll kill her, Cross. I'd do it in a heartbeat. I'll kill her. Even the boys. It's not a problem for me. That's who I am.'

The look on Caitlin Sullivan's face wasn't so much surprise or shock as terrible sadness and disappointment in this man whom she probably loved, or had loved at one time anyway. The youngest boy was screaming at his father, and it was heart-wrenching. 'No, Daddy, no! Don't hurt Mommy! Daddy, *please*!'

'Put the guns down!' Sullivan yelled.

What could I do? I had no choice. Not in my mind, not in my ethical universe. I dropped my Glock.

And Sullivan took a bow.

Then a shot exploded from his gun.

I felt a hard punch in the chest, and I was lifted halfway off the ground. For a second, maybe, I was standing on my tiptoes. Dancing? Levitating? Dying?

I heard a second explosion – and then there wasn't much of anything. I knew that I was going to die, that I would never see my family again, and that I had no one to blame but myself.

I'd been warned enough times. I just didn't listen.

The Dragon Slayer no more.

Chapter One Hundred and Twenty

I was wrong. I didn't die that night outside the Butcher's house, though I can't exactly say that I dodged another bullet.

I got shot up pretty bad, and spent the next month at Massachusetts General Hospital in Boston. Michael Sullivan took his bow, but then Sampson shot him twice in the chest. He died right there at the house.

I don't regret it. I don't have sympathy for the Butcher. And that probably means I haven't changed as much as I wanted to, that I'm still the Dragon Slayer at least.

Nearly every morning these days, after I see patients, I have a session with Adele Finaly. She handles me as well as anybody could. One day, I tell her about the final shootout at the Sullivan house, and how I wanted the satisfaction of revenge, and justice, but didn't get it. Adele says she understands, but she doesn't have any sympathy, not for Sullivan and not for me, either. We both see the obvious connections between Sullivan and me. Then one of us dies in front of his family.

'He told me that he didn't kill Maria,' I tell Adele during the session.

'So what, Alex? You know he was a liar. A psychopath. Killer. Sadist. Piece of dog shit.'

'Yes, all of that and more. But I think I believe him. I do. I just don't understand what it means yet. Another mystery to solve.'

In another session, we talk about a road trip I made to Wake Forest, North Carolina, which is north of Raleigh. I took the new R350, the family car, the crossover vehicle. I went down there to visit Kayla Coles, to talk to her, to stare into her eyes when she talked to me.

Kayla was in great shape, mentally and physically, and said that she liked her life down there more than she'd expected. She told me that she was staying in Raleigh. 'Lots of people to help down here in North Carolina, Alex,' she said. 'And the quality of life, for me anyway, is better than in Washington. Stay around a while and check it out.'

'Was that an invitation Kayla was giving you?' Adele asks after a silence between us.

'Could have been. An invitation she knew I wouldn't accept.'

'Because?'

'Because? Because . . . I'm Alex Cross,' I say.

'And that isn't going to change, is it? I'm just asking. Not as a therapist, Alex, as your friend.'

'I don't know if it is. I want to change some things about my life. That's why I'm here. Besides the fact that I kind of enjoy shooting the breeze with you. All right, the answer is *no*. I'm not going to change all that much.'

'Because you're Alex Cross?'

'Yes.'

'Good,' says Adele. 'That's a start. And Alex—'

'Yeah?'

'I enjoy shooting the breeze with you too. You're one of a kind.'

Chapter One Hundred and Twenty-One

One more mystery to be solved.

On a night in the spring, Sampson and I walked on Fifth Street, just hanging out together. Comfortable, like it's always been between the two of us. We were brown-bagging it with a couple of beers. Sampson had on Wayfarer sunglasses and an old Kangol hat I hadn't seen on his big head in years.

We passed old clapboard houses that have been here since we were kids and didn't look all that different now, though a lot of DC has changed tremendously, for good and bad, and something in between.

'I was worried about you up there in that hospital,' he said.

'I was worried about myself. I was starting to get

a Massachusetts accent. All those broad *a*'s. And I was becoming politically correct.'

'Something I need to talk to you about. Been on my mind a lot.'

'I'm listening. Nice night for a talk.'

'Little hard to get into it, to get started. This happened maybe two, three months after Maria was killed,' Sampson continued. 'You remember a neighborhood guy, Clyde Wills?'

'I remember Wills very well. Drug runner with lofty aspirations. Until they got him killed and dumped in a trash bin behind a Popeyes Chicken, if I recall.'

'You got it right. Wills was a snitch for Rakeem Powell when Rakeem was a detective in the 103.'

'Uh-huh. I'm not surprised Wills played both sides of the street. Where is this going?'

'That's what I'm going to tell you, sugar. That's what I'm trying to do. Clyde Wills found out some things about Maria – like who might have killed her,' Sampson went on.

I didn't say anything, but a chill ran down my back. I kept walking forward, legs a little unsteady.

'It wasn't Michael Sullivan?' I asked. 'Just like he said.'

'He had a partner those days,' Sampson said. 'Tough guy from his old neighborhood in Brooklyn, name of

James "Hats" Galati. Galati was the one who shot Maria. Sullivan wasn't there. He may have put Galati up to it. Or maybe Galati was gunning for you.'

I didn't say anything. To be honest, I couldn't. Besides, I wanted to let Sampson finish what he had come here to do. He stared straight ahead as he walked and talked, never once looking at me.

'Rakeem and I investigated. Took us a few weeks, Alex. We worked the case hard. Even went to Brooklyn. But we couldn't get any hard proof against Galati. We knew he did it, though. He'd talked about the hit to friends in New York. Galati had been trained as a sniper in the army down at Fort Bragg.'

'You met Anthony Mullino back then, didn't you? That's why he remembered you.'

Sampson nodded. 'So here's the thing, here's the thing I've been carrying around ever since. I have a lot of trouble just saying it now. *We put the mutt down, Alex.* Rakeem and I killed Jimmy Galati one night in Brooklyn. I could never tell you, 'til right now. I tried back then. I wanted to when we started looking for Sullivan again. But I couldn't.'

'Sullivan was a killer, a bad one,' I said. 'He needed to be caught.'

Sampson didn't say any more than that, and neither did I. We walked for a while more; then he trailed away and headed home, I guess, down those same streets where we grew up together. He'd taken care of Maria's killer for me. He'd done what he thought was right, but he knew that I couldn't have lived with it. So he never told me about it, not even when we were chasing after Sullivan. I didn't quite understand that last part, but you never get to understand every-thing. Maybe I'd ask John about it some other time.

That night at home I couldn't sleep, and I couldn't think straight. Finally, I went in and bunked with Ali again. He was sleeping like an angel, not a care in the world.

I lay there, and I thought about what Sampson had told me and how much I loved him, no matter what had happened. Then I thought about Maria and how much I'd loved her.

You helped me so much, I whispered to my memory of her. *You knocked the chip off my shoulder. Taught me how to believe in love, to know there is such a thing, no matter how hard it is to come by. So help me now, Maria . . . I need to be over you, sweet girl. You know what I mean. I need to be over you so I can start up my life again.*

Suddenly I heard a voice in the dark, and it star-tled me because I'd been somewhere else in my mind, far away from the present.

'Daddy, you all right?'

I hugged Ali lightly against my chest. 'I'm all right now. Of course I am. Thanks for asking. I love you, buddy.'

'I love you, Daddy. I'm your little man,' he said.

Yeah. That's all there is to it.

EPILOGUE

SOMEBODY'S BIRTHDAY PARTY

Chapter One Hundred and Twenty-Two

So this is how my new life begins, or maybe just how it continues from story to story. Mostly it's pretty good and nice today, because it's Nana's birthday, though she refuses to say which one or even what *decade* we're talking about.

I would think she might be at a stage where she'd want to brag about her longevity, but that's not the case.

Anyway, it's definitely her night, her birthday *week*, she says, and she can do whatever she wants. *Just like on every other day of the year,* I think to myself – and keep it to myself.

It is her highness's command that 'the boys' prepare dinner, and so Damon, Ali, and I take our family car to the market and use up some of the eighty-five cubic feet of cargo space. Then we spend the better part of the afternoon making two kinds of fried chicken, biscuits from scratch, corn on the cob, butter beans, tomato aspic.

Dinner is served at seven, and it includes a nice Bordeaux, even a sip for the kids. 'Happy one hundredth!' I say, and raise a glass.

'I have some toasts of my own to make,' Nana says, and rises at her place. 'I look around our table, and I have to say that I love our family more than ever, and I feel proud and lucky to be a part of it. Especially at my age. Whatever age that may be, which is *not* one hundred years.'

'Hear, hear,' we all agree, and clap our hands like those little toy monkeys with the clangers.

'Here's to Ali, who is reading books all by himself, and who can tie his shoelaces like a real champion,' Nana continues.

'To Ali! To Ali!' I chant. 'Way to tie those shoelaces.'

'Damon has so many wonderful options to consider in life. He is a beautiful, beautiful singer, an excellent student – when he applies himself. I love you, Damon.'

'I love you, Nana. You forgot the NBA,' says Damon.

'I didn't forget the National Basketball Association.' Nana nods his way. 'You have a weak left hand. Work on it like a demon possessed if you want to play at a higher level.'

Then she goes on, 'My girl, Janelle, is another excellent student, and she doesn't do it for me or for her father – she does it all on her own, for herself. I'm proud to say that Janelle rules Janelle.'

Then Nana sits down, and we're all a little surprised, but especially me, since I didn't even get a mention. I didn't even know I was in her doghouse until now.

Then she pops up again with a sly smile spread across her small, angular face. 'Oh, I almost forgot someone.

'*Alex* has made the most profound changes of anyone this year, and we all know how hard it is for that man to change. He has his practice again and is giving of himself to others. Working in the kitchen at St A.'s too, though it's hard to get him going in *my* kitchen.'

'Who cooked this dinner?'

'The *boys* did a splendid job, all of you. I'm so proud of our family, and I *know* that I'm repeating myself. Alex, I'm very proud of you. You are a puzzle. But you are a constant delight to me. You always have been. God bless the Crosses.'

'God bless the Crosses!' we agree in unison.

Later that night I put Ali down as I usually do

lately, and I stay in his bed for a few extra minutes. The boy has had a big day, and he goes right off.

Then the phone sounds like an alarm, and I jump up and hurry out into the hall. I grab it off the wobbly stand.

'Cross family residence,' I answer, in the spirit of the day.

'There's been a murder,' I hear, and my stomach falls.

I pause a beat before I say anything. 'Why are you calling me?' I ask.

'Because you're Dr Cross, and I'm the murderer.'

Turn the page for a preview of the next
compelling thriller featuring Alex Cross . . .

JAMES PATTERSON

DOUBLE CROSS

PROLOGUE

IN YOUR HONOR

One

At the time of his formal sentencing in Alexandria, Virginia, for eleven known murders, the former FBI agent and pattern killer Kyle Craig, known as the Mastermind, was lectured and condescended to by US District Judge Nina Wolff. At least that's the way he took the judicial scolding, and he definitely took it personally, and very much to heart.

'Mr Craig, you are, by any criteria I know, the most evil human being who has ever come before me in this courtroom, and some despicable characters have come—'

Craig interrupted, 'Thank you so very much, Judge Wolff. I'm honored by your kind and, I'm quite sure, thoughtful words. Who wouldn't be pleased to be the best? Do continue. This is music to my ears.'

Judge Wolff nodded calmly, then went on as if Craig hadn't spoken a word.

'In reparation for these unspeakable murders and repeated acts of torture, you are hereby sentenced to death. Until such sentence is carried out, you will spend the remainder of your life in a supermaximum-security prison. Once there, you will be cut off from human contact as most of us know it. You will never see the sun again. Take him out of my sight!'

'Very dramatic,' Kyle Craig called to Judge Wolff as he was escorted from the courtroom, 'but it's not going to happen that way. You've just given yourself a death sentence.

'I will see the sun again, and I'll see you, Judge Wolff. You can bet on it. I'll see Alex Cross again. For sure, I will see Alex Cross. And his charming family. You have my word on it, my solemn promise before all these witnesses, this pathetic audience of thrill seekers and press hyenas, and all the rest of you who honor me with your presence today. *You haven't seen the last of Kyle Craig.*'

In the audience, among the 'thrill seekers and press hyenas,' was Alex Cross. He listened to his former friend's empty threats. And yet he couldn't help hoping that ADX Florence was as secure as it was supposed to be.

Two

___

Four years to the day later, Kyle Craig was still being held, or perhaps *smothered* was the more apt description, in the maximum-security prison in Florence, Colorado, about a hundred miles from Denver. He hadn't seen the sun in all that time. He was cut off from most human contact. His anger was growing, blossoming, and that was a terrifying thing to consider.

His fellow inmates included the Unabomber – Ted Kaczynski; Oklahoma City conspirator Terry Nichols; and Al Qaeda terrorists Richard Reid and Zacarias Moussaoui. None of them had required much sunblock lately either. The prisoners were kept locked away in soundproof seven-by-twelve concrete cells for twenty-three hours every day, completely isolated from anyone other than their lawyers and high-security guards. The

solitary experience at ADX Florence had been compared to 'dying every single day.'

Even Kyle admitted that escaping from Florence
was a daunting challenge, maybe impossible. In fact,
none of the prisoners inside had ever succeeded, or
even come close. Still, one could only hope, one could
dream, one could plot and exercise the old imagination. One could most definitely *plan* a little revenge.

His case was currently on appeal, and his lawyer from
Denver, Mason Wainwright, visited once a week. This
day, he arrived as he always did, promptly at four p.m.

Mason Wainwright sported a long silver-gray pony-
tail, scuffed black cowboy boots, and a cowboy hat
worn jauntily back on his head. He had on a buckskin
jacket, a snakeskin belt, and large horn-rimmed glasses that gave him the appearance of a rather studious
country-and-western singer, or a country-and-west-
ern-loving college professor, take your pick. He
seemed a curious choice as an attorney, but Kyle Craig
had a reputation for brilliance, so the selection of
Wainwright wasn't seriously questioned.

Craig and the lawyer hugged when Wainwright
arrived. As he usually did, Kyle whispered near the
lawyer's ear, 'There's no videotaping permitted in this
room? That rule is still in force? You're sure of it, Mr
Wainwright?'

'There's no videotape,' answered Wainwright. 'You have attorney–client privilege, even in this pathetic hellhole. I'm sorry that I can't do more for you. I sincerely apologize for that. You know how I feel about you.'

'I don't question your loyalty, Mason.'

Following the hug, Craig and the lawyer sat on opposite sides of a gray metal conference table, which was bolted securely to the concrete floor. So were the chairs.

Kyle now asked the lawyer eight specific questions, always the same questions, in session after session. He asked them rapidly, leaving no time for any answers by his attorney, who just sat there in respectful silence.

'That great consoler of mass-murdering prisoners, Truman Capote, once said that he was afraid of two things, and two things only. So which of these is worse, betrayal or abandonment?' Kyle Craig began, then went right to the next question.

'What was the very first thing you forced yourself not to cry over, and how old were you when it occurred?'

And then, 'Tell me this, Counselor: what is the average length of time it takes a drowning person to lose consciousness?

'Here's something I'm curious about – do most murders take place indoors or out?

'Why is laughing at a funeral considered unacceptable, while crying at a wedding is not?

'Can you hear the sound of one hand clapping if all the flesh is removed from the hand?

'How many ways are there to skin a cat, if you wish it to remain alive through the entire process?

'And, oh yes, how are my Boston Red Sox doing?'

Then there was silence between Kyle and the lawyer. Occasionally, the convicted murderer would ask a few more specifics – perhaps additional detail about the Red Sox or about the Yankees, whom he despised, or about some interesting killer working on the outside whom the lawyer had informed him about.

Then came another hug as Mason Wainwright was about to leave the room.

The lawyer whispered against Kyle's cheek. 'They're ready to go. The preparations are complete. There will be important doings in Washington, DC, soon. There will be payback. We expect a large audience. *All in your honor.*'

Kyle Craig didn't say anything to this news, but he put his index fingers together and pressed them hard against the lawyer's skull. Very hard indeed, and he made an unmistakable impression that traveled instantly to Mason Wainwright's brain.

The fingers were in the shape of a cross.

PART ONE

ALL THE WORLD'S A STAGE

Chapter One

Washington, DC.

The first story, a thriller, involved an Iraqi soldier and a crime writer. This soldier was observing a twelve-story luxury apartment building, and he was thinking, *So this is how the rich and famous live. Stupidly at best, and very dangerously for sure.*

He began his checklist of possibilities for a break-in.

The service entrance at the back of the super-luxury Riverwalk apartment building was rarely, if ever, used by the residents, or even by their sullen lackeys. More secluded than the main entry or the underground parking garage, it was also more vulnerable.

A single reinforced door showed off no external hardware. The frame was wired on all sides.

Any attempt at forced entry would trigger simultaneous alarms at the Riverwalk's main office and with dispatch at a private security firm based just a few blocks away.

Static overhead cameras monitored all deliveries and other foot traffic during the day.

Use of the entrance was forbidden after seven p.m., when motion detectors were also engaged.

None of this was a serious problem, the soldier believed. Actually, it was an advantage for him.

Yousef Qasim had been a captain for twelve years with the Mukhabarat under Saddam. He had a sixth sense about such things, anything to do with the illusion of security. Qasim could see what the Americans could not – that their love of technology made them complacent and blind to danger. His best way into the Riverwalk was also the easiest.

Garbage was the answer. Qasim knew it was carried out every Monday, Wednesday, and Friday afternoon, without fail. American efficiency, so valued here, was another of the luxury building's vulnerabilities.

Efficiency was predictability.
Predictability was weakness.

Chapter Two

Sure enough, at 4:34 p.m. the door to the service entrance opened from inside. A tall black lackey in stained green coveralls and a silver Afro latched a chain from inside the door to a hook on the outside wall. His flatbed dolly, loaded with bulging plastic garbage bags, was too wide to negotiate the opening.

The man moved slowly, lazily, carrying two bags at a time to a pair of commercial Dumpsters at the far end of a covered loading dock.

This man is still a slave to the whites, Qasim thought to himself. *And look at him – the pathetic shuffle, the downcast eyes. He knows it too. He hates his job and the terrible people in the Riverwalk building.*

Qasim watched closely, and he counted. Twelve paces away from the door, nine seconds to throw the garbage bags in, then back again.

On the man's third trip, Qasim slipped by him unnoticed. And if his own cap and green coveralls weren't enough to fool the camera, it was no crucial matter. He'd be long gone by the time anyone came to investigate the security breach.

He found the poorly lit service stairs easily enough. Qasim took the first flight cautiously, then ran up the next three. Actually, the running released pent-up adrenaline, which was useful to get under control.

On the fourth-floor landing was an unused utility closet, where he stashed the garment bag he had carried in, then continued up to twelve.

Less than three and a half minutes after entering the luxury building, he stood at the front door to apartment 12F. He gauged his position relative to the peephole in the door. His finger hovered over the buzzer, a recessed white button in the painted brick.

But he went no further than that. He didn't actually push the buzzer today.

Without making a sound, he turned on his heels and left the way he had come. Minutes later, he was back out on the street, busy Connecticut Avenue.

The drill, the rehearsal, had gone fairly well. There were no major issues, no surprises either. And now Qasim jostled along with the rush-hour pedestrian traffic. He was invisible here, just as unseen in this herd as he needed to be.

He felt no impatience for the execution up on the twelfth floor. Patience and impatience were irrelevant to him. Preparation, timing, completion, success: those were the things that mattered.

When the time came, Yousef Qasim would be ready to do his part.

And he would.

One American at a time.

You've Been Warned

James Patterson and Howard Roughan

Internationally bestselling author James Patterson delivers the most haunting thriller of his career.

YOU'VE BEEN NICE, VERY NICE

Kristin Burns has lived her life by the philosophy, 'don't think, just shoot' – pictures that is. Struggling to make ends meet, she works full time as the nanny for the fabulously wealthy Turnbull family, looking after their two children and waiting for her life as a New York fashion photographer to begin. When her photographs are being considered at an elite Manhattan art gallery, it seems she might finally get the chance that will start her career.

YOU'VE BEEN NAUGHTY, VERY NAUGHTY

But Kristin has a major distraction: forbidden love. The man of her dreams is almost hers for keeps. Breathless with an inexhaustible passion and the excitement of being within reach of everything she wants, Kristin ignores all signs of catastrophe brewing.

NOW, YOU'VE BEEN WARNED

Fear exists for a reason. And Kristin can only dismiss the warnings for so long. Searching desperately for the truth through the lens of her camera, she can only hope that it's not too late. This novel of psychological suspense is a stunning new achievement for the man the *Sunday Telegraph* called 'the master of the suspense genre'.

Praise for James Patterson's bestselling novels:

'Pacy, sexy, high-octane stuff' *Guardian*

'A novel which makes for sleepless nights' *Daily Express*

978 0 7553 4956 2

headline

Step on a Crack

James Patterson and Michael Ledwidge

First came ALEX CROSS.

Then the WOMEN'S MURDER CLUB.

Now meet Detective Michael Bennett, NYPD
– and his ten children.

The world's most powerful people have gathered in St Patrick's Cathedral, New York, to mourn the unexpected death of a former first lady. Then suddenly they find themselves trapped within one man's brilliant and ruthless scheme.

Detective Michael Bennett – *father of ten* – is pulled into the fray. But as the danger escalates, Michael is hit with devastating news – his beloved wife has lost her battle against cancer. Grief-stricken, he has no choice but to carry on and try to save the 34 hostages – and raise his ten children.

With the entire world watching and the tension boiling to a searing heat, Bennett must face the most ruthless man he has ever dealt with – or face responsibility for the greatest debacle in history.

From the man the *Sunday Telegraph* called 'the master of the suspense genre' comes his most fiendishly terrifying thriller yet.

Praise for James Patterson's bestselling novels:

'Pacy, sexy, high-octane stuff' *Guardian*

'Brilliantly terrifying . . . so exciting I had to stay up all night to finish it' *Daily Mail*

'James Patterson does everything but stick our finger in a light socket to give us a buzz' *New York Times*

978 0 7553 4954 8

headline

Now you can buy any of these bestselling
books by **James Patterson** from your bookshop
or *direct from his publisher*.

FREE P&P AND UK DELIVERY
(Overseas and Ireland £3.50 per book)

Miracle on the 17th Green *(and Peter de Jonge)*	£7.99
Suzanne's Diary for Nicholas	£7.99
The Beach House *(and Peter de Jonge)*	£7.99
The Lake House	£7.99
Sam's Letters to Jennifer	£7.99
Honeymoon *(and Howard Roughan)*	£7.99
Lifeguard *(and Andrew Gross)*	£7.99
Beach Road *(and Peter de Jonge)*	£7.99
Judge and Jury *(and Andrew Gross)*	£7.99
Step on a Crack *(and Michael Ledwidge)*	£7.99
The Quickie *(and Michael Ledwidge)*	£7.99
You've Been Warned *(and Howard Roughan)*	£7.99

Alex Cross series

Cat and Mouse	£7.99
Pop Goes the Weasel	£7.99
Roses are Red	£7.99
Violets are Blue	£7.99
Four Blind Mice	£7.99
The Big Bad Wolf	£7.99
London Bridges	£7.99
Mary, Mary	£7.99
Cross	£7.99
Double Cross	£7.99

Women's Murder Club series

1st to Die	£7.99
2nd Chance *(and Andrew Gross)*	£7.99
3rd Degree *(and Andrew Gross)*	£7.99
4th of July *(and Maxine Paetro)*	£7.99
The 5th Horseman *(and Maxine Paetro)*	£7.99
The 6th Target *(and Maxine Paetro)*	£7.99

Maximum Ride series

Maximum Ride: The Angel Experiment	£7.99
Maximum Ride: School's Out Forever	£6.99
Maximum Ride: Saving the World and Other Extreme Sports	£6.99

TO ORDER SIMPLY CALL THIS NUMBER
01235 400 414
or visit our website: www.headline.co.uk

Prices and availability subject to change without notice